America Gilt

America Gilt

BOOK II

ABSINTHE

J.D. Peterson

"America Gilt "
"Absinthe"
Volume Two of the 'America Gilt ' Trilogy

Previously published as:
'Swan Song Trilogy'

Bibliography and Photographic credits located at the back of this book.

AMERICA GILT – Absinthe
Volume 2 in the *America Gilt Trilogy*
ISBN 13 978-1535560306

Previously Published as *Swan Song - Absinthe* 2015
ISBN-13:9781535560306 (J.D. Peterson Media)
ISBN-10:1535560304
Library of Congress Control Number: 2015917098
J.D. Peterson Media, Laguna Niguel, CA

Published by J.D. Peterson Media
California, U.S.A.

www.americangilt.com
www.jdpetersonmedia.com

This book is dedicated to you, dear reader.

SARA SWAN WHITING BELMONT
JUNE 22, 1861 - MAY 20, 1924

TABLE OF CONTENTS

CHAPTER ONE

January 10, 1883
Le Havre, France

A SHARP WINTER WIND SEARED Sara's eyes as she gazed at the clear skies over France. Following her new husband down the gangplank, she stumbled, steadying herself on sea legs that wobbled on the hard cobblestones of the city street. Oliver slipped his arm around her waist, his body strong and warm, steadying her while she adjusted to the earth beneath her feet.

Laughter bubbled up inside her as she tried to walk. "It's been a long week on the Atlantic," Sara giggled, holding tight to his arm.

"Fortunately for you, I've had a lot of practice from my experience in the navy." Oliver met her eyes warmly, "Not to worry, my sweet. You'll be fine in a bit." Glancing at the street he eyed the line of horse-drawn taxis awaiting the passengers. A transfer coach to the train was a complimentary perquisite offered by the steamer company. Noticing Oliver, a driver dressed in fine livery quickly approached the newlyweds.

"Good afternoon, sir," he said, his diction laced with a French accent, "Welcome to Le Havre. Can I give you a lift to the train?"

"Good afternoon," Oliver smiled. "Yes. Thank you."

"Very good, sir. Off to Paris, then?" the man asked, making pleasant conversation.

Oliver nodded in reply, "My new bride and I are here on our honeymoon."

The driver gave them a wide smile, "Well then, congratulations are in order! Paris is a lovely place for a honeymoon, very romantic indeed." He surveyed the sailors, hoisting the luggage onto the dock. "Why don't we get the lady into the carriage, out of this wind? The company will take care of your trunks." He gestured toward their transport parked near the docks. A lad in matching uniform stood holding the reins of the horses, steadying them against the crush of disembarking travelers bustling about the port.

"I think I'd prefer to take the luggage with us now," Oliver told him.

"Very good, sir. As you wish. Point out which suitcases are yours and we'll get them loaded up right away."

Still holding Sara firmly, Oliver steadied her as they followed the man to the carriage. The driver threw open the door, and she climbed inside, glad to be out of the weather. She wrapped her coat closely and tucked her hands into her fur muffler, watching her breath turn to mist in the chilled air.

"Sit tight, while I take care of things," Oliver instructed. "We'll be off before you know it."

Sara nodded, watching through the window as he returned to the dock with the driver, the lad following both men. She leaned back on the cushioned seat, closing her eyes for a fleeting moment of rest.

The journey across the Atlantic had been brilliant – dinners and dancing every evening. But the most fabulous part was sleeping at night in the arms of her new husband, snug and safe against the winter seas. She had never been happier.

Waiting in the coach she reflected on their protracted courtship, particularly Oliver's parents' misgivings to the union. Mr. and Mrs. Belmont had made a concerted effort to discourage the marriage. They'd separated the two sweethearts by ordering Oliver to Germany for well over a year where he was to learn the banking business in the Rothschild's house in Bremen. Sara wasn't quite sure what had caused them to acquiesce to their wedding, but they had finally allowed Oliver to return to Newport, and she'd been more than grateful.

The wedding was held a few days after Christmas at her family's estate, Swanhurst. It was attended by the elite of society, most noticeably, Mrs. Caroline Astor. Recognized by the upper class as the reigning queen of the Four Hundred, Mrs. Astor's favoritism had secured Sara's place among society's *beau monde*. Her daughter, Carrie Astor, was Sara's dear friend, along with Edith Jones and Anita Tiffany. Carrie had agreed to be Sara's maid of honor, and Anita her bridesmaid along with her cousin, Charlotte Whiting. Edith missed the celebration as her family was traveling, but she'd sent a lovely gift of a silver tea set for the newlyweds.

Sara and Oliver had departed after the reception for New York, where they boarded a steamer headed for their extended honeymoon in Paris. Her family often vacationed there, as did many of society's families, but this time it was different. She was a married woman traveling with her husband, no longer a débutante.

She had first come out to society three years earlier, completely enjoying the fanfare and attention of her débutante status. But as the months turned to years without Oliver's parents' approval of an engagement, Sara secretly feared she would face the fate dealt her older sisters, Jane and Milly. Neither had married, and both still lived with their widowed mother at Swanhurst.

In a nod to a family honeymoon custom, the three Whiting women would be joining the newlyweds in Paris soon to introduce them amongst their European friends as Mr. and Mrs. Oliver Hazard Perry Belmont. There had been whispers of disapproval from some that the newlyweds should be left alone to better acquaint themselves with each other, but Sara's mother pooh-poohed them, saying her own family had added much joy and celebration to her marriage to Sara's father, Augustus Whiting. Sara rather liked the idea as well, and Oliver had voiced no objections to the arrangements. In fact, he'd negotiated them a large apartment on the Champs-Élysées until springtime. Sara smiled to herself, the thought of spring in Paris a pleasant one.

The carriage jostled as the men boosted the trunks onto the roof for the drive to the train station. Huge workhorses stomped the ground from the movement, seeming eager to leave the busy port with its noise and activity. Sara glanced outside, her eyes searching for Oliver who had disappeared in the crowd. When he didn't appear after ten minutes, a quiver of abandonment threatened her good mood. Waiting in the coach on the busy dock, Sara began to feel very alone.

I'm being childish, she thought, and quietly chastised herself for such wild thoughts – especially after all they'd been through to get to this point.

Still, she breathed a sigh of relief when the carriage door opened and Oliver climbed in beside her, carrying a cotton sack.

"Where have you been? I was starting to think you were lost."

"Not at all," he chuckled, opening the bag. "I went into the cheese shop and got us a little snack for the trip, as well as some libations." He pulled a wheel of Brie and a freshly baked French baguette from the cloth bag, along with a bottle of fine champagne. "We are still celebrating, you know."

"I should hope so," Sara gave him a playful poke on the arm. "We've only been married two weeks. What else have you got there?" she asked, noticing another item in his bag.

Oliver lifted a bottle from the sack. She read the label: Absinthe.

"This is for me," he proclaimed happily, "It's an acquired taste I developed while in Germany. I'm sure you would much prefer the bubbly. We'll open it once we board the train. I know they offer refreshments, but this is an aged bottle. Only the best for you, my sweet."

There was a twinkle in his eye that quickly put her mind at ease. Sara heard the driver shout to the horses, and the coach rumbled away from the curb en route to the train station.

Five days later
January 15, 1883
Atlantic Ocean

Glancing across the dining table at Jane and Milly, Mrs. Whiting considered her daughters. Even though she tried not to show it, they had so disappointed her by not marrying properly into society. That was every mother's dream for her daughters - in fact, the unspoken goal for their future. Unfortunately, the outbreak of the civil war had left few available bachelors in the set for her older daughters to court.

There were times in the past when she grew weary of hoping for the grandchildren she had so dearly wished for. Finally, her son Gus had married Florence Green, and they had given her a grandson, but sadly, he died as an infant. The couple tried again and had recently delivered a granddaughter: Charlotte. Mrs. Whiting was delighted with the little girl, who appeared to be thriving, but with four grown children of her own, she had secretly dreamed of being surrounded by oodles of grandchildren. Now, aboard the ship traveling to meet with Sara and Oliver in Paris, she anticipated that the situation might soon be cured.

It no longer mattered that Jane and Milly were well past débutante status. Thanks to Sara, the Whitings were now a part of the exquisitely wealthy Belmont family. Their place was secure in high society, and she intended to make the most of their new position.

"I am feeling surprisingly weary," Jane mumbled to no one in particular. "I suppose it's the result of weeks of excitement from the wedding. I think I'll go to my cabin and rest after lunch."

"The ocean has been rather choppy with this winter weather," Mrs. Whiting scrutinized her. "You don't suppose you're coming down with a case of seasickness, do you? That would surely put a damper on our holiday."

"No Mother, I'm not getting ill, just fatigued from all the fuss over Sara's nuptials." Jane grimaced at her mother disapprovingly, "So much entertaining and now we're sailing across the ocean again. I'm simply tired."

"Have you ever thought of purchasing our own place in France?" Milly asked out of the blue, "We're in Paris nearly as much as Newport and New York."

Mrs. Whiting grew thoughtful at her daughter's idea. "Actually, I have dreamed of retiring in France in my old age. Paris is such a lovely city, the quintessence of culture. There's always so much to do."

"With our own place, we could shop for art and beautiful French furniture and always be surrounded by our personal things," Milly smiled, encouraged. "We'd be certain of the comfort of our own suite every time we came to France."

"The idea does have its merits," Mrs. Whiting agreed, "although I am drawn more to Pau, than to Paris. But for now Paris is the place to be. And I do enjoy the adventure of staying in a hotel suite. It gives me a chance to meet people and I don't need to bring extra servants. I suppose there are advantages to both."

The waiter brought their lunches, placing the sizzling plates of grilled chicken before the women, the aroma stirring their appetites to life.

"Can I get you anything else right now?" he asked them in a formal tone.

"I would like some more tea," Jane said sharply, pointing at the carafe in the center of the table. "Very hot, please."

"Of course, ma'am," he nodded. Removing the cold teapot, he left for the galley.

"Well, Jane," Mrs. Whiting said. "Get your rest while we're traveling. We'll be in Paris in three days."

"It seems the journey grows shorter with each crossing," Milly noted, purposely ignoring her sister's disagreeable mood. "I suppose that's a good thing."

"Well, the steamer is full of its own entertainments. There's a Captain's Dinner tonight I would like to attend, and I expect you to come along." Mrs. Whiting glanced earnestly at her daughters. Distracted with their meals, Milly nodded in agreement while Jane shrugged, indifferent. "Keep in mind that once we get to Paris, I'll be hosting dinner parties for the newlyweds to introduce them to European society, and you both shall be required to attend."

Clearly bored at the prospect, Jane nodded, wearing a distinct frown.

To the contrary Milly perked up, pleased with the idea of mingling in French society. "Do you think it's too late for me to wish for such a happy ending as Sara has found with Oliver?" Her eyes danced at the thought. "I know I'm past my prime, but there are many men who've been left widowed and may be hoping for such a match." She reached for the butter crock and broke a piece of bread off the crusty loaf in the basket.

"You're nearly forty years old," her sister grimaced. "Stop daydreaming and deal with the reality of your life." Jane was in a cruel mood. "We're spinsters, plain and simple. And that's a fact we have little hope of changing at our age."

"I suppose…" Milly mused, but her eyes shone with a far-off look.

Abruptly, Jane put down her fork. Pushing back her chair, she rose from the table. "I seem to have lost my appetite," she announced coolly.

"I'll be in my cabin." And with that she gathered her pocketbook and left the dining room.

Mrs. Whiting and Milly looked at each other in surprise.

"Seems she's got a real bee in her bonnet," Milly sighed.

"Not to worry about your sister," Mrs. Whiting kept her voice calm. "She's just adjusting to life without Sara. She'll conform to the new order in time."

Milly considered her mother's words. "I suppose you're right," she nodded, returning her attention to her lunch.

Three days later
January 18, 1883
Belmont Mansion, New York City

The crisp beams of a new day cascaded through the windows, burnishing the home in bright sunlight. Caroline found August in the morning room, where he stood absently gazing out the French doors.

"Lost in thought I see." She walked over, joining him at the window. "At least the sun is shining in spite of the cold."

August turned, roused from his ruminations. "Good morning, my dear. How are you today?" He kept his tone light, not wanting to seem too anxious about her health.

"I'm happy to announce that I feel wonderful." Caroline moved to the jacquard sofa, gracefully relaxing into the seat. "Now that this situation with Oliver and Sara has been resolved, I must admit, I'm experiencing great relief."

Shaking his head in agreement, August settled into the leather armchair beside her. "I was having similar thoughts in regard to the matter. I'm most hopeful this marriage will finally bring some maturity to Oliver and encourage him to settle down. He has serious responsibilities now that he's taken a wife."

"Whatever he does," Caroline sighed, "it'll concern us much less now that he's married. My worries these days have more to do with getting

Raymond back on the right track." A troubled look clouded her eyes as she contemplated their youngest son. "I'm afraid Oliver has had a very negative effect on his conduct, schooling him in his playboy ways. Now that Oliver's married, I'm hoping Raymond will focus on his education with more effort." She grew quiet, toying with the ruby ring on her finger. "But, regarding Oliver, I do hope Sara has the influence on him that we're hoping for. I've grown quite weary trying to handle his affairs, first with the navy and then with the Rothschilds. I should like nothing more than to wash my hands of his problems."

A servant walked into the room with a tea service, skillfully placing it on the sofa table in front of them. The mouthwatering aroma of sugar and cinnamon drifted from a plate of warm muffins, croissants, and scones. The maid carefully poured two cups full of the hot brew, then stepped back.

"Is there anything else I can get you?" she asked with formal precision.

"No thank you, Marie. This is fine for now." Caroline nodded her dismissal.

The room lapsed into silence with the servant's departure. August reached to stir his tea, the spoon clinking on the edge of the porcelain. "How long are the newlyweds planning to stay in Paris?"

"I'm not certain, but I believe for several months." Caroline lifted her steaming cup, "At least until springtime." She grew thoughtful, and leaning her head a bit, turned to him. "What do you really think about this business of Sara's family staying with the newlyweds while they're on their honeymoon?"

August scratched his temple, feeling like he was being backed into a corner.

"Honestly, I find it a bit odd. I'm not familiar with the tradition of family joining in on the honeymooners' holiday. I doubt if we would have given our parents any grandchildren if they'd been in the adjoining room."

Caroline smiled, too mature to be shocked by his frankness. "I doubt if you would have stood for it, August. Even as a young man you stubbornly insisted on having things your way."

"Is that true?" he asked with a playful grin. "Me? Stubborn?"

She raised an eyebrow, entertained by his response. "Not that I mind, I admit. That's what makes you the powerful king of Fifth Avenue commerce," she flattered him, tongue in cheek. Caroline chose a scone, and nibbled gently at the steaming pastry. "Oliver doesn't seem to mind the Whitings visiting them on their honeymoon. Or if he did, he didn't say anything to the contrary. I hope it doesn't turn out to be a problem once he realizes the day-to-day realities of living with his new family."

"I'm sure they'll work it out just fine, Caroline. Now, please, once and for all, stop worrying about Oliver."

"Of course, you're right. Oliver's life is now on the perimeter of my concerns. If going on honeymoon with Sara's family doesn't bother him, why should it bother me?"

And with that she took another bite of her pastry.

CHAPTER TWO

Ten days later
January 28, 1883
Paris, France

"My dearest petite-mere, Oliver and I are writing to you side-by-side in the most romantic manner…" [1]

Sara reviewed the letter they'd written earlier. Pleased by its happy content, she folded the papers and slid them into the envelope addressed to Mrs. Belmont in New York. Rising from her writing desk she walked to the foyer and placed the note in a basket on the entry table reserved for mail. Overflowing with letters and thank-you cards addressed to family and friends in the States, she made a mental note to have Bridget, her maid, take them to the post office.

Returning to the parlor Sara glanced at the gilt clock ticking away on the fireplace mantel, and snuggled onto the velvet love seat, wondering what was keeping Oliver away for so many hours.

After a lovely morning together he'd stepped out after lunch, saying he needed to take care of a few errands. Sara didn't mind really, as it left her some quiet time to savor the moments they'd been sharing since arriving in Paris as husband and wife.

The entire apartment staff had been very hospitable, making deliveries of bouquets, bottles of champagne, and other necessities they'd ordered to their room. A fabulous restaurant on the ground floor accommodated them by sending an errand boy to their suite with elegant meals when requested. They'd spent many days in the apartment enjoying their time together, disturbed only by the deliveries. She smiled to herself, content.

The newlyweds had transformed the apartment into their nuptial love nest. For her, their honeymoon was a happy wish come true.

Relieved to discover her pre-wedding fears of lovemaking had been unwarranted, Sara found Oliver very sweet and gentle. He sensed her innocent shyness, soothing her anxiety, tenderly making love to her. She breathed in a sigh of pleasure. It was wonderful to finally be an initiated woman, having experienced the secrets of intimacy. She'd heard many differing opinions from society's matriarchs, ranging from delight to distaste, depending on who was speaking. Her own mother had remained silent on the subject, leaving Sara twined in confusion as to what to expect on her wedding night.

As it turned out, it had been completely wonderful. Sara loved Oliver even more now that they had consummated their marriage, not once, but over and over again as newlyweds. Their wedding night in Fall River had been like a dream. Her dream. Her very own lover's fantasy come true, complete with rose petals on the bed. The two had proceeded to laugh and love their way across the Atlantic while traveling on the ship. And now in the privacy of their Paris apartment, Sara found herself relaxing even more into Oliver's touch as they explored every detail of passion.

Glancing at the clear sky through the suite window, she felt sweet and mellow from their romantic hours of intimacy. They'd written together to her mother-in-law that their marriage was a wonderful thing and had been well worth waiting for. Sara knew now without doubt or regrets that Oliver was the man of her dreams.

The key clicked in the lock, rousing her from her reflections as the door to the suite opened. With a quick look at the mantle clock Sara noticed a full half-hour had passed while she'd been lost in thought. Now six o'clock, it was nearing time for dinner. She rose from the seat and walked to the entrance with an eager smile, greeting her handsome husband as he entered.

"Hello, my sweet," he smiled, giving her a serene kiss on the forehead. "Writing to our family back home?" He glanced at the stack of letters waiting in the basket. "Here's today's mail." He nonchalantly threw a few envelopes on the table.

"Yes. I want them all to know how perfectly dreamy our honeymoon has been." She smiled flirtatiously, showing new confidence in her sensuality.

Moving to the table Sara went through the recent mail, coyly letting her lace dress fall low on her décolletage.

"What's this from the Vanderbilts?" she asked, flipping the gold-trimmed envelope over in her hand. Sara enjoyed a twinge of pride to see it addressed to 'Mr. and *Mrs.* Oliver H. P. Belmont'.

They walked together to the parlor where she found the scrimshaw letter opener on the desk and eagerly opened the note. Her eyes quickly scanned the contents. "How wonderful! It's an invitation to a party," she announced. "It seems Alva has finished the new house on Fifth Avenue and they're celebrating with a fancy ball. Costumes required."

"When is it?"

"The end of March. Nearly two months from now." The dimples in her cheeks showed her delight. "Perhaps we should accept the invitation and return to New York for the festivities. There's been some talk about Alva wanting to throw the party of the season. I wouldn't want to miss it, and it would give us the perfect chance to make an appearance as husband and wife back in New York society."

He reached for the note, quickly examining the invitation. Turning to meet her gaze he offered an eager smile.

"If you'd like," he nodded. "It only takes a week to cross the Atlantic on these new ships. We could leave the middle of March and be there in plenty of time for the ball."

"I should like that very much." Sara lowered her lashes alluringly.

The look was not lost upon him. He answered by leaning down and kissing her deeply. That wonderful warm glow began moving through Sara, intoxicating her again, and they dwelled in their devotion. Oliver punctuated the kiss by another tiny one on the tip of her nose. As he pulled away, she noticed he carried a cloth sack.

"Have you brought me a gift?" she teased, "or has the honeymoon already worn off?"

Oliver opened the bag and pulled out a bottle of absinthe bearing a different label than the one he'd purchased in Le Havre.

"More absinthe?" she raised a brow. "Don't tell me you've already finished the first bottle?"

"There's still a bit left," he shrugged. "But *Pernod Fils* is the original brand. There weren't many choices in the port." He threw an easy smile her way, "Absinthe is one of my favorite liquors, and I can only get the best variety here in Europe, so I thought I'd indulge myself."

"Isn't this the drink that makes men go insane?" Sara grimaced, eyeing the bottle. "They say it's made with wormwood. Isn't that a poison?"

"Not at all – wormwood is an herb. It's said to cure malaria," he chuckled. "Besides, anything and everything will make you go insane if you partake of it too much. You know what the Romans say, 'everything in moderation' or something to that effect."

Smiling at his breezy manner, Sara's mind was put at ease by his certainty. Oliver was so different from her mother and older sisters with their constant fretting and fussing. Sara found his sanguine demeanor irresistible. It took a lot to upset Oliver, or at least he hid his displeasure well, she decided. Perhaps it had been his upbringing. His life was so carefree compared to most. He was always cool and confident, regardless of the problem or conflict. And Oliver always found an agreeable way out of unpleasant situations. Just like the navy. And just like Bremen.

"Are you hungry?" He glanced at her, changing the subject. "It's getting near time for dinner."

"Yes. Very," Sara nodded. "Do you mind if we go out tonight? I'm growing a bit weary of these rooms."

His brows peaked in mock horror. "Now it's my turn to wonder if the honeymoon is over?" After a moment his expression gave way to a smile.

"Don't be silly!" she gave him a gentle push on his shoulder. "You know I've never been happier than I am right now."

Oliver pulled her into his arms with a quick swoop, cupping her chin in his hand.

"Then we shall go wherever you like, and indulge in whatever epicurean delight you desire." He kissed her again, lingering.

"Perhaps you can save the seduction for after dinner?" she said, breathlessly. "I don't want to faint on you during the throes of lovemaking from a lack of sustenance."

Throwing his head back, he laughed heartily. "I certainly cannot have that happen to my beautiful, young bride. Imagine the rumors we'd start."

Sara giggled freely. Yes, she thought, wedded bliss is a very appropriate description for the joy they were sharing in their Paris suite.

"I'll go and dress, then you can surprise me with dinner plans. You know how I love it when you surprise me."

"Hmmm," Oliver eyed her curiously. "Leaving the burden of choice on me, are you? Perhaps I've misjudged your cleverness."

He moved in for another kiss, the two melting into each other's arms. The heat between them ignited and swirled like a mysterious current. After a long and deep moment he released her, still gazing into her eyes.

"Sara…" he whispered. "You've made me so very happy. Happier than I ever thought I could be. I'm looking forward to building our life together as I've never anticipated anything before."

She blushed furiously at his words of devotion, meeting his eyes. "I never knew that love could be so wonderful. Make it last forever will you, Oliver? I never want this feeling to end. Never. Ever."

"And it never will, my sweet. We'll show all those busybodies that they were wrong about us. We'll be the paragon of wedded bliss."

Not waiting for him to initiate, Sara leaned in and boldly kissed him again. He squeezed her, the room quiet except for the sound of the clock ticking above the fireplace.

At last, she drew away. "I'll go and change," she whispered, warm with desire. "I must look my absolute best now that I'm Mrs. Belmont."

Oliver's eyes were glued to her every movement as she disappeared into the bedroom. Sighing happily he went to the sideboard across the parlor, grabbed the spoon and glass sitting on the tray, and began louching himself a drink of absinthe.

One week later
February 3, 1883
Paris, France

Stifling a laugh, Carrie wondered at Marshall's antics as he pulled her through the hallway. Escaping the party in the ballroom he led her to the library on the other side of the Hôtel Ritz. Holding her hand firmly, she sensed he had a deeper purpose.

"You grip my hand like a man possessed. I won't run away," Carrie promised in a hushed voice. "I can only disappear for a minute, or Mother will come looking for me. I don't think she'd be too pleased to find us sneaking off alone."

"I just want a moment with you, away from the crowd," Marshall assured her. "Is there anything wrong with that?"

"As long as you're a gentleman," Carrie smiled flirtatiously, "I suppose there's no harm at all."

Guiding her toward the blaze in the library fireplace, he turned to face her, "Have I ever been anything but a gentleman with you, Carrie?" Marshall feigned offense. In the stillness of the room he drew her into a close embrace.

Meeting his eyes Carrie grew modest. "Do stop teasing me," she said, her heart beating faster.

He kissed her hand gently, gazing at her. "I'm not teasing you," he whispered. "I've brought you here to talk for a bit. I didn't want the night to finish without some time alone." He kissed her lightly on the lips, holding her hands captive in his own. "There's something I want to tell you. I assure you, now, I am being perfectly serious."

"Oh?" Carrie searched his face. "You're being very dramatic." Sensing a nervous excitement in his demeanor, she grew shy.

Marshall squeezed her hands tighter. "I want to talk about us, Carrie. You and me."

"What about us?"

"We've always enjoyed each other's company, haven't we?" He reached to brush her check gently, searching her eyes.

"Of course. There's no one I'd rather spend time with. Certainly, you must know that by now."

"It's reassuring to hear, just the same." Marshall smiled, relief passing over his face like sunlight darting from behind a cloud. "But, I must admit, being with you means more to me than just sharing a dance with a lovely woman," he paused, shifting on his feet as the fire crackled warmly. "In all honesty, I find my thoughts preoccupied by you. I want to spend every free moment in your company. That's why I followed you here to Paris."

She broke his gaze, glancing at the embers under the burning logs. "I must confess the same," she said softly, as if allowing the words to be spoken would break the enchantment.

"Carrie..." he turned her face to meet his eyes, "Don't you know that I'm in love with you? It's a feeling that grows stronger every day."

The room faded, and Carrie saw nothing but her beau. "Oh, Marshall..." she whispered, "I'm in love with you, too." It was liberating, speaking the words she'd held prisoner in the secret places of her heart.

His delight at her reply was obvious in his wide grin. "The time isn't right, but one day soon Carrie Astor, I'm going to ask for your hand in marriage. In the meantime, I hope you'll keep your dance card open only to me."

Smiling coyly, Carrie tilted her head, "I might be able to arrange that," she whispered.

Pulling her closer, Marshall kissed her again in the soft fire light.

CHAPTER THREE

Three days later
February 16, 1883
Paris, France

THE MELODIOUS STRAINS OF VIOLINS floated across the ballroom. Voices rose over the music, trilling with laughter and merriment. Crystal chandeliers sparkled, while flickering candles perched on immense candelabras cast shadowed light over the moving bodies of dancers engaged in a cotillion on the parquet floor. The scent of flowers and French perfume filled the expansive room, airy but warm, in spite of the frosty weather, and Sara sighed blissfully, delighted to be in the presence of Paris society.

"I've really been enjoying your visit," she said to her family, who were accompanying the newlyweds to an evening ball. "I was happy to know you had a pleasant journey."

"For the most part, it was," Mrs. Whiting spoke from across the large round table. "A bit choppy at times, but after all, it *is* winter."

"The new steamers are very fine," Milly offered. "The dinners and evening entertainments were quite lovely. They made the time pass quickly. We were here before I could blink an eye."

"I'm so glad to hear it," Sara gave a congenial smile to her sister. "Winter travel can prove to be unpredictable. Now that you're settled in, we can socialize properly."

"Indeed," Milly smiled. "There are so many new faces this season."

"I must say you look lovely this evening, Sara," Mrs. Whiting nodded her approval. "Are you pleased with the gowns you chose for your honeymoon trousseau?"

"Very much," Sara smoothed a gentle hand over the silk ruffles of her emerald dress. The fabric matched the color of her sparkling eyes. "They're beautiful, and quite in vogue here in France."

"I'm going to order a few more gowns while I'm here," Milly asserted.

"If you don't mind, I'll go with you," Sara offered. "I feel a constant need to stay chic now that I'm married. It's almost worse than being a débutante. Would you like to tag along, Jane?"

"Perhaps," her sister shrugged. "I'd like to stop at the millinery shop, if it's not too much trouble. I'm interested in a new hat. Perhaps a fur style, to keep the cold wind at bay."

"That sounds lovely," Sara agreed, glad to see her oldest sister in a happy temperament.

"Sara – I thought that was you!"

Startled from the conversation, Sara turned to see her dear friend, Lady Lister-Kaye, née Natica Yznaga, join them at their table. Natica's beauty was enhanced by her bright, open smile. She wore a gorgeous gown sewn in layers of fine yellow lace and silk that contrasted beautifully with her beige skin.

"Natica!" Sara rose and gave her old friend a hug. "You've been in England for so long, we've lost touch."

"How lovely to see you again, Lady Lister-Kaye," Mrs. Whiting joined the greeting. "Congratulations on your marriage," she added. Jane and Milly echoed her sentiments, also happy to see their old friend from New York.

"Yes! Congratulations! You've been married for a year now," Sara chimed in. "How does it feel to be British royalty?"

Lady Lister-Kaye was one of the Yznaga sisters. Her father, Antonio Yznaga was Cuban, descended from Spanish aristocrats. He'd immigrated to New York as a young boy and became an American citizen a few years later. In 1849 Mr. Yznaga married Ellen Clement, the beautiful débutante of a wealthy merchant family.

Mr. Yznaga held the deeds to a considerable amount of real estate in Cuba and the United States. Owner of a large sugar plantation near Trinidad and another in Louisiana, Mr. Yznaga had also opened a business on Broad Street in New York where he imported Cuban goods to America – which, of course, included sugar. Antonio was very successful in his endeavors and had become quite prosperous.

Natica and her sisters, Consuelo and Emily were very beautiful. They also had a brother, Fernando, but the three sisters were the life of the party. Spunky and vivacious, they quickly became favorites among the set. Unable to find a suitable match for her daughters, Mrs. Yznaga took them abroad in search of husbands, bringing along a sizable dowry for each of the young ladies, generously provided by their father.

Consuelo had married the Duke of Manchester and settled in Ireland, while Natica had married Sir John Lister-Kaye, securing both women royal titles. Before they'd left for Europe, the sisters were frequently in the company of Sara, Edith and Carrie. The ladies formed close friendships, creating a lovely alliance among the débutantes of society.

"Thank you so much…" Lady Lister-Kaye nodded, "John and I have been getting settled on his estate in Yorkshire. It's been quite an adventure after living in New York."

"How are your sisters doing? Is the Duchess here?" Sara asked.

"I'm afraid not," Natica shook her head to the contrary. "But John and I thought we would travel to Paris for a holiday to brighten the winter season. Such wonderful luck to run into you – my old friends from America." She gave Sara an impish smile. "And may I congratulate you as well, my friend – married to Oliver Belmont!"

"Thank you," Sara smiled warmly. "We're in Paris on our honeymoon. My family is joining us for a visit."

"How wonderful," Natica said, "I really must have a dinner party in your honor to celebrate your marriage."

"How gracious of you," Sara agreed. "And I want to know all about your new life as part of English nobility. It must be so exciting hobnobbing with kings and queens and princesses."

Smiling demurely, Natica made light of her new position. "As you know, the gentry comes with its own set of decorum, my dear. It is wonderful, but it can also prove tiring at times."

"What a delightful problem," Sara teased, and they both burst into happy laughter.

"Where are you staying?" Natica asked. "I'll send an invitation for our dinner party as soon as I make the arrangements."

"We have an apartment on the Champs-Élysées," Sara told her. Using the pencil from her dance card she jotted down the address for her friend, and handed her the note.

"Wonderful," Natica said, taking the address. "Well, I must rejoin my group. Perhaps we can find some time later to talk more." Giving Sara another hug, Natica left the table with promises to get together very soon.

Returning her attention to the dancers, Sara noticed Oliver returning, accompanied by a well dressed couple. An air of royalty surrounded them; walking with heads held high, they carried themselves proudly. The attractive woman looked older than Sara – thirty or so, her hair arranged in soft curls under a glittering ruby and diamond tiara, offset by the rich jewels around her neck. Coordinating bracelets and earrings sparkled as she moved under the flickering lights. The gentleman at her side was finely dressed in the requisite dinner jacket. He had a round face, sporting a full beard. Sara adjusted her posture, preparing for the introduction.

"This is my wife," Oliver gestured, arriving at the table. Sara stood and curtseyed. "Prince Albert and Princess Marie, the Duke and Duchess of Edinburgh, visiting from England," Oliver introduced.

"A pleasure," Sara softly bowed her head, glimpsing her family rise from their seats.

"Lovely to meet you," the Duchess said graciously, her upper class accent proclaiming origins other than England – perhaps Russia.

"Congratulations on your marriage," added Prince Albert in a thick baritone. "We wish you many happy and prosperous years together."

Continuing the proper introductions, Oliver acknowledged Sara's family around the table, each offering their welcome to the Duke and Duchess with a befitting curtsey. Sara thought the princess a bit aloof, but was pleased to make her acquaintance. After a few moments of trite conversation the two dispersed for their seats where companions awaited their return.

Oliver grinned at Sara, "They've invited us to stay with them at their castle. Perhaps when spring arrives we can take a trip to England. Would you like that?"

"That would be wonderful," Sara nodded. "I haven't traveled much outside of London. I'm sure we'd meet many interesting people in their circle of friends." Nodding towards Natica's table, she continued, "This must be the night for British royalty. My friend Lady Lister-Kaye is here as well. She's going to have a dinner party in our honor. Won't that be lovely?"

"Indeed it will," Oliver agreed. He waved down a passing servant balancing a tray of bubbling champagne coupes. "Anyone need a fresh drink?" he asked, settling into his seat with the others.

"Oh, why not?" Mrs. Whiting nodded. "Now that we've arrived in Paris, I feel a need to enjoy myself a bit more. It's been quite a hectic year and it's only the end of January." The servant set a glass in front of her, bowing as he left the table.

"One of my colleagues from Bremen is in attendance this evening, a Mr. Harper. I was talking with him about the Rothschild's bank. I hope I didn't keep you women waiting long."

"Not at all," Mrs. Whiting assured him. "We were catching up with our friends. I'm sure you would have been quite bored."

Oliver gave her an easy smile, "Then I'm grateful for my escape from such a discussion."

"Oh look," Mrs. Whiting peered across the ballroom. "I believe that's Mrs. Hitchcock! How lovely to find her in Paris, too. What a wonderful party this is turning out to be. If you'll excuse me, I think I'll go over and visit with her for a bit."

"Of course," Sara waved her mother off. "We'll meet up with you later. Oliver and I have some dancing to attend to." She gave her husband a sweet smile. He responded by discreetly taking her hand under the table.

Mrs. Whiting got up from her heavy chair with the assistance of a footman standing in close attendance.

"Do you mind if we join you?" Jane asked, with a glance at Milly.

"Not at all."

Taking Milly by the hand, Jane followed after Mrs. Whiting, the three ladies melting into the crowded ballroom.

The orchestra finished their tune, and dancers scattered their separate ways. Some moved toward the bounty of food offered on the buffet tables, while others headed for their chairs. A moment later the musicians began a new waltz, and couples reformed on the dance floor.

Oliver held out his hand to Sara, "May I have this dance, Mrs. Belmont?"

"Absolutely," Sara smiled, rising. The footman again assisted with the chair, and she followed Oliver to the ballroom floor, her lovely silk dress rustling as she moved.

Four days later
February 10, 1883
Paris, France

Cigar smoke fogged the dimly lit pub, fusing with the musty smell of mold and opium in the dank basement room. Candles sat on the rickety tables in cheap blue glass jars, flickering shadows hiding the faces of the anonymous patrons. Oliver stared at the dilapidated square of lumber used for a stage, where women swiveled and flexed in their salacious dance. Seductively stripped to expose their voluptuous breasts, leering eyes observed them in the darkened room, ravishing their bodies with lewd imaginations.

Whispers emanated from a back corner next to a rough and weathered door. An unkempt man in tattered clothes sporting a scraggly beard spoke to another man, well dressed, then motioned for an idle dancer sitting near the stage to come toward them.

Focused on their exchange, Oliver watched the dancer and well-dressed man disappear behind the creaking door while he poured himself a drink of absinthe, easily louching the concoction, practiced. He downed it in a swift, easy gulp, his eyes returning to the shabby stage. Watching in lustful fascination, his thoughts drifted.

It had been several weeks since his mother-in-law had arrived with her two daughters. "I thought I could handle it," he murmured, pouring another drink. Tiring of the constant presence of so many women he became frustrated by the arrangement, and left the suite under the ruse of meeting a nameless friend. Instead, he'd sought the solace of the taproom. His tastes in entertainment usually drew him to more upscale establishments, but tonight, he yearned for a break from propriety, wanting to blend in with the commoners.

Sipping his absinthe, he reviewed the events of the past few months; it had been such a whirlwind of travel and celebration. This marriage has afforded me freedom from my Bremen assignment, not to mention a higher allowance from Papa, Oliver thought. If he could endure his mother-in-law's visit, all would be well. Why he had ever agreed to such an arrangement he could not recall, but after being exiled in Germany, he remembered thinking that he was ready to agree to just about anything that would bring him an escape from the drone and drudgery of the bank.

A gaunt and skinny man smelling of urine roused him from his thoughts, stumbling against Oliver's chair on his way to the street. Oliver shifted and sat up with a lazy effort, his feet cold against the stone floor.

A rumbling under Oliver's shoes made the room tilt and he worked to steady himself. Thinking for a moment that there was an earthquake, he stabilized his hands on the table, but the movement continued, finally settling into stillness. Working to control his labored breath, he anxiously remembered stories of the catacombs beneath the city where the graves of millions lay buried in a mass of bone and skulls. Fighting the thought, he clutched his glass, but the idea persisted causing a chill to run down his spine. Oliver was gripped with the certainty that the souls were lurking nearby this deep basement in the subterranean tunnels.

Sweat dripped down his forehead, and he carelessly wiped at it with the back of his hand. A queer sensation moved through his body, a pounding pulsation, and he leaned back into the chair, cramped and uncomfortable. Loud ringing and buzzing grew sharp in his head and he tugged at his ears in an effort to make it abate. The pub took on a freakish green glow and he reached again for his glass. With sick fascination he watched his hand separate from the flesh, as if vaporized, like wax from a burning candle.

Overcome with a peculiar vibration in his limbs, Oliver surrendered to the sensation. It felt as though his soul had detached from his body, leaving him a ghostly, omnipotent entity. Floating above the room, he keenly observed the activity of the hall from the ceiling, shape-shifting into a macabre raven perched in hiding. Hypnotized by the phenomenon, he allowed the feeling to grow. A moment later his entire consciousness merged with the room, the hall itself mutating into a catacomb before his open eyes.

Enthralled, he witnessed the skin melting from the faces of his fellow patrons in the fluctuating glow of light, slowly transforming the men into leering skeletons that smoke and drank, ogling the dancers. Panicked at first, he relaxed, bewitched by the scene, and became one with the dead. One with the sins of the room. The sound of laughter mutated into the wail of tortured souls, the haunting echo roaring in his ears. Cigar smoke swirled and twisted, specters forming out of the curling shapes. Peering in silence at the tormented phantoms, his heart beat as hard and cold as the stone beneath his feet, and he snickered, offering no sympathy for their plight.

Raucous laughter rose from the group seated beside him, breaking the spell, bringing the dance hall back to its original darkened form. Oliver was once again planted in his chair. Shaking his head, he let out a delusional chuckle, entertained by the vision, and poured himself another drink of absinthe while keeping his eyes focused on the nudity of the stage.

Ten days later
February 20, 1883
Paris, France

The fire blazed warmly through the parlor where the family had gathered, sipping tea from fine English china. A pleasant sunny morning had given way to a cloudy afternoon, and the sound of raindrops patted against the window-pane. Sara and Oliver arranged themselves cozily on the love seat, perfectly sized for two people. Jane sat primly in the Queen Anne chair, while Milly relaxed next to Mrs. Whiting on the comfortable, overstuffed sofa.

"Last night's dinner was another success in your introduction as husband and wife to our European friends," Mrs. Whiting took command of the conversation. "Everyone seems very happy with the news of your nuptials."

"Yes," Sara smiled. "Count Turenne seemed very pleased at the course of events. He was so helpful during our courtship."

"He was a supporter of your marriage from the beginning," her mother agreed, bobbing her head. "There are many who were, and I've been delighted to tell them that all has ended well for the two of you."

Sara glanced at Oliver, an air of boredom emitting from his direction. "Don't you agree, Oliver?" she asked, trying to include him in the discussion.

Absently stirring his tea with an ornate silver spoon, Oliver seemed fascinated by the activity. Roused at her question, he worked to feign interest. "Of course my dear," he said lethargically. "It's a delight to be able to parade you around at these parties as my wife."

For a moment Sara wondered if she accurately sensed sarcasm coming from her new husband.

The room grew quiet, a sudden chill charging the atmosphere. Jane adjusted a pillow, but remained silent.

"Well…" Mrs. Whiting set her empty cup ceremoniously on the table beside her. "Jane and Milly and I have luncheon plans. I'm sure you'd be welcome, if the two of you care to join us?"

Sara looked to Oliver for an answer. She was having a hard time deciphering his mood lately, as he'd been pensive. The honeymoon had started off so perfectly, yet she couldn't help noticing he'd grown distracted and remote since the arrival of her family.

He caught her cue. "Thank you, no," Oliver was quick to reply. "I'd like some time with my wife, if that's acceptable to you."

Certain she'd heard an edge in his voice, Sara fought a wave of embarrassment. It was true, their time together had been frequently interrupted by her mother's insistence they engage in social activities, but he'd always enjoyed the entertainment. Besides, things would not always be this way. After a while the parties they were required to attend would be less frequent, and they could return to the romantic evenings they'd shared before her family's arrival in Paris. Surely he knew that.

"Girls, gather your things," Mrs. Whiting instructed. "We're expected at the Rodgers shortly."

"I'm not looking forward to venturing out in this rain," Jane grumbled, but did as she was told.

"You're not made of sugar," Milly smiled, as she rose from her seat. "I'm sure you won't melt." It appeared to Sara that her sister had definitely grown more cheerful since the wedding, while Jane remained her crotchety self.

Ten minutes later the three ladies shuffled out of the suite leaving Sara and Oliver to each other's company for the first time in a week.

She smiled demurely at him, working to lighten the mood, but he did not smile back. Puzzled by his response she tried to ease the tension. "You seem troubled by something, Oliver. Have I displeased you in some way?"

Sluggishly he rose from the seat and walked to the fireplace, its blaze growing weak. "No, my sweet, you have not displeased me." He spoke deliberately, as if it were too exhausting to talk.

"I couldn't help but notice that you seem somewhat gloomy," she continued, watching his heavy manner.

He turned toward the fire, his back to her, and grew quiet.

"Oliver…" her voice was sweet and gentle. "Please tell me what's bothering you." Sara felt the whisper of foreboding and pushed it aside, offering him a soft smile.

Spinning around to face her, Oliver's expression was grim. "Well…" he answered with obvious trepidation, "I scarcely know how to approach you on the matter for fear of offending you."

"Please tell me the problem," she encouraged, although uneasy at his remark. "I should like to help in any way I can."

Returning to the love seat he sat down, rigid, and took her hands in his own. "My dear, I am being most selfish, I suppose…" He paused, glancing around the parlor as if searching for words. "I don't imagine I'll find an easy way to say this, so I guess I should simply be out with it." He hesitated again, taking a breath. "The problem is simply this: I want you all to myself. I've grown uncomfortable sharing our honeymoon suite with your family."

"Oliver!" A gasp escaped her. "You agreed to this months ago. I don't understand what has suddenly changed?" Sara stared at the carpet, her mood shifting to displeasure. "I'm completely enjoying their visit. Mother is making a very concerted effort to proclaim our marriage amongst society, and I for one, am most appreciative of her efforts. Aren't you?"

"Of course I am, Sara," he said quickly, trying to allay her fears. "It just seems that our privacy has been compromised. Have you not noticed that you kiss me less now that your mother is here?"

"Well, I certainly can't be flaunting our romantic encounters in her face," she scoffed. "That would be completely inappropriate."

"What is inappropriate is their very presence in our suite," he frowned. "Your family has distracted us from our honeymoon revelry, and it seems to be taking a toll on my happy mood."

Sara pulled her hand from his, pretending to brush her hair aside. With effort, she spoke in an even tone. "As I said, you were previously in agreement of them sharing our suite."

"At first I was," he assured her. "But now I feel that it's put a damper on our personal activities. We've scarcely been alone since their arrival." His lips were tight, his eyes glazed with discontent. "Sara, I'm the man of the house. I should be the one making the decisions in regard to our affairs and activities. I feel as though I'm a little boy, constantly taking instructions from your mother. It's as though I've jumped from the frying pan into the fire. I'd had enough with my own parents controlling my life. Now your mother has replaced the position. It's emasculating at best."

Stunned by his admission, Sara wavered. "It won't be long-lived," she argued, working to understand his position. "They only plan to be here for a month or so, then they'll be returning to the States. We can follow at our leisure and take up housekeeping at that point. You'll not have to concern yourself over such matters then."

"I don't want to wait!" Oliver's voice was hard, unyielding. Throwing his hands in the air, he got up from the seat, frustrated. Pacing the carpet in front of her, he glanced around the room, exasperated with the conversation. The liquor decanters on the sideboard caught his attention and he reached for a bottle. Carelessly he splashed scotch into a glass, then gulped it in one long breath.

Watching him, Sara grew cautious of his demeanor. He reached for the bottle again, and quickly downed another drink. Baffled and leery of his behavior, she flinched when he spun on his heel, stepping quickly toward her.

"Why not let me lease them an apartment of their own?" he asked point blank, hoping to find a solution that would suit them both. "I'd be happy to cover the rent. Perhaps there's an opening in this very building."

"You must be joking," Sara's eyes grew wide at the proposal. "That would hurt my mother's feelings very deeply – and embarrass me. They've traveled here to announce us to society. She would most certainly be offended. I really can't agree to that."

"Then you and I will get another apartment." His eyes beseeched her, perspiration beading on his forehead. "They can stay on in this suite, with absolutely no inconvenience to them."

"I simply cannot believe what you're suggesting," Sara objected. "I thought you liked my family." She stared at him, confused by her allegiances.

"I do. I do..." he assured her. "It's just that I miss our special moments together. Surely you can understand how I feel. They've cramped our honeymoon. I just don't feel it's appropriate for them to be sharing the suite with us now. How can I make you understand?"

She fought against the shrillness in her voice, "But you agreed to this!"

"Now I'm changing my mind," Oliver's jaw clenched. "This is a special time in our lives, and a very private time as well. I simply do not want to share it with your mother and your sisters. It's perfectly reasonable to want you to myself on our honeymoon. Your mother's attention to a long-dissolved family tradition is wearing on my peace of mind. I should be much happier if we were to have a place of our own to continue our holiday. We can still see them often, but we'd be afforded more privacy to devote to matrimonial pleasures."

"Is that what this is all about?" Sara spat the words. "Are you not getting your physical desires fulfilled in a way you would prefer?"

"My dear…" Oliver began earnestly, "Is that so unreasonable, or so difficult for you to understand? I'll be most happy to pay for another apartment out of my own pocket."

"My mother does *not* need your charity!" Sara's anger peaked. "I simply must refuse your request."

"And I must insist upon it!" Oliver barked.

Sara recoiled, suddenly wary of him. She had never heard him direct that tone toward her before.

"You are my wife! And I will make the rules that dictate our decisions."

Losing her patience, Sara rose from the love seat and fiercely threw a pin-tucked pillow back onto the sofa.

"And I will *not* ask my family to leave our apartment. Now that you've escaped your father's leash, it appears you have no further need for my family. Well, I *do* – particularly now that you've become so unpredictable."

She walked toward the bedroom, her loud, deliberate footsteps reverberating through the hallway. Oliver followed quickly behind. He reached to grab her arm, angry and rough, bruising her delicate skin.

"I will make arrangements for another suite immediately," he commanded. "And you will do as I say in this matter, so pack your things. It's what's best for both of us. And for our marriage!"

Sara jerked her arm free of his grasp, growing frightened of him. "How dare you detain me in such an ungentlemanly fashion." She rubbed her arm to ease the pain. "The only problem I can see is all the liquor you've been drinking! That poison, absinthe, you're consuming night and day is affecting your judgment! It's making you crazy – causing your very personality to change! I'm afraid to be alone with you for fear of your conduct. For that reason alone, I prefer my family remain here." [2]

"You're being impertinent!" he growled.

"It's the truth! You've never behaved this way in all the time I've known you!" She glared at him, holding her ground. "My family is not imposing on us in any way, and they will stay here with us according to our original plans."

She headed for the bedchamber, and Oliver grabbed her arm again, pulling her back.

"You're hurting me!" she cried, struggling to escape his hold. "You brute, let me go!"

Breaking free of his grasp she rushed toward the bedroom, fearing for her safety.

"How dare you treat me in such an abhorrent manner!" Sara yelled, "and don't think you'll be sharing my bed after treating me so cruelly!" [3]

"You're my wife now – I'll treat you as I wish! And I'll sleep wherever I choose!" Oliver's tone boomed with belligerence. "And you will take instructions from me! Not the other way around!"

Tears streaming down her face, Sara escaped to their bedchamber, slamming the door behind her. Oliver heard the lock latch, the sound echoing throughout the apartment.

Overcome with rage, he grabbed a delicate Chinese vase sitting on the hallway table, and slammed it with all his might against the locked door. Shards of ceramic splintered onto the floor in noisy disarray. He stood there, sweating, a victim of his temper, his breath surging in heavy gasps. Turning for the foyer, he grabbed his hat and stormed out of the suite, slamming the door even louder than Sara had done just moments before.

CHAPTER FOUR

The next day
February 21, 1883
Paris, France

MOVING ACROSS THE COLD BEDROOM floorboards, Sara caught her reflection in the vanity mirror and absently raised her hand to swipe the hair from her face. Studying her image, she was dismayed at the sight of dark circles under her eyes, unwelcome guests on her countenance. I look as though I've aged ten years, she thought in chagrin, patting at her cheeks. Pulling up the sleeve of her nightgown, she examined the painful bruises on her arm, purple and swollen.

The gray light of morning was just beginning to peek through the shades. Gloomy, it held no promise of affection. A perfunctory glance across the room revealed the undisturbed side of the bed where Oliver had previously slept, now conspicuously noticeable.

The clock read six-thirty, still too early for her mother or sisters to be awake. Impulsively, she decided to slip out of the suite for a while, the idea of French coffee coaxing her on. Perhaps a walk in the fresh air would help to clear her head, to better consider what had transpired.

Splashing her face with cold water she slipped on a clean morning dress. Working to unlock the door quietly, she left her chamber on tiptoe. Moving stealthily toward the sitting room, she frowned at the sight of Oliver dozing, rumpled and sprawled on the sofa. He wore the same clothes from yesterday, his hair oily and mussed. The curdled smell of liquor and cigar smoke filled Sara's nostrils, apparently coming from his direction. Oliver stirred, sensing her, and opened an eye. She stared at him with harsh judgment from the doorway. Scowling, he returned her look of displeasure, while brushing at his lapel.

"A bit early for you, isn't it?" he asked, in a tone thick with aspersion.

Folding her arms across her chest in a protective stance, she wondered if he was still drunk. "Where did you go all night?"

He arched an eyebrow, "I don't see where that's any concern of yours, especially since you've refused me entry into our bed – in a suite I'm paying for, by the way." His voice was deep and rough. He sat up, running his hands through his hair in an effort to straighten his appearance. "I'll sleep where I wish under such circumstances."

"I suppose it's no use trying to talk reasonably with you, Oliver." Sara frowned at his foul mood while summoning her courage. Working to appear bold, she hid the fear he'd instilled in her as a result of his mistreatment. "I suppose you need time to sleep it off." Turning for the door, she said, "I'm going down to the bakery. I need some fresh air." Taking a step, she paused, "But I must remind you, this isn't the navy. You're a gentleman – at least I thought you were," she accused, "and a married man. That entails responsibilities – marital responsibilities." She cut short, surveying him with fresh eyes, realization dawning on her. "I hope you weren't back at that brothel that disguises itself as a casino." [4]

He shook his head and quietly smirked, "What do you know of such matters? An innocent such as yourself is only a pawn for gossip and rumors."

Insulted, she shook her head, lips turned in a frown. "I've had quite enough of this conversation," Sara said coldly.

She stepped to the door, refusing to endure another moment of his indignities, and left the apartment. Once in the corridor, Sara gulped away the tears searing her eyes. "A walk alone in the morning air is just what I need," she whispered. Some time away from everyone would allow her to collect herself, and figure out how to deal with her predicament.

Reaching the sidewalk a cool breeze hit her face, and she walked faster. *Who is that man sitting in my suite, disguising himself as my husband?* He certainly didn't resemble the Oliver she'd traveled to Paris with only a month before. *How could things have taken such a nightmarish turn* within such a short time? Had Oliver only married her to escape his father's control? Could the presence of her family really be the cause of these bad feelings between them, or was there something more going on that she wasn't aware of?

Blind to the beauty of the morning sun rising over the Paris rue, a memory flashed of the absinthe bottle, as icy fear struck her heart in confirmation.

Four days later
February 24, 1883
New York, New York

Ringing the bell on the porch, Mrs. Belmont was promptly greeted by an English butler. Wearing a perfectly pressed suit, he stood tall, holding his spine straight.

"Good afternoon, madam. Mrs. Cushing is expecting you. If you'll follow me into the parlor."

"Thank you," Caroline said, stepping into the foyer. She removed her coat, handing it off to the butler, then followed him into the opulent sitting room, decorated like so many others of her New York friends.

"Please, make yourself comfortable and I'll let Mrs. Cushing know that you're here." The butler bowed, leaving the room. Caroline removed her gloves, and settled into the comfortable sofa.

"Mrs. Belmont..." her hostess breezed into the room. "How lovely it is to have this chance to visit."

Mrs. Cushing greeted her guest with a warm handshake. A maid carrying a tray laden with a teapot and all the necessary accoutrements followed her closely.

"It was lovely of you to invite me," Caroline smiled. "I don't socialize much these days, but you and I have always been friends."

"True enough," Mrs. Cushing nodded. "We're both cut from the same societal cloth. That in itself breeds a welcome comfort to us both."

The maid poured the tea, ceremoniously placing a cup in front of each woman.

"How is August?" Mrs. Cushing asked, quickly adding two heaping teaspoons of sugar, and a dab of fresh cream to her tea. "He and Thomas are always making the newspapers regarding politics or banking."

"Yes, the reporters grow rather tiresome," Mrs. Belmont acknowledged, catching the eye of her hostess. "August is fine, but as you said, he keeps very busy."

"Yes, as does Thomas," Mrs. Cushing fought a devilish grin, "but they do tend to keep us surrounded by the style we're most accustomed to."

"Indeed," Mrs. Belmont agreed, returning her smile. She sipped her tea, enjoying its brisk flavor.

"And the newlyweds? Have you heard anything from them? On honeymoon in Paris, I understand."

"I just received a letter from them yesterday. I'm happy to announce that they seem quite well. Just between us, I think we narrowly avoided a scandal over that engagement."

"Oh, pish-posh," Mrs. Cushing brushed away the comment. "Sometimes young people just need a little shove in the right direction."

"Whether they like it or not!"

"True," replied her friend with a nod. "The wedding was quite lovely. I've never traveled to Newport in the winter, but the town was very festive at Christmas time. Perhaps you've started a new trend."

"I'm not sure about that, but the ceremony did turn out nicely. I tried to persuade them to hold the wedding in New York, but Sara wanted to have the celebration in her family home."

"All's well that ends well," Mrs. Cushing offered. "I'm glad to find they're enjoying a pleasant honeymoon. When I heard the bride's family was joining the couple, I had some misgivings." She pursed her lips, tsking softly. "Such an odd idea… Perhaps Mrs. Whiting finds it hard to release Sara to marriage."

The ladies shared a chuckle. "I couldn't tell you. I expressed my concerns, but Oliver didn't seem to mind, so why should I? I'm relieved now that they're away, I can focus on other matters."

"I couldn't agree more. By the way, Thomas and I are going abroad in a few months."

"Where are you off to?" Mrs. Belmont asked politely.

"He has some business in London, and then we're going to take a holiday in Spain. Madrid and Barcelona beckon us. It will be a nice change of scenery. How about you? Any plans for travel?"

"No, not currently. I think I'll stay in the States for a while. I thought I'd go up to Newport when the weather breaks and open the house. Right now, I'm more in the mood to rest. The rigors of travel can be exhausting at times, as you well know."

"Indeed I do," Mrs. Cushing agreed. Setting her empty cup on the table, she assessed Mrs. Belmont. "I'm delighted to see you looking well. We really should try to get together more often. It seems like time is just flying by these days."

"Yes, we must make plans to visit again soon," Mrs. Belmont said, rising. Her hostess walked her to the parlor door where the butler appeared out of thin air, prepared to escort her to the home's entrance. "I'll write next week and we'll plan a lunch. How does that sound?"

"Wonderful," Mrs. Cushing confirmed. "I'll check my schedule and we'll arrange a time."

The next day
February 25, 1883
Paris, France

With a glance over her shoulder, Mrs. Whiting noticed Sara trying on a buckram hat. "That one is a lovely color," she said, "and very much in vogue. It would make a perfect addition to your wardrobe."

"I already have one this shade of blue," Sara shrugged. Her voice was hollow as she replaced the hat on its display stand. Moving from the mirror, she meandered listlessly around the store, indifferent to the wares on display. "Can we go now?" she asked. "I'm growing bored with the shops."

"You? Bored shopping?" her mother replied, but acquiesced, following her daughter out into the hectic Paris street. Moving down the sidewalk, Mrs. Whiting eyed her with concern.

"Sara... dear," she began gingerly. "I don't want to pry, but I can't help noticing that you and Oliver have been spending much less time together. He seems to be frequently absent from the apartment." With new determination, Mrs. Whiting continued, "To be honest, I'm getting worried about your health. You don't look well. With those circles under your eyes, I wonder if you're not sleeping well."

Sara blushed, embarrassment showing on her cheeks. "I'm fine, Mother." She tried to make light of the question. "It's nothing for you to concern yourself with."

"But I *am* concerned," Mrs. Whiting insisted. "I must admit that I've overheard you and Oliver arguing, and one can't miss the fact that he's been sleeping on the sofa instead of with you in your bedroom, the way young married couples should do."

Staring at the ground, Sara knew if she looked at her mother her misery would become obvious to her maternal inspection. "I'm sorry if we've disturbed you in some way, but I assure you, it's nothing for you to worry about."

Sara's head started to pound, her memory fresh from the argument of the night before. In the middle of the night a loud banging coming from the sitting room had awoken her. Sara went to check on it and found Oliver slamming his absinthe bottle on the table, apparently frustrated that it was now empty. It was clear to her from the crazed look in his eyes, that he'd consumed all the liquor.

The memory of their dispute flashed through her mind...

"Oliver – whatever are you making such a ruckus about?" she asked in an urgent whisper, rubbing the sleep from her eyes. "You're going to wake the entire family with your noise."

"Oh my!" Oliver responded loudly, sarcasm thick in his words. "I should never want to disturb your precious family."

"Shhh!" she insisted. "You've been drinking again. Why on earth do you continue to conduct yourself in such an ungentlemanly fashion? Are you determined to humiliate me in front of my mother and sisters, not to mention the servants?"

In response, Oliver stared at the empty bottle in his hand. "I would never want to cause you humiliation, my dear." With that he threw the bottle against the wall in one quick and violent movement.

Sara started to tremble, frightened by yet another act of his unpredictable temper. She wondered for a brief moment if she was safe, alone in this room with him. It was most certain that the noise had disturbed her family, and she worried they would try to intervene. Desperately she sought a way to quietly calm him from his agitated state.

Like a jack-in-the-box, he sprang from his seat, startling her, and moved quickly to her side. "Do I humiliate you, now?" he leered in front of her face, his breath foul, his expression contorted and grotesque. "I thought you would love me forever – and obey me. Isn't that what you said?"

"Oliver, please calm down! You're drunk, again." Sara tried to control the fear flooding her mind. Never in her entire life had she been exposed to such inebriation. It left her stunned and confused as to how to handle him.

"Why don't you lay down and sleep," she said in the sweetest voice she could muster.

"Certainly. As long as I'm sleeping in my own bed! Not on this lumpy sofa!" Oliver narrowed his eyes, giving her an accusatory look. "But, clearly you've chosen your mother and sisters' comfort over your husband's needs."

"That is absolutely not true! Must I remind you again, you agreed to this arrangement. Now that you've escaped your father – you've changed your mind and want to throw my family out. Frankly, I'm too frightened to be alone with you now!"

"Oh, you think you've got this all figured out, don't you?" he sneered.

Afraid to broach the subject further in his current state of mind, she took a deep breath and worked to cajole him, "Just try to sleep. Can't we talk about this in the morning when you've had some rest?"

Who was this stranger, stinking of liquor? Where had her loving husband disappeared to?

He grabbed her arm again and squeezed hard. "If I can't share your bed, then you're not my wife. Divorce is always an option," he threatened. "Perhaps I should go find a new wife who is more accommodating to her husband, concerning herself less with her mother's business. Time to cut the apron strings, don't you think Sara?"

He flung her arm free with a force that sent her reeling back a few steps and she'd stumbled, laboring to regain her balance. Realizing too late the extent of his irrational mood, Sara accepted that she wouldn't be able to do anything with him until the absinthe had released its grip on his brain.

Oliver had turned, frowning as he stumbled back toward the divan. Sara quickly took the opportunity to escape, stealthily slipping into their bedroom, soundly locking the door behind her from the demon he'd become.

Her mother began to speak again, rousing Sara from the bitter recollection.

"There's a period of adjustment after vows are exchanged," Mrs. Whiting began. "It's a time for a husband and wife to learn more of each other, oftentimes things are revealed that they'd never known before. It takes some effort to accommodate each other's quirks and temperament." Sara felt her mother glance at her, but again, she avoided meeting her eye.

"I'm sure you're quite right, Mother," Sara wanted to be agreeable, but devoutly wished for a change of discussion. "I'm certain it's nothing more than a marital adjustment period. Don't worry, Oliver and I will work this through just fine."

Mrs. Whiting began to speak again, but Sara interrupted her, raising a hand for silence. "Please Mother – if you don't mind, I really would prefer changing the subject. This topic is growing rather tiresome."

Mrs. Whiting restrained her words, mouth drawn tight, and said nothing. Silent, she continued to walk in step next to her troubled daughter.

CHAPTER FIVE

Three days later
February 28, 1883
Paris, France

THE BEAUTIFUL SINGING VOICES OF the two women rose from the stage, enchanting the audience with the strains of the 'Flower Duet'. The music resounded gloriously through the large, darkened concert hall of *Salle Favart*. Sara sat in the velvet chair beside Oliver, witnessing the Paris debut of Leo Delibes' opera *Lakmé* with her family.

They'd all been invited to dine last night with the Rothschilds. The banking tycoon had graciously offered his opera box for an evening of entertainment. Mr. Rothschild had been called back to Germany today unexpectedly, where he was needed on business, preventing him from catching the premier. He had insisted they attend tonight's performance for the opera's opening rather than leave the box empty, especially since the show was being touted as the best of the year.

Oliver had accepted the invitation, much to Sara's delight. And he was in a pleasant mood this evening, smiling and happy like his old self, leaving Sara hopeful things would return to the way they'd been at the start of their holiday. Perhaps her mother was right; a period of adjustment was needed for newlyweds. Sara certainly wished as much, although it seemed that Oliver was frequently absent since their argument over her family's visit.

She pushed the bad times from her mind, happy he was here now joining them at the opera's debut. Perhaps it was Mr. Rothschild's involvement that caused him to be agreeable to the outing. It didn't make a difference why, she thought, happy to be attending the concert.

She glanced at him in the darkness, and he smiled back, bringing a sigh of relief to her heart. This was the man she'd fallen in love with and married. Listening to the beautiful music she felt hopeful of better times between them and allowed herself to enjoy some peace – a welcome relief from Oliver's moodiness.

Stealing a silent look at her family she could see they were engrossed in the opera's music as well. Jane watched the stage captivated, a soft smile on her face. Milly sitting beside her, looked quite lovely in her new Chantilly lace gown and hat. Her sisters passed the spyglasses back and forth, taking turns to view the show up close through the lens. The curtain fell, and the house lights went up, her quiet thoughts returning to the realities of life outside the theatre.

"What a wonderful performance," Mrs. Whiting chirped, rising from her seat. "It's certain to be a classic. I really do enjoy the arts so much more here in France."

Oliver nodded in agreement, lending a hand to help Sara from her seat. "Very nice indeed," he said, "and I don't usually care much for opera."

He was being wonderful, she thought, as he offered his arm. Her family departed the theatre box, and he paused, pulling her aside.

"Did you enjoy the performance?"

"Yes, very much," Sara nodded, her eyes smiling. "It was lovely. The *Flower Duet* was my favorite part. Among all the instruments, the human voice is the most expressive."

"Those women certainly did the composition justice. Their voices were marvelous." He helped her with her cloak. "How do you feel about getting some dinner?" he asked, "just the two of us?"

"That might be nice." The idea of spending some private time with Oliver in his good mood was very appealing. Although she didn't want to offend her family by going off without them, she didn't think they'd mind.

"I'd like to have some time with you, alone," Oliver professed. "Your family is amicable, but we're on our honeymoon. I'm sure they'll understand. There's a lovely restaurant just around the corner on the Rue Peletier that I think you'd really enjoy. The food is fantastic. What do you say?"

Pleased by the invitation, Sara decided to focus her attention on her bridegroom this evening, instead of her visiting family. "I'd like that very much, Oliver," she consented, smiling demurely. Finally, she thought, my sweet husband is back.

Returning her smile, he wrapped her arm around his and led her from the theatre box into the carpeted hallway. Mrs. Whiting was talking to an old friend from New York, Mrs. Plunkett, recently arrived in Paris for the show. As Sara approached, she overheard Mrs. Plunkett invite the family for cocktails and supper at the Hôtel Ritz.

"That sounds like a lovely idea," Mrs. Whiting accepted. "It'll give us a chance to catch up on the newest gossip from New York."

"Well, your daughter's wedding was certainly on everyone's lips," she heard the older woman say, discreetly keeping mum that part of the scuttle-butt pertained to Mrs. Whiting herself, roosting in the newlywed's apartment. "It was the news of the season – at least for a while," Mrs. Plunkett dangled this last tidbit.

"Oh?" Mrs. Whiting's face perked up in curiosity. "Do tell."

"Alva Vanderbilt's causing quite a stir – who else? That woman lives to be the center of attention," Mrs. Plunkett rolled her eyes. "She's captured everyone's imagination with plans for an enormous masquerade ball at the end of March – the twenty-sixth, I believe – the day after Easter. Excitement for the party is spreading like wildfire. The set is all abuzz, curious to see the inside of the new house she's built on Fifth Avenue. It's simply spectacular from the street – a regular castle, if I do say so myself."

Catching sight of Sara on Oliver's arm, Mrs. Plunkett waved them over. "Here are the two lovebirds now," she cooed. "Sara, Oliver – how are you enjoying your honeymoon?"

"We're having a lovely holiday, thank you." Sara smiled politely, and for the first time in days it was true. "Paris is the city for romance, you know."

"Indeed it is," Mrs. Plunkett agreed. "And you, Oliver? How is married life treating you?" She flashed him a warm smile, searching his demeanor for any hint of discord, hoping for fuel to fire up the gossip grapevine.

"Married life is wonderful Mrs. Plunkett, thank you for asking," he answered in a syrupy tone. He turned to Sara, patting her arm with no sign of discontent.

"You must join us for some refreshments at the Ritz," she insisted. "I should like to raise a glass of champagne – a toast in your honor."

Oliver turned to Sara, his expression unfathomable. Knowing he'd just asked her to a private dinner, she was torn between the two invitations. In his good mood she was loathe to upset him by changing their plans, and hesitated. But, if the truth be told, she didn't want to miss a chance to join the party either, as the night was still young.

"Thank you, but not tonight. I hope you'll excuse us," Oliver answered. "We've made plans for the evening, but we'd love to join you another time."

Disappointment passed over Mrs. Plunkett's face, her eyes jumping from Oliver to Sara. "What terrible luck. Well, perhaps we can arrange a celebration sometime next week."

"That would be most agreeable, Mrs. Plunkett," Oliver said. "Send a note and we'll make plans that accommodate both our schedules."

Sara caught Mrs. Whiting's questioning look. Her mother, unaware Oliver had invited Sara for a private dinner, eyed him curiously, as if trying to remember what their prior engagement might be. "Are you absolutely certain you won't join us?" she asked, entreating first Sara, then Oliver.

"No, thank you." Oliver was firm. "Not tonight."

In a flurry of polite 'good-byes' the group dispersed, the Whitings bustling off with Mrs. Plunkett, who joined her husband at the bottom of the staircase. Watching them leave, Sara obediently followed Oliver out to the street.

"I should have liked to have gone with them," she said wistfully. "And catch up on the news."

"But we've made dinner plans…" Oliver's smile faded. He studied her face quietly under the street lamp. "I understand…" he shook his head impatiently, "You'd prefer to be out and about with your family, rather than spending time alone with me." The atmosphere shifted between them, turning tense and chilly. "My dear, you really must decide where your loyalties lie. Now that we're married, of course I think they should be with me, and most certainly while on our honeymoon."

"I didn't think marriage would dictate that I had to choose between the two, when both are a priority to me. Nor did I realize you'd become so disagreeable concerning socializing with my family. Of course, you have no such concerns, coming and going as you please. I'm beginning to think I don't have any say in how I spend my days – or with whom." She regarded him, coolly, "You've changed, Oliver. It's as though you've become a stranger to me."

His eyes grew dark and brooding, his mouth sealed in a tight smile, "That's precisely why we're going to dinner – alone. It'll give us a chance to rekindle our romance without being surrounded by others. Then perhaps we can rent a hotel suite near the restaurant and share a quiet night together, reminiscent of the start of our holiday."

"I told you, I'm fine with the living arrangements as they are," Sara's anger sparked to life. "My mother will worry if I don't return this evening. Besides, I don't have any luggage for an overnight stay."

"It's easy enough to send a note – and a footman to collect your things. Your maid can pack you a bag."

"Is that why you've invited me to dinner?" Sara glared at him. "Are you trying to trick me into having your way with things?"

Oliver remained silent.

She pulled on her gloves, refusing to meet his eye. "If I were to agree to a separate apartment, this isn't the way I'd go about it. I'd much prefer speaking to my mother in person, so as not to hurt her feelings."

A brisk wind blew at the couple confronting each other on the sidewalk. Oliver turned and waved his arm for a taxi.

"Have it your way, then," he snapped. Not waiting for the driver, Oliver pulled open the coach door, ushering her inside.

Sara climbed into the carriage, and Oliver followed. "*Café de la Paix*," he ordered to the driver in a sharp tone. The coach instantly hurdled into motion.

Sara took pause, surprised to hear him instruct the driver to take them to the wine bar, in the opposite direction of Rue Peletier and the restaurant he'd raved about, as originally planned. She didn't speak and Oliver didn't offer any explanation. Sitting with him in thick silence she felt resentful, too cross to question or argue.

The carriage pulled up to the curb at their destination, and Oliver jumped out in a flash. Sara moved to join him, when the coach door slammed in her face. Oliver's voice reached her, instructing the driver to return her to the apartment. Before she could object, the horses began trotting off into the winter night, snorting at the cold.

Turning, she watched through the window as Oliver sauntered into the club. Furious tears filled her eyes. Her only consolation was the knowledge that her family was out, and she wouldn't have to explain why she'd returned home alone.

The ride to the apartment was spent in a jumble of emotions. Letting herself into the suite, she removed her coat, hat and gloves, haphazardly throwing them in a pile on a chair near the foyer. Struggling with anger and sadness, she ceased to try to understand the events of the evening.

Changing into a housedress, Sara endured a now-pounding headache. Casually glancing at the clock on the mantle, she noted the time, only ten o'clock; still early compared to the all-night balls of New York. Yet here she was, alone at home. Perusing the books on the shelf for entertainment, she found nothing that interested her, so decided to write a few letters instead.

Sitting at the desk, Sara opened the drawer and removed a piece of new stationery embossed with her married name. She gazed at the paper bearing the title she'd so long coveted. Dipping the pen into the inkwell, she began to write a note to Oliver's mother.

After a few moment's consideration, she thought it best to be direct and honest. Carefully choosing her words, she relayed to Mrs. Belmont the dilemma emerging from Oliver's moods. Sara explained the situation, concluding it appeared to be the result of a problem with liquor. She disclosed her tale, and admitted to Mrs. Belmont that, "I can do absolutely nothing with him. I have tried my best, but he is past listening to reason." [5]

The words on the page blurred as she fought against her confusion, working to be strong. Bitter tears fell on the wooden desktop, unbidden, and she threw the pen on the desk, surrendering to her grief. Allowing her emotions to flow unrestrained, Sara quietly sobbed. What use was it to keep her despair caged inside her? Such a chore required too much effort for her weary mind. Alone in the suite, she freely released her dismay at the unhappy evening, and the condition of her new marriage.

Not expecting Oliver's return, as had become his habit, Sara heard the clock strike midnight, and wondered when her family would get back, imagining the fun time they must be enjoying. Drying her face, she composed herself, and headed to the kitchen for a drink of water.

Walking through the hall past the sitting room, she heard the sound of the key in the door. Expecting her mother and sisters, Sara grew wary when Oliver entered the room. It was clear he'd been drinking, and he carried another sack under his arm which she assumed was more absinthe.

"Good evening, my sweet," he said in an overly polite voice. "I've decided to return early and enjoy my refreshments here at home tonight, in our little love nest. After all, I'm paying the rent." He opened the bag and removed the liquor.

Just as she'd thought: absinthe.

Cautious, Sara regarded him with growing uneasiness. He was being too friendly, considering their argument, making her nervous and suspicious. She now knew enough not to agitate him in this mood, mentally comparing him to a stick of dynamite – dangerous, and ready to explode.

"Why don't you let your guard down for just a moment," he wheedled, "and join me for a drink? I think you'll find it enjoyable, and most delicious."

He looked at her, waiting for an answer, but Sara only shook her head 'no'.

"As you wish," he shrugged. Ambling over to the sideboard he mixed the concoction with precision.

Sara quietly left the room and went to the kitchen. Her hands trembled as she filled a glass with water, spilling half the contents on the countertop. Taking a sip from the glass she paused, then returned through the hallway. Passing the sitting room, she moved toward the bedroom with a sideways glance at Oliver.

"Sara!" he nearly shouted. "We really must talk."

"What would you like to talk about, Oliver?" she asked, pausing at the edge of the parlor. His pupils were dark and dilated, and his eyes were unfocused, seeming to spin wildly in his head. It gave him the appearance of a caricature, not unlike an ugly newspaper cartoon. Cold fear washed over her, giving her pause. With the absinthe coursing through his blood, Sara braced herself, knowing he wouldn't speak rationally.

"I've decided to forgive you your rudeness this evening, not to mention refusing me permission to join you in our bed," he slurred. "Tonight we'll begin fresh, as though it's our wedding night."

Sara recoiled, repulsed and terrified by his words. She could never allow this monster to come near her, let alone kiss her. Her mind raced for an escape and she viewed the bedroom door with its strong lock.

Oliver sensed her loathing, and swiftly rose from the sofa, moving toward her.

"Yes, that's exactly what we'll do..."

He reached to embrace her. Sara moved to dodge him. He caught her arm, pulling her back hard against him, and began kissing her on the neck. Her hands in fists, she fought to evade him, but his hold was too strong.

"Kiss me the way you did on our wedding night," he growled.

"Stop!" Her voice was weak as she worked to free herself, wrenching her shoulder as she struggled against his strength. "How could I ever kiss you in this state, Oliver? You reek of spirits. Let me go!" she cried in vain. "I know you've been spending your nights in brothels – a place no man in your position should go!" She fought against his hold, sickened by the sour odor of alcohol.

"Then you are not my wife!" he shouted, his hot breath on her face. "You are *not* my wife!" [6] He released her from his grip, throwing her against the wall.

She reeled from his force, bounced against the wainscot and fell to the floor, battered. His anger unleashed, he approached her with hand raised, and slapped her hard, again and again. Sara fought against his strength, screaming in protest.

The door to the apartment opened and Mrs. Whiting stood there with Jane and Milly, shocked by the scene playing out before them.

"Oh, how perfect!" Oliver sneered, lowering his hand. "Here's your rescue party."

He stomped to their bedroom, slamming the open door against the wall, all the while yelling at Sara.

"You are *not* my wife!" he shouted. "I'll see to that, you can be sure!"

"What's going on in here?" Mrs. Whiting asked, although no explanation was needed. "Girls, go to your rooms," she ordered Jane and Milly. "I'll handle this." Mrs. Whiting quickly closed the apartment door in an effort to keep the argument private.

Stunned by the assault, Sara worked to get up, her back aching, her face swollen and red. Ashamed, she felt debased in front of her family, and whimpered quietly.

This was her fault. If only she'd gone to dinner with Oliver, she thought in retrospect. He'd seemed like his old self tonight, for just a bit; perhaps his fury could have been avoided. Sara stood in the hallway like a rag doll, catching her mother's eye. Mrs. Whiting cast her a warning look, motioning for her to stay still.

Oliver shouted from the bedroom, "Sara, I must insist we move into an apartment of our own, or I'll create a scandal for all of you to deal with," his furious threats now aimed at Mrs. Whiting. "I'll hire a lawyer and file for a divorce. Then let society decide if a mother should follow her daughter on her honeymoon." [7]

Mrs. Whiting recoiled, initially insulted, then cautiously worked to pacify him.

"Try to calm down," Mrs. Whiting said softly, "and think more prudently about what you're saying. Perhaps you should speak with your father before making such a rash move." [8]

Sara watched Oliver throw his clothes in a suitcase, ignoring his mother-in-law.

"I simply cannot endure this a minute longer!" he yelled. "I only agreed to marry one woman – not four!"

Having seen many a man in a drunken rage, Mrs. Whiting knew from experience the best thing to do was to stay out of his way.

Marching from the bedroom, Oliver dragged the packed suitcase behind him. "If you won't stand beside me like a proper wife, instead choosing your mother, then I'm forced into only one solution – and that is to leave here immediately! I won't have you ganging up on me." He glared from one woman, to the other. "I'm leaving for a few days to think things over. I suggest you do the same." [9]

"Where are you going?" Mrs. Whiting intervened.

"London, or Nice – anywhere but here!"

"Oliver – wait!" Sara pleaded, "you're being irrational! Stay and get some rest."

She reached for his arm in an effort to stop him, but he shook her off, snarling like an angry dog, and threw her again with great force. Sara's body banged against the wall and she crumpled, hitting the floor with a cry.

"Let me know if you change your mind about your loyalties!" he sneered.

Mrs. Whiting rushed to Sara's side. The two women looked up in time to see the apartment door slam.

CHAPTER SIX

Two days later
March 2, 1883
Paris, France

"THIS IS A TRAGEDY, EDITH," Sara fought against her bitterness. "How could Mr. Stevens' mother cancel your wedding like this? I can't believe the nerve of that woman."

She handed her friend a cup of strong, steaming tea.

Edith dabbed at her eyes, her lace handkerchief damp. "The engagement was announced and the wedding date was set for next year. Everything was perfect, or so it seemed. The next thing I know, Henry's mother was pushing back the date. I went along with it to appease her. But now this!" She shook her head in disbelief. "Mrs. Stevens invited us to dinner and announced that the wedding has been postponed indefinitely. In my book, that's as good as cancelled!"[10] Edith sipped from her cup, the china rattling under her shaking hands. "The next thing I knew I'd received your letter explaining what'd happened between you and Oliver. Well, I was just horrified at the news!" Edith paused, giving her friend an apologetic look. "Oh Sara, I'm the one who should be comforting you."

"I suppose we can comfort each other," Sara replied in resignation.

"But you're already married! What are you going to do if word of this gets out?"

"I really don't know. I must confess, I'm at a perfect loss as to how to handle this mess. There's only so much I can do to prevent the truth from getting into the hands of the gossipmongers – or worse, the newspapers.

I don't have to tell you, that could prove to be disastrous for both the Whiting and the Belmont families."

"How could Oliver just up and leave you like this – on your honeymoon, no less." Edith shook her head, outraged. "It is simply inexcusable conduct for a man of his stature."

"Oh Edith, he was perfectly horrible after my family arrived, constantly complaining about them, even though he'd agreed to let them stay with us. I was so embarrassed. I tried to hide it, but his outbursts grew more frequent – and violent. His behavior became totally unpredictable." Sara kept quiet about Oliver's visits to the city's brothels, too ashamed to speak of it. "I've never seen a man's personality change so markedly. I simply didn't know how to handle it."

Edith turned, concern in her eyes, "He didn't hurt you did he?"

Pulling at the cuff of her long-sleeved sweater, Sara bristled, "I was bruised and sore. The truth be told, I'm terrified of the man – my own husband!" She leaned forward, imploring her friend, "What should I do if he does return and asks for my forgiveness? I am in perfect terror of what he might do.[11] Oliver's moods are as changeable as the weather – suppose he turns violent again, this time seriously injuring me – or worse?" Sara rubbed her temple, working to ease her mind. "I want my marriage back, really I do. But Oliver is prone to acting like a madman at times, and I don't think I can endure another of his episodes."

"You shouldn't have to!" Edith exclaimed, indignant. "No woman should have to live in fear of her husband harming her. I can't imagine what's caused such a change in Oliver's temperament. He always seemed so easy going and fun-loving. He's never shown any sign of an ugly temper before." [12]

"I know the reason," Sara divulged. "Absinthe. He was always drinking it. He must have discovered it while working in Germany.[13] Perhaps drinking spirits soothed his dismay with his father's orders. There was always a bottle of it around the apartment – that, and aged scotch. It started to become common for him to begin each afternoon with a cocktail. That wasn't the Oliver I knew when I married him."

"I had an uncle that drank himself insane," Edith quietly shared. "His condition put a heavy burden on our family. No amount of discussion could get him to give up the habit. In the end it brought him an early death." Edith grew thoughtful, staring into her empty teacup. "Perhaps you should consult a doctor? See what his opinion is regarding Oliver's behavior."

Sara reached for the porcelain teapot and refilled their cups, pondering Edith's words. Rain started to fall. Pinging against the windowpanes, it brought a chill into the sitting room that leached into Sara's heart.

She worked to be cheerful, "Well, I'm happy to discover that you're here with your family in France. I haven't been accepting visitors for fear of starting rumors, claiming illness."

"I'd be inclined to do the same if I were in your shoes."

"But to hear your engagement's been canceled – how perfectly awful."

"At least we make equally miserable company for each other," Edith offered.

"By the way, I received your gift," Sara gave her friend a weak smile. "It was so thoughtful of you. She motioned toward the silver basket filled with roses sitting on the sideboard.[14]

"I suppose I'd hoped it would console you, if even for a moment."

"It did brighten my mood. Thank you."

Her friend smiled, settling back in the chair. "I have an idea," Edith said.

"Let's hear it. I'm open to anything."

"Why should we sit around moping over things we can't control, for now, anyway? Let's go out and try to be happy, take things a day at a time."

"What do you propose?"

"Shopping, of course!" Edith gave her a mischievous wink. "We're in Paris, for heaven's sake. Let's go have some lunch, and afterward visit the boutiques. We'll make a day of it."

"What an excellent idea!" Sara perked up, "Shopping is always a wonderful distraction.[15] Oh, Edith, I'm so glad you've come to France!" Sara paused, hesitant, "But I do run the risk of bumping into people fishing for gossip."

"I can certainly understand your concerns," Edith commiserated. "Just stick to your story that Oliver's away on business. No one will be the wiser. Who knows – maybe he'll come to his senses and see what a catch you are and come running back, begging for forgiveness."

"You're so sweet Edith, to anticipate a favorable outcome."

"Stop worrying Sara, things will work out. I'm sure of it. How about tomorrow – I could stop by around noon?"

"Okay, let's do it. Tomorrow at noon. By the way, how long are you staying in France?"

"It's a short visit, only a week, maybe two," Edith replied. "My family is sailing for New York on the fifteenth. We're attending the Vanderbilt Fancy Ball at the end of March. As humiliated as I am by my wedding's cancellation, I suppose by then I'll feel better about things. My mother's insistent that I go, she wants me to find a good husband – and soon."

"Mothers can sometimes be difficult with their demands," Sara conceded. "But I must admit, my mother's been a great comfort to me as of late. I don't know what I'd have done if I'd had to face Oliver's temper alone."

Edith became quiet, then grew a rascally smile, "I have another idea."

"You're full of them this afternoon."

"It's a wild one," Edith admitted, "but I rather like it. Why don't you come to New York for the Vanderbilt ball?"

"Without Oliver?" Sara exclaimed, "You must be joking!"

"Not at all," Edith took her hand. "Why should you miss out on the fun, just because Oliver would rather lose himself in a liquor bottle. Just keep telling people he's off on business in some distant land. Not only will it bring you some enjoyment, but if word reaches Oliver, it might send a clear message you're not going to sit around sulking while he lives his life."

"You make a good point." Sara paused, considering her argument, "I was really looking forward to the ball. Everyone is talking about the new house." Warming to the suggestion she rose and walked over to the desk. Reaching into a drawer, she pulled out the invitation. "The note *is* addressed to Mr. and Mrs. Oliver H. P. Belmont."

"And you most certainly are Mrs. Belmont," Edith responded with authority. "You should go. Get out of Paris. You know Alva – I'm sure she'll do her best to make it the event of the season, if not the entire year."

"Or the century," Sara giggled.

"You can come back right after the party. It only takes a week to cross the Atlantic. If Oliver returns in the interim, you'll only have been gone a few weeks at the most."

Sara fingered the invitation, "Oliver and I were planning on attending, in fact I sent a response back to New York accepting, while he was still here." Concern clouded her face, "What will I tell my mother?"

"Tell her you're visiting me in Italy. My family is renting a house there. She'd be none the wiser. Besides, you're a married woman now, and an experienced traveler. You should go," Edith said with conviction. "Who knows, maybe Oliver will think he's lost you. That'll make him come running home. Men hate losing."

Edith made an excellent case in her favor, and Sara considered the real possibility of going back to New York. There was a lot of good sense in the idea and the more she considered it an option, the more she felt herself getting excited.

"I would need a costume. It's a masquerade ball," Sara eyed the light flickering in the chandelier. "Hmmm… Perhaps I could go as a geisha."

"You would look lovely as a geisha," Edith smiled victoriously.

The next day
March 3, 1883
Paris, France

Closing the door to her bedchambers, Mrs. Whiting sighed quietly to herself. It's been a very long day, she reflected, placing her hat back in its box. Changing into nightclothes, she mulled over everything that'd happened to Sara since the wedding. What a sham of a man that Oliver was! She couldn't help being disgusted with him. Every day he continued to be absent, her heart grew colder toward him. 'Absent absinthe Oliver', she thought. A spoiled little rich boy is what he is, unable to attend to his wife and marriage for even a few months!

Mrs. Whiting had not been prepared for the shocking scene that she and the girls had witnessed when they'd returned from the opera. It was one thing to find the newlyweds arguing, but completely another to watch Oliver strike Sara. She knew he'd been drinking a lot of spirits, but she'd never expected to stumble in on such a disturbing display of brutality as the one playing out in the apartment. The level of violence Oliver had inflicted on her daughter was reprehensible. No man should treat his wife that way – but a newlywed! Shocking! And a man of his social upbringing, no less!

It was clear Oliver blamed her, Jane and Milly for his bad demeanor, but Mrs. Whiting knew that liquor played a major role in his deplorable conduct – and that was hardly an excuse, as far as she was concerned. Then for him to just up and leave! Deserting Sara on their honeymoon. That young man was too accustomed to getting his own way in life, she grumbled. He needs a strong dose of moral accountability.

But how to get Oliver to own up to his responsibilities was an unanswered dilemma. Mrs. Whiting gazed out at the street lamps, the French evening quiet. She found herself wishing her own affairs were as tranquil as the night.

Turning, she fought the dread growing in her mind, worried by the possibility that Oliver might never return to his wife or his marriage. Maybe it would be just as well, Mrs. Whiting considered, remembering Oliver's state of mind and the force of his rage. The disdain left her bitter.

Perhaps I need to step back and reassess the situation, Mrs. Whiting deliberated. After all Sara was a Belmont now. Her new social ranking brought with it a great deal of privilege and respect. Then another possibility ran across her mind.

Divorce.

It would most certainly cause a scandal, not to mention much heartache for Sara, Mrs. Whiting realized with regret. But she would still retain the Belmont name and most probably be presented a nice cash settlement in light of Oliver's desertion – not that money was the issue. Perhaps his parents would intercede and try to keep Sara out of the Belmont coffers. Or they could do the opposite and give her an even larger sum to protect the family's integrity in an effort to keep the matter quiet.

Either scenario was repugnant at best. Mrs. Whiting shook her head with chagrin. This was not at all the happy outcome she'd wished for her youngest daughter when she'd married Oliver at Swanhurst last Christmas. Mrs. Whiting's heart ached for Sara in the way only a mother's could.

Only three months ago her future looked so bright. How had things taken such an awful turn, and in so short a time? This was beyond appalling. With each passing day Mrs. Whiting felt it was growing more important to create a line of defense and protect Sara from Oliver's moodiness. There was a dark side to him that certainly surprised everyone who bore witness to it.

She's in over her head, Mrs. Whiting thought decisively. Sara is too inexperienced in such matters. I think it's best for me to handle any correspondence with Oliver, she silently resolved. Sara needs someone to run interference from him.[16] She's terribly hurt and simply not thinking straight. This situation should be handled with experience and proficient finesse. It's a lot like a game of chess, Mrs. Whiting determined, a grim scowl growing on her face as she compared her daughter's fate with a board game.

A soft knock on the chamber door interrupted her contemplation.

"Come in," she called quietly. "Sara, why are you still up and about?"

"I couldn't sleep," Sara answered, moving to sit on the edge of the bed. "I have something on my mind I want to discuss with you."

"Has something happened I should know about?" Mrs. Whiting stiffened. "Have you heard from Oliver?"

"Not a word," Sara shook her head. "But, as you know, Edith came to visit. Her fiancé's mother cancelled her engagement to Henry Stevens."

"I heard the news at lunch today," Mrs. Whiting frowned. "I'd imagine the two of you found comfort with each other." [17]

"Yes. Very much so," Sara offered a soft smile. "And that's what I want to discuss with you."

"What's on your mind?"

"Well…" Sara began, "Edith and her family have rented a house in Italy, and I've been invited to visit. At first I wasn't fond of the idea, but I must admit, it's starting to grow on me."

"You can't just leave Paris," Mrs. Whiting narrowed her eyes. "What if Oliver returns to find you gone?"

"I'm growing sick and tired of waiting for Oliver to make a move," Sara's voice cracked with harshness. "He considers no one but himself. You do realize he's controlling the entire marriage – and me – by his absence? The least he could do is write." She wiped a hand over her face, "I'm past the point of tolerance."

Mrs. Whiting shifted closer. "I know how hard this has been on you, but going to Italy is a rash move, don't you think?"

"At first I did," Sara gazed absently out the window. "But the more I mull over the invitation, the more I like the notion. I'd only be gone a few weeks, maybe three. If Oliver shows up, you could wire me, and let me know. I'd return to Paris at once."

Mrs. Whiting's misgivings were evident in her expression, "It's Lent, dear, Easter is almost here. Don't you want to attend mass with our family? We've been invited to dinner at Mrs. Plunkett's along with other friends in the set."

"I really don't think I'll be missed. I can attend mass in Italy. Honestly, I think if I don't get out of Paris soon, I'll go mad."

"I don't know about this…" The bedchamber fell quiet while Mrs. Whiting considered her request. A trip could help break the melancholy she'd watched Sara battle. Being with Edith might be a very good idea for both of them right now. If word got to Oliver she'd left Paris, perhaps it would be the impetus needed to get him back to the apartment, and hopefully, make amends.

Or maybe it would have the opposite effect.

Divorce entered her thoughts again, but she didn't speak of it, hiding the possibility from Sara. It was too soon to talk of such matters, anyway. Why add to her worries?

"Perhaps it *is* a good idea. Of course you will be taking Bridget with you as a companion," Mrs. Whiting turned to her daughter. "Are you sure this is what you want to do?"

"Yes. After long consideration, I think it would prove very helpful to me in many ways." Sara met her eye, "I won't be gone that long, and I relish a change of scenery – I think it will do me good."

"Would you like me to write to Mrs. Jones?"

Sara's heart pounded with fear at the thought of her mother discovering her true plans. "Oh no!" she said hurriedly. "I can handle all the details myself. I've just received another letter from Edith and my visit is fine with her family."

Mrs. Whiting detected something unusual in Sara's voice, something that seemed out of character. She surveyed her daughter, wondering if there wasn't more to this trip than she was saying. She hesitated, rethinking her position. In light of everything Sara had been through, maybe it was a good idea. In the end, it really was her decision. After all, she was 'Mrs. Belmont' now. By rights Sara didn't have to ask her permission to do anything. But Mrs. Whiting was gratified that her daughter had deferred the decision to her, if even as a courtesy.

"Well… if you're sure that's what you want to do," her mother consented. "I'll go with you tomorrow to purchase tickets."

"That won't be necessary, Mother," Sara dissuaded her. "I'm quite capable of tending to the travel arrangements myself."

"Are you certain?" Mrs. Whiting frowned, "You've never taken care of such matters before. Travel arrangements can prove complicated."

"Mother, I'm a married woman, even if my husband is absent. It's time I learned to handle these matters on my own – but thank you for the offer."

Getting up from the bed, Sara landed a light kiss on her mother's cheek. "I'll finalize the plans and purchase my tickets in the morning." She headed for the bedroom door, "Sweet dreams."

"Good night," Mrs. Whiting said, watching the door close.

Left alone again with her thoughts, Mrs. Whiting reconsidered her decision, unsure if the trip was a good idea. Something seemed a bit out of place, although she couldn't quite put her finger on it.

"What can it hurt?" she whispered as she climbed into bed, extinguishing the lamp.

Two days later
March 5, 1883
Barcelona, Spain

The banquet room was filled with partygoers, growing a bit rowdy and wild as they enjoyed the festivities. The ballroom was decorated with candles and bouquets, while flower garlands hung from the ceiling in lovely loops. Oliver wasn't sure how he'd ended up in Spain, but the question left his mind as quickly as it'd entered when he heard the sound of the musicians launching into the opening notes of one of his favorite waltzes.

"Come on, my dear," he grabbed Lily's hand. "Let's take a twirl around the ballroom, shall we?" He gave her a brief scan. She really wasn't unattractive, but definitely not the kind of woman his mother would approve of. A smug feeling of defiance matched his gait as he led her onto the dance floor.

Lily let out a drunken laugh, "How long do you plan on torturing me with all this fun?" she joked. "We haven't taken a rest since we left France."

"Never!" he retorted. "You're much too fine a traveling companion. We'll attend party after party until we're exhausted. Only then shall we rest, and just enough to get up and start again."

Their laughter pealed through the room, mixing with the sounds of the party revelry. Men bowed at the knee of ladies, inviting them to dance, while others refilled their glasses with wine and ale. The group was a mixture of aristocrats and women of questionable background, but the level of intoxication was such that no one really seemed to notice or care who the men brought to the party. As long as they had money to spend, they were welcome to enjoy themselves however they pleased.

Oliver and Lily danced with drunken abandon, stopping only when the violins played the last note of the song. As the music faded, Oliver took Lily's hand and led her back to their table. He sat down smoothing his jacket, and started drinking a fresh glass of wine.

"I'm going to the powder room," she informed him. "Don't you dare think of dancing without me."

"Why on earth would I do such a thing?" he asked, mustering up his most innocent expression. "I'll be right in this chair when you return, waiting with bated breath."

Oliver watched her depart in a flourish of cheap lace, shaking his head at her wild ways. There was something delectable in their forbidden fun, and he was totally enjoying his holiday. All protocol and rules were thrown out the window around Lily, and if he was honest about it, at times he became quite reckless. Romantic relations with her were more adventurous than any he'd ever experienced with a woman. Oliver smiled to himself, reaching to refill his glass. It's certainly a far cry from the life of a naval officer, or, he thought in a moment of contrition, a newly married gentleman.

He quickly ignored the twinge of guilt, turning his attention back to the party. Distracting himself, he casually looked through the crowd. There shouldn't be anyone here I know – drat that Mr. Cushing, he thought, feeling a nudge of remorse.

A brief encounter with him a few weeks ago in the hotel lobby had left Oliver wary that word of his whereabouts would reach his parents, as Mr. Cushing was a family friend. He really didn't want anyone to know he'd left Sara in Paris, not until he was good and ready to disclose the information himself.

"Oh well," he whispered. "There's nothing I can do about it now."

Watching the dancers, Oliver came to full attention, surprise slapping him sober.

"What the devil..."

It was Sara.

The woman was turned away from him talking to her friends, but the way she held herself, the style of her hair and dress...

Oliver sat up straight in the wooden chair, fighting the dread pumping through his veins. How could he possibly explain himself? Staring at the woman across the room, his mind swirled with questions. Why in the world would she do a crazy thing like follow him to Spain? A surge of panic gripped his stomach as he watched her glide toward chairs on the opposite side of the room. Drunken guffaws erupted from the people in her group as she joined them. Her white dressed flowed as she spun around, finding her seat with a twitter of laughter.

Relief poured over him, sweat breaking on the back of his neck.

"It's not Sara..."

He watched the English woman closely, thinking she could've passed for Sara's twin. Gathering his wits he grabbed his glass, taking a long, deep gulp of cabernet. Emptying the bottle, he ordered the waiter to bring another.

"Try and be quick about it," he called after the server, taking his turmoil out on the man.

I must be getting paranoid, he thought, rubbing his forehead. But, why should he be? He'd had the perfect right to leave the apartment back in Paris. I really worked for a compromise with Sara, he assured himself; I tried to persuade her to get our own suite. Hell, he'd even offered to pay for both places. If things turned sour, the burden of responsibility was with the Whitings – not on his shoulders. Forget the fact that he'd originally agreed to the arrangement. He'd changed his mind, and had put up with their presence way past the breaking point. If it hadn't been for the relief of the absinthe, he'd probably have given up a lot sooner than he had.

Letting his thoughts wander back to his new bride, Oliver rallied in defense of his actions. The marriage had started out so happily. And they'd gone through so much hardship to make the wedding happen. Memories of their arguments ran through his mind, and he felt a tiny pang of regret. Releasing a guilty sigh, Oliver admitted to himself, however briefly, that he'd let his temper get the best of him. He grabbed the glass sitting on the table and filled it with fresh wine, sloshing down its contents.

Maybe he should return to Paris and try to make things right. He certainly didn't want to be labeled a blackguard. Maybe he'd overreacted by leaving for such a distant city as Barcelona. He considered his actions and his options, then remembered Mrs. Whiting, Jane and Milly, hunkered down in his apartment. He couldn't hope for the situation to improve, not unless the living arrangements changed.

"What has you all serious?" Lily asked, returning to the table. She sat down on his lap with aplomb. "Where is that smile I left you with?"

Startled, Oliver wrapped his arm around her bare shoulders. "Oh, nothing for you to worry your pretty little head over." He gave her a weak grin, "I just thought I saw someone I knew, that's all. It was a mistake."

"Good!" she said jumping up from his lap. "Let's dance again." She grabbed him by both wrists, pulling him to his feet.

Oliver wobbled for a moment, then gained his balance, throwing her a shrewd look.

"You'll soon be begging me to let you stop," he said, leading her to the center of the ballroom.

When the violins started playing, Oliver found he'd forgotten all about Sara and her meddlesome mother, vowing to dance with Lily long into the night hours.

CHAPTER SEVEN

Three days later
March 8,1883
Paris, France

THE EARLY MORNING SUNLIGHT IN the gothic cathedral had evolved into the warmth of afternoon, bathing the church with a holy aura. Beautiful stained glass windows flooded multi-colored prisms of light through the sanctuary, filling Sara's heart with a flush of happiness. Though she'd heard nothing from Oliver since he'd left their suite several weeks before, today she was calm. Deciding to push their conflict out of her mind, she let herself enjoy the feeling of renewal that had touched her while being confirmed today in the sacrament.

After Oliver's outburst she'd fallen ill, weak from the physical and emotional trauma he'd inflicted upon her and the Whiting family. Edith had brought some welcome relief, but she'd left Paris, and Sara's melancholy had returned with full force. Fighting her humiliation, she searched for solace, and found it in the comfort of the church. Thinking this was the perfect time for her confirmation, she'd asked to have the ritual performed in the Episcopalian cathedral while visiting Paris.[18]

"Getting confirmed here in Paris was a lovely idea, my dear," Mrs. Whiting looped her arm through her daughter's. "How are you feeling?"

"I feel surprisingly peaceful," Sara answered, "considering everything that's happened."

"I'm so glad to hear it."

They walked outside, down the church steps and onto the sidewalk. Sara looked over her shoulder to see her sisters following several yards behind. She'd labored to hide her embarrassment over Oliver's absence, knowing full well Jane and Milly were clearly aware of Oliver's words and actions. The two hadn't said much to her on the subject, and for that she was grateful. She was having enough difficulty coping with events, without having to listen to her sisters' opinions about her troubled marriage.

It seemed as though her life had been caught up in a terrible storm, a tornado of disastrous proportion. Little more than three months had passed since her wedding, Sara realized in dismay, and nothing had gone as planned. The degradation and pain she'd experienced from Oliver's alcoholism were the worst of her entire life. Now abandoned by her groom on her honeymoon, she fought against the agony. There were moments when her heart physically ached, as though shot by a piercing bullet. Shame and humiliation hung from her like a dark, heavy shroud.[19] Sara wondered how long she could invent excuses for societies' mothers when they asked why Oliver wasn't by her side? She certainly didn't want word of this to start making the gossip buzz, and she was determined to avoid any slander or scandal, regardless of the circumstances.

Strolling with her mother down the sidewalk, Sara admired the Parisian architecture, lost in her ruminations. She was a new bride – yet now, she was alone. Her groom had transformed into a 'Doctor Jekyll and Mr. Hyde' character before her very eyes. Seeking some peace in her religion, her decision to be confirmed had been a wise one. At least now she felt the protection of the church, sheltering her soul in this dark hour.

"Mrs. Wilson is hosting a luncheon to commemorate your confirmation," her mother said. "Are you up to socializing?"

"Yes. For a while," Sara nodded. "We'll have to make light of Oliver's absence, but I feel new hope and strength for the effort." She turned to her mother, smiling with bravado, "I think lunch with our friends will be a good distraction to help me sustain my happy mood. Besides, I suppose one must keep up appearances."

The Whiting family continued the short promenade down the city block to the restaurant where Mrs. Wilson, recently arrived in France, was waiting with Mrs. Plunkett and other family friends. The Whitings entered the establishment, and were met by the wonderful smells of French cuisine. Roasting meats and the scent of herbs filled Sara's senses and she became aware of dull pangs of hunger.

It'd been hard to eat in the past weeks; her stomach was not up to the challenge of digestion. Sara had had no appetite, and the food she'd tried to eat seemed to lie in her belly for days. She found it easier to skip meals, much to her mother's dismay. But today in light of her confirmation, she was hungrier than she'd been in days.

As the festivities got underway Sara glanced around the table, surrounded by friends celebrating the occasion with her. The luncheon was a welcome relief from disappointment. It felt good to be happy, if only for the day.

Mrs. Cushing sat across the dining table, and Sara overheard the woman mention Oliver's name. An unfortunate tremble moved through her, and Sara took a sip of wine to calm herself. Oliver had brought her new anxiety with his harsh treatment. She'd never been struck by a man before, not even by her father when misbehaving as a child. Sara discovered that Oliver's violent rages weren't something she could easily forget. Regardless, she did hope to get Oliver back home. If only he would stop drinking, there was a chance they could work through the situation, before things developed into a full-blown scandal. Casually, she leaned a little closer toward Mrs. Cushing in an effort to hear if there was any knowledge of his whereabouts.

"You didn't tell me Oliver was on business in Spain," Mrs. Cushing said to Mrs. Whiting. "My husband and I just returned from Barcelona. Mr. Cushing happened to cross paths with Oliver himself while meeting with clients." She pulled a fresh roll from the platter on the table. Turning, Mrs. Cushing lowered her voice, "I'm sorry to break your heart with this news, but it appears he's attending to more than business. He was seen traveling with a *dancer* - a French dancer, no less." [20] Innuendo oozed from her words. "I'm not sure of all the details. We didn't have a chance to finish our discussion before Mr. Cushing was called away to London."

"A dancer!" Mrs. Whiting quietly hissed. "Surely, there must be some mistake. He's newly married. A man of his position taking up with a woman like that would cast shame not only on himself, but on his entire family."

"I assure you, it *is* true," Mrs. Cushing asserted. "We're close friends with the Belmonts and I'm certain my husband wouldn't say such a thing if he hadn't seen it with his own two eyes. We're loath to spread rumors – unless, of course, it's the truth – then it's considered news. Mr. Cushing believes it's his duty to let Mr. Belmont know of Oliver's activities, and I to you, since the young man is supposed to be tending to business matters." She looked from Mrs. Whiting to Sara, "Will he be returning to his new bride soon?"

"Oh yes, he's only been gone a little over a week." Mrs. Whiting labored to make light of Oliver's travels. "He assured us it would be a short trip."

Hearing enough, Sara pushed the chair back from the table, politely excusing herself for the powder room. Reeling from what she'd just heard, she retreated from the distressing conversation. She wasn't sure if it made her happy or sad to know where Oliver was. Secretly, she'd hoped he was closer than Spain – at least still somewhere in France. To discover he was gallivanting around Barcelona with a woman of ill repute was news she was not prepared for. I don't know why I'm so surprised, she quietly seethed. It's not as if this is the first time he'd engaged in that sort of activity; she thought back to his trips to the seedy cabarets and men's clubs in Paris.

In the safety of the washroom Sara looked at her reflection, and scarcely recognized herself. Although with Bridget's faithful assistance she'd gone through all the usual motions of dressing, somehow she looked nothing like her old self. Decidedly pale, her eyes were bloodshot and red from lack of sleep, her countenance whispering of illness. Suddenly weary from the day's activities, Sara decided to make an excuse and escape the party. Instead, she'd return to the suite for an afternoon rest.

In spite of their grievances, Sara desperately wished that when she woke up from her nap, Oliver would be laying beside her, whispering it had all been a very bad dream.

That same day
New York, New York

Walking over to his wife, August Belmont gently rubbed her shoulders. "You really shouldn't worry yourself, Tiny.... Things will work out fine, I'm sure of it."

"I wish I could share your optimism," she replied glumly. "I must admit I've grown fond of Sara, in spite of my reservations. Her letters have been very affectionate and sweet. My initial misgivings on the marriage have given way to sincere affection.[21] I'd truly hoped the marriage would inspire Oliver to settle down into a responsible lifestyle." She set the letter from France on the escritoire. "I suppose I was hoping for too much."

"Nonsense. Give the boy some time," August settled in to the leather chair he favored. "He's probably upset over the intrusion of her family. I'm sure Oliver will return to France in the very near future and make things right." He hoped his voice didn't betray his skepticism. Sadly, he thought, a horse doesn't change its colors, and Oliver had always had a taste for the obstreperous life.

"I had my doubts about the Whitings traveling to Paris. How could Mrs. Whiting have thought staying with the newlyweds a good idea? I can't fathom her reasoning," Caroline bristled. "Sara shouldn't have allowed it. At the very least, she should have asked her family to make separate living arrangements so the two could've enjoy their honeymoon in marital privacy."

A quiet filled the room as husband and wife each fell into their own thoughts.

Caroline opened the desk drawer and slipped out a piece of stationery. "I'm obliged to write a response to Sara's letter, although I'm not quite sure how I will state my opinion. The last thing I want to do is discourage her even more at such a troubled time. But Sara really must be made to see that her family has had a definite influence on the course of events."

"So it would seem," August frowned. "I imagine she won't appreciate your criticism. Perhaps it's her mother you should be writing to. I believe she's meddled too much in their affairs. If the Whitings would bow out of the picture, there's a chance the newlyweds will work through their differences."

"Whatever the solution, I hope it presents itself soon." Caroline shook her head in weary resignation, "If not, I fear we'll find ourselves in the throes of a scandal worse than the one we've just avoided over their engagement."

She doused the quill in ink and began to write. The scratching sounds of her efforts echoed through the room, cold from a winter storm. August watched her from his chair, trusting she'd find the right words to express their concern.

Abruptly, she stopped writing and turned to him. "Perhaps you should travel to Paris…" She spoke as if it were a question, "Or go to Spain and try to locate Oliver?"

An expression of aversion draped August's face. "That's a horrible idea," he said bluntly. "Isn't it bad enough her mother is intruding in their personal affairs? My presence runs the risk of complicating things even more than they already are." He rubbed his muttonchops, continuing. "As for going to Spain… Well, I don't think that would do a bit of good. Oliver doesn't listen to me these days, anyway. Let them know our advice and opinion through letters. I really believe the two need to work things out for themselves. After all, they've gotten themselves into this mess."

Caroline gazed absently into the fire. "I suppose you're right," she said, resuming her draft. "It's just that I feel so powerless to help from three thousand miles away." [22]

"Perhaps being three thousand miles away has advantages that you can't see at the present moment," August cocked an eyebrow. "Why walk into the center of a hornet's nest? I assure you, you'll have much more influence through your letters. And, I believe we can be considerably more impartial from where we sit here in New York."

"You're right, of course," Caroline nodded in agreement. "Traveling to Europe might bring undue attention to the discord, creating just the kind of scandal I hope to avoid. I'll settle for sending a letter and try to give the best counsel I can."

She returned again to her writing, carefully voicing her opinion to Sara.

Twelve days later
March 20, 1883
New York Harbor

The frozen wind blew across Sara's face, causing a shiver to run through her body. She knew it was foolish to stand on the ship's deck in the cold, but she didn't care. It was worth being uncomfortable to catch the first view of New York harbor. It was a skyline that couldn't be fully enjoyed from the cabin window and despite the stormy weather, she'd gone on deck to relish their arrival in the States.

"Such a beautiful sight," Bridget sighed, holding her coat close. "Even though I've been terribly dismayed to discover that you lied to your mother about our true destination."

Glancing at her devoted servant, Sara knew she could count on Bridget to protect her secret. "Don't worry yourself about that now," she instructed her maid. "I'm attending the Vanderbilt Fancy Ball and that's final. It'll be our little secret."

"Most certainly the newspapers will be printing detailed reports on the party – and the guests," Bridget warned.

"At that point, I really don't think it'll matter," Sara shrugged. "Mother already knows Oliver and I were invited to the ball, though she'd never dream that I'd take such a journey on my own. I must admit it feels liberating to be doing things for myself. I'm a married woman now and I'll make my own decisions."

Bridget gave her a doubtful look. "Forgive me for saying so, miss, but I'm afraid you'll be under the power of your mother until her dying breath."

"I suppose to some degree you're right," Sara laughed at her candor, "but at this particular moment I'm the master of my fate. And I say I'm going to the Fancy Ball – and no one can stop me. Especially not now that we're here in New York."

"Yes ma'am," Bridget acknowledged. "I'll pick up your costume from the theatre shop when we arrive. You'll have to try it on, so I can see if it needs any alterations. I'm sure you'll look lovely, and no one will be the wiser as to why Oliver isn't at your side."

"That's the spirit!" Sara cheered. "I'm delighted you've found your sense of adventure. This is much more fun than lounging around in some dreary Paris apartment." She turned a fond eye to Bridget, "I'm not sure if sitting around hoping for Oliver's return has done any good to rectify the situation anyway, and I'm completely frustrated with waiting for him."

"The circumstances are most unfortunate," Bridget agreed, taking in the sight of the city. "Well, we're here now, I suppose we should make the most of the trip, and enjoy ourselves. But with all due respect miss, I must insist we head back right after the ball, like you promised. I won't rest easy till we're back with your family in Paris." Bridget's face told of her concern. "Is your stomach still unsettled? I've never seen you with such an awful case of seasickness."

"It passed with the storm," Sara said, flicking her wrist. "I feel wonderful, especially now that we're here in New York." Sara smiled at her loyal maid, then turned her attention back to the approaching port.

"And yes, Bridget, to address your concerns, the tickets have already been purchased for the cruise home. We're returning two days after the ball."

"I'm relieved to know it."

"I must say, I'm so disappointed that Edith won't be making it to the ball after all. Especially since this was her idea." Sara frowned, "I was discouraged to hear her family was detained in Italy. But Lady Lister-Kaye will be there, which will be lovely. And I can spend time with Carrie. She wrote that she's doing a special quadrille with some of the ladies. Won't that be fun?"

"I'm sure it will be very nice," Bridget assured her. "All your friends will be at the ball and I'm certain they'll be delighted to see you."

A loud horn erupted from the stack of the steamer, echoing over the harbor as the ship pulled into port.

"Come on," Sara waved. "Let's get down to our stateroom and make sure our luggage is being handled properly."

Three days later
March 23, 1883
Barcelona, Spain

Oliver stared at the letter gripped tightly in his hands, working to shake off the ring of reproach his mother had woven through her words. She has no right to judge my actions, he thought bitterly. How could Mamma possibly know what'd occurred in the honeymoon suite? She simply couldn't, but she'd written as though she was there for every disagreement. He supposed nothing would stop her from sending him pages of advice. I'm certain Papa was helping her draft this note, he thought, and that can't be good. Oliver was frustrated by their meddling in his personal affairs. How did she get his address anyway? I suppose it's challenging for a Belmont to disappear into the crowd, especially with such a big wallet, he thought, frowning quietly in the soft chair of his suite.

"Sara's letters to me lately, while very affectionate and sweet," his mother wrote, "Seem to evince restlessness and unhappiness." [23]

What about his restlessness or his unhappiness? The bitter taste of indignation caught in his throat. I'm sick and tired of hearing about Sara's feelings, Oliver thought sullenly. No one seemed to care how the turn of events had affected him. But, one good thing had been accomplished by this matter – his father had finally stopped hounding him about a career. And I'm getting a nice fat allowance as a married man, he reminded himself. It'd been easy to push Sara far from his mind. But in the end, Oliver supposed he must decide on a course of action… What exactly was he going to do?

"I don't have a clue," he murmured quietly, staring at the artwork covering the walls of his hotel room. Was there any possibility that Sara and he could patch things up? Especially with the opinions and influence of their parents hanging over them? It seemed an impossibly high hurdle to jump.

Oliver let his thoughts drift back to their departure from New York as newlyweds. I should've planned a trip to India or Japan for our honeymoon, he chided himself. He doubted Mrs. Whiting would've felt inclined to follow them halfway around the world hauling her older daughters along for the ride. Refusing to accept his responsibility in the fiasco, or his problematic penchant for drinking absinthe, he staunchly laid the blame of his troubled marriage on the shoulders of the Whiting family.

Returning his attention to the letter, he reviewed the words again.

"Take into consideration the fact that women, particularly those of a nervous nature, are sometimes subject to serious misgivings in the most unaccountable ways." [24] He re-read his mother's words written in her flourishing script, then in a surge of angry frustration, crumbled the paper into his clenched fist.

It was Sara – not he, who should be apologizing. "Fat chance," he laughed with rancor. "Not as long as Sara's mother is by her side coaching her every action."

Oliver had once considered Mrs. Whiting to be his best ally in persuading his parents to announce their engagement. Now she was proving to be a strong adversary, working against him.

Should he write back and defend himself? Would it do any good? He hated the thought of airing the couple's issues, especially in light of his parents' resistance to their engagement. So far, there'd been no 'I told you so'. Thank goodness. But there was the matter of avoiding a scandal, and Oliver knew that'd be high on his mother's list of priorities. He remembered how he'd threatened Sara with a separation, or worse, a divorce. But he'd been angry – and admittedly inebriated. He'd spoken from his fury. Is that what I truly want, he wondered quietly to himself.

"Damn," he griped under his breath. "I don't know what to do about this mess, and until I do, the entire world can go to hell."

Indignant, he threw his mother's letter into the fire, the hot flames igniting the paper. Reaching for his glass of scotch, he watched grimly as the note turned to ash.

CHAPTER EIGHT

Three days later
March 26, 1883
New York, New York

"OH WHAT A JOY TO be back with my friends in New York," Sara laughed openly, while giving Carrie a gentle hug so as not to muss their costumes. "I've missed you so much."

"I've missed you too, Sara."

The ladies entered the grand foyer of the new Vanderbilt mansion, amazed by its size. The vast vestibule was purported to be sixty feet long and twenty feet wide, very grand under the light of stained glass windows. From their vantage point they could view the wide, massive staircase that rose to the upper floors, built with stone imported from Caen, France. The building was so impressive that *The New York Times* had written a large article about its unveiling in the morning newspaper. [25]

Sara and Carrie were greeted by a footman in a powdered wig who led them to their place in the receiving line. Impressed by the sight of the party already in full swing, they surveyed the costumes. Men dressed as sheiks and generals escorted ladies masquerading as Marie Antoinette and Little Bo Peep. Other than in the theatre, Sara had never seen so many elaborate outfits under one roof. Hundreds of guests had already been received. The sound of tuning violins emanated from the direction of the ballroom, causing a pulse of excitement to grow with each newly arrived guest.

"I really admire your geisha costume," Carrie said, battery powered lights twinkling in her hair.

"Thank you. I had to rush to pull it together, having just arrived in New York. Your costume is lovely too, the lights are a spectacular touch!"

"I hope they hold up through the evening." Carrie gently patted her wig as they stepped into the receiving line. "We're all wearing them for the quadrille." She leaned in close to Sara and continued in a whisper, "Unfortunately, there was a bit of a confrontation between Alva and my mother over securing my invitation."

"What do you mean?" Sara frowned in disbelief. "Your mother's the undisputed queen of society. Of course you were invited!"

"Alva seems to be vying for the position as monarch of the set. As you know, Mother's never included the Vanderbilts on her guest list. She has a disdain for the nouveau riche, and only invites families from the Four Hundred to her balls. You know, those with aristocratic bloodlines going back at least three generations, and all that propriety."

"Ah yes, I know your mother keeps a tight hold on such matters, with the help of Mr. McAllister. But the Vanderbilts have become one of the wealthiest families in America. They won't be easily ignored, especially not now, with this new house."

"I feel certain that was Alva's plan," Carrie wore a shrewd smile. "Anyway, while you were in France on your honeymoon, I was preparing the Star Quadrille with Anita, Miss Marie and some other ladies who *had* received invitations to the ball. As time passed it became clear that my invitation was not going to be forthcoming, even though I'd been rehearsing with the other dancers. Clearly, Alva was making a point."

"What finally happened?"

"Mother got in her carriage and paid Alva a visit. She had her footman leave her calling card," Carrie divulged.[26] "Alva all but forced Mother to acknowledge the Vanderbilts into society. I received an invitation the very next day, although I was secretly planning to come regardless," she giggled mischievously. "It would be hard to imagine a doorman preventing an Astor entrance to the party – any party."

"You never know with Alva. She may have had you singled out to her footman to drive home the point. Anyway, I'm glad it worked out, particularly without a confrontation. Things could have gotten messy."

"You're probably right – but it's not an issue any longer." Changing the subject Carrie announced, "I understand there are scores of wonderful entertainments planned, and Mora Photographers are here doing portraits of the guests in their costumes."

"How fun," Sara said, her eyes lighting up at the news. "I think I'll have my photograph taken to commemorate the occasion."

At last they reached the front of the receiving line where they were greeted by Mrs. Vanderbilt. She was accompanied by her sister-in-law, Mrs. Alice Gwynne Vanderbilt, the Duchess of Manchester, elaborately dressed as 'Lady Light'. She was adorned with enough diamonds to light up all of New York, with or without electricity. Apparently, the duchess was the guest of honor, which explained her prestigious place in the receiving line.

"Hello, Miss Astor," Alva greeted Carrie with a victorious nod. She turned to Sara, "and the new 'Mrs. Belmont'. Welcome to our home."

Carrie and Sara curtseyed. "Thank you for the invitation, Mrs. Vanderbilt," Sara said, eyeing her hostess's fabulous costume.

Declaring herself dressed as a Venetian princess, Alva wore a magnificent gown, sewn with lavish white and yellow brocade. The rich fabric had colors blending from deep orange to the palest yellow. Hand-sewn iridescent beads outlined flowers and leaves in gold and white on the bodice. A long pale-blue train puffed at the side and draped behind her, embroidered all in gold. Alva had topped the costume with a Venetian cap adorned with opulent jewels, which included a peacock broach fashioned out of many colors of gold. The jewel was clearly custom-made to go with the costume.

"The house is magnificent," Sara flattered her hostess, "and so is your costume."

"Thank you for saying so. Where is Oliver tonight?" Alva asked.

"Unfortunately, he's on business in Spain. He sends his apologies," Sara fibbed.

"How regrettable," Alva said, unfazed. "But, I'm glad you could join us tonight in his absence. We have some lovely entertainment arranged, as Miss Astor knows." She tossed the gibe at Carrie, triumphantly. "The Hobby Horse quadrille has spectacular costumes consisting of life-size horses made with genuine hides, manes and tails. Then there's the Mother Goose quadrille and the Opera Bouffe which my sister, Mrs. Yznaga, organized." Alva finished in a flourish of smugness.

"I'm sure it will be lovely," Carrie said, working not to bristle under the woman's boastfulness.

"Thank you, again, Mrs. Vanderbilt." Sara curtsied, preparing to leave the receiving line. In spite of the duchess's place welcoming guests, it was clear Alva was the queen of tonight's party, even if it was purportedly held in honor of her sister.

The two friends left the receiving line. Behind them they heard a torrent of congratulations and 'thank you's' enthusiastically erupting from the guests that followed, praising Alva on the Vanderbilt's magnificent new home.

"That woman has enough arrogance for five queens," Carrie whispered through gritted teeth.

"Don't let it bother you Carrie," Sara offered. "You've got more class than her any day."

"I hope my mother and Alva don't have words – they've both dressed as Venetian princesses! Can you believe the coincidence?"

"Your mother has too much sophistication to let that bother her," Sara asserted. "Besides, you never know – she may have done it on purpose to trump Alva at her own game."

The ladies drifted with the crowd toward the ballroom, caught up in the celebratory mood. "I must tell you, Sara, I think it's very bold of you to come to New York with only your maid as your chaperone. Especially during Easter season. I'm surprised your mother let you travel during Lent."

"It took some convincing, but Mother finally allowed it, although she thinks I'm in Italy with Edith and her family."

Carrie looked at her with wide eyes, "Well, you *are* growing bold!"

"I'm a married woman now, I'm trying to learn to assert myself against my mother – and sisters."

"Good luck with that," Carrie moaned. "As you know, I face the same challenge."

"Mothers can be hard to deal with sometimes," Sara commiserated. "Besides, what my mother doesn't know won't hurt her."

The only dilemma that concerned her was if Oliver returned, then the cat would be out of the bag. But she refused to worry about that unless it happened. She was determined to make an appearance in society tonight, regardless of the obstacles – and she planned on enjoying herself to the fullest, if she died trying.

Their conversation lulled, while they watched the scene before them. Miss Kate Strong sauntered by wearing a stuffed cat on her head, catching the attention of the Count of Monte Cristo. The friends exchanged a look of disbelief, stifling laughter.

"Poor kitty," Sara whispered.

"Maybe it's her deceased pet," Carrie chuckled. "Preserved forever by a taxidermist." They both laughed, prepared to bear witness to anything at the masquerade. "I'm surprised Alva had the ball so soon after Lent." Carrie continued. "She certainly didn't waste a single moment, seeing as how yesterday was Easter Sunday."

"Alva probably would've thrown the party after Easter mass if she thought she could get away with it," Sara whispered back. The two ladies released a burst of giggles, the sound mingling with the hubbub filling the hall.

"Well, I'm glad you came, regardless of the subterfuge needed to get you here. I'm certain you would have regretted missing it, especially due to Oliver's business responsibilities." Carrie waved a gloved hand at the grandeur of the festivities. "I understand over twelve-hundred invitations were sent. I doubt if anyone sent regrets."

Sara was relieved that Carrie hadn't lingered on the topic of Oliver's absence. She'd given her friend a simple, albeit well-rehearsed, explanation that he was abroad on pressing business. Thankfully, Carrie was too interested in the ball to talk about Oliver.

"As far as housewarming parties go, this is the most splendid one I've ever had the pleasure of attending," Sara admitted. "Such a large invitation list would explain my difficulty getting to the house. When I arrived the street was backed up with a long line of carriages ferrying guests to the residence. My own coach joined the line, with spectators filling the sidewalks and blocking the road trying to catch a glimpse of everyone in their fancy costumes."

"I saw it myself," Carrie's voice bubbled with excitement. "The throng was so huge, I understand the police had to be called in to help with the crowds jamming Fifth Avenue." She turned to her friend, lowering her voice, "The gossip mill says that commoners were heard complaining about the city's poverty in the face of what they claim is conspicuous wealth." Carrie frowned at Sara in disbelief. "There've even been rumors circulating that the communists are planning an attack on the house with the intent of robbing the Vanderbilts of their jewels and priceless art." Carrie finished, breathless from the melodrama.

"I doubt that will happen," Sara smiled, caught up in the adventure. "But the ball has certainly caused a lot of rumors. It's sure to be a night everyone will remember."

They ambled into the ballroom, passing a servant who handed them each an elegant leather dance card embossed with a gold letter 'V" on maroon leather; maroon being the Vanderbilt family color. Garlands of orchids and greenery were draped around the ballroom, highlighted by countless baskets and vases, all silver, filled with glorious, and innumerable, red roses – American Beauty and Jacqueminot, their delicate scent drifting through the banquet hall. [27]

The grandeur of the mansion's architecture and furnishings easily rivaled that of a museum. Alva apparently had no qualms in demonstrating her admiration for French interior design. Gold and brocade draperies sewn from costly fabric hung over immense windows, a stylish and modern flair that matched well with the classic Louis XV trend. Priceless tapestries, artwork and sculpture, as well as carved and gilded furniture imported from Europe, filled the house in accordance with these styles. The Vanderbilt fortune was obvious throughout every inch of the residence.

"This isn't a house," Carrie murmured, "it's a palace. Certainly one of the most impressive places I've ever seen – including Europe."

"It's a breathtaking sight," Sara agreed. "I've never seen so much gilt work or marble, except in a cathedral. It's absolutely spectacular. I wonder how William feels about Alva spending so lavishly."

She fought a twinge of jealousy. *My future is so uncertain,* Sara thought. *Would she ever be the grand lady of the Oliver Belmont house, like Alva and Mrs. Astor were the grand dames of their homes?*

"It's a pity Oliver couldn't be here. This party would be such a wonderful chance for you to be introduced as a married couple. The guest list is filled with the names of societies' most prominent members." Carrie voice had the tone of someone in the know.

"Most of the guests arrived in full costume, while others asked to bring their valets and dress at the Vanderbilt home. Alva frowned upon the idea, requesting that valets and maids not be present – can you imagine? It created quite a disturbance among those used to the assistance of their servants, but Mrs. Vanderbilt was adamant in her 'request'."

"I'm sure her request was not well received by some," Sara chuckled, "especially in light of the detail on these elaborate costumes."

"I'm quite sure you're right!"

The two friends drifted through the rooms, taking a short tour of the main floor. They admired the paneled walls and gilded boiserie of the music room, imported from a Parisian castle. Each room they entered was more fabulous than the last.

"The dancing has started," Carrie announced, "let's get back to the ballroom."

"I'm right behind you." Sara followed her to the main hall. Along the way she discreetly aimed her fan toward a particular guest. "I recognize that man," she whispered. "He's the Duke of Edinburgh, Prince Albert. I met him at a ball in Paris."

The gentleman promenaded past them, his wife at his side. "I think you're right. Princess Marie isn't very well liked," Carrie gossiped, holding her fan over her face. "She's thought to be quite arrogant and aloof. I suppose she has a right to be – apparently she's descended from Russian royalty and was given a very large dowry."

Sara watched a man dressed as a knight wearing full armor chat with Lady Washington, who cackled while toasting wine glasses with her friends. Mother Goose talked with a gypsy, as a Turkish arnaut joined them; all the while the orchestra played under the exquisitely hand-painted ceiling depicting the marriage of Cupid and Psyche. The fresco was ablaze in the light of majestic crystal chandeliers, sparkling high above the ballroom.

"I have more news," Carrie broached the subject gently. "Mr. Wilson and I are growing quite close. I'm hopeful for an engagement sometime in the near future."

"Oh Carrie! How wonderful!" Sara exclaimed. "Why didn't you tell me sooner?"

"You're a newlywed. I didn't want to seem gauche talking about a wedding so soon after your own."

"You needn't have worried," Sara assured her. "I'd be delighted if you and Mr. Wilson got engaged."

A twinge of guilt rumbled in Sara's heart for withholding the troubled state of her marriage from her friend. But as long as there was a chance things could work out between she and Oliver, why bring it up? Particularly in light of Carrie's misgivings about the marriage.

"Is Mr. Wilson here? You must go and dance with him. Please don't think you have to chaperone me. I know a lot of the guests – I'll be fine on my own."

The pair reached the far end of the ballroom where their attention was drawn to a group of men breaking into exuberant laughter. Sara smiled, catching sight of George Rives and William Vanderbilt among the circle. They were talking with Woodbury Kane and Perry Belmont, her brother-in-law. She grew cautious, unsure which of the men caused her more apprehension; Oliver's oldest brother, one of his wedding ushers, or William and George. Just as she was thinking of making an impromptu visit to the powder room, George glanced their way, spotting her and Carrie.

"Ladies!" he called with a wave. "Please, come and join us."

Carrie turned to Sara, whispering, "Let the games begin."

Standing tall, Sara composed herself, prepared for the questions regarding Oliver's absence. With head held high she gave her friend an impish smile, "Let's not keep the gentlemen waiting."

"I wouldn't dream of it," Carrie laughed, as they sauntered over to join the men.

George, dressed as a prince in an outfit complete with a sword, bowed as they reached him. It was only then that William recognized Sara in the geisha costume. He was also dressed as a prince, although, as the host of the ball, his costume was more elaborate than George's.

"Well, what have we here? Sara, you made it back from France – what a nice surprise," William smiled. "I thought you were on your honeymoon in Paris." He gave a cursory glance at her costume, "You make a lovely geisha. How are you Mrs. Belmont?"

"I'm well," Sara smiled cordially.

He turned to Carrie, "I see you made it as well, Miss Astor."

"Yes, indeed." Carrie ignored the undertone in his voice, and curtseyed in greeting.

Sara caught the mischievous glint in William's eye as he regarded her friend. It reminded her a little of Oliver's demeanor after drinking too much absinthe. She felt herself become vigilant of the conversation.

"Mrs. Belmont," Mr. Kane greeted. "How nice to be in your company. Where's Oliver?"

"He's on business in Spain. I came alone, not wanting to miss the fun."

"Hello Sara," Perry said politely. "I didn't know Oliver had business in Spain." He eyed her curiously.

Sara's heart pounded, wondering how much Perry knew about their situation. Did Mrs. Belmont tell him Oliver had left her alone in Paris? She fought against her fear and uncertainty, worried he would expose her in front of everyone. She took a deep breath, striving to stay calm.

"I must say, it's nice to see you both again," George welcomed the ladies.

"Thank you, Mr. Rives." Carrie smiled, enjoying the attention.

"There you are," Marshall Wilson joined the group, "I've been looking for you, Carrie. Gentleman, unless you're up for a duel, hands off this one."

"It's very clear Mr. Wilson, that Miss Astor will be chaperoned solely by you this evening," George smiled good-naturedly at the couple.

Extending his palm, Marshall asked, "Miss Astor, would you like to join me for a waltz?"

"Very much so," Carrie said, taking his hand. "If you'll excuse me…" she said to the group. Smiling brightly, the pair took to the ballroom floor.

"Well," Perry said. "I must arrange a waltz with Miss Langdon before her dance card is full. I'm afraid if I don't act now, I may lose my opportunity." He turned to Sara, "It was nice to see you again."

"You too," she smiled, as he turned and left the circle.

"I'll come with you," Woody said, following close behind Perry. "If you'll all excuse me…"

Watching them disappear into the crowd, Sara wondered again how much Perry knew. Searching through the multitude of faces, she looked for Mr. and Mrs. Belmont. Knowing they must surely be in attendance, she kept alert in an effort to avoid them. Catching her preoccupation, she chided herself and pushed aside her worries. Let Oliver explain himself to his parents, she thought, refusing to dwell on his absence. Taking into consideration the happy news of Carrie's courtship with Mr. Wilson, she decided to focus on more pleasant subjects.

"So, Oliver's in Spain on business?" William asked pointedly. "I've never known him to miss a good party – or to be one to put business before pleasure. How very brave of you to come alone." There was an air of skepticism in his comment.

"I simply didn't want to miss the ball tonight, so Oliver suggested I go without him." The fib tumbled off Sara's tongue quite easily.

"How very benevolent of him," William noted. "Considering your beauty and the fact that he's a newlywed, I'd think he'd be here with bells on his feet." He glanced around the hall, "Where's your family?"

"They stayed behind in Paris," Sara explained in an even voice.

"It seems you've become quite independent Mrs. Belmont. Well, your new mother and father-in-law are here tonight. I'm sure they'll be delighted to see you."

Sara smiled congenially. "Yes, of course – I must catch up with them," she said, silently vowing to avoid their company at all costs. The last thing she wanted was a confrontation, particularly without her mother at her side for support.

"May I get you a drink?" George interjected, changing the subject, much to Sara's relief. She wondered if he sensed her discomfort.

"That would be wonderful," Sara replied. "Excuse us, Mr. Vanderbilt."

"I'll catch up with you later, William," Mr. Rives called, leading Sara toward the beverage table.

"Is your wife here tonight?" Sara asked as they skirted the dance floor.

"As a matter of fact, she is." George smiled, glancing through the crowd for his spouse. "She's around her somewhere. You'll have to say hello. My wife's been a big fan of yours since hearing you sing at the Stevens' party."

A smile crossed Sara's face, recalling her first Newport ball. She'd been such an innocent then, happy to be introduced into society. "I'll have to thank her properly," she said appreciatively.

George took two glasses from a tray on the drink table and handed one to Sara.

"A toast," he said.

"A toast," Sara said, clinking her coupe against his. "I'm glad to hear your wife's health has improved. It would be a shame to miss this ball." Sara took a sip from her glass. "And you, George? How have you been?"

"Very well, Sara," he said. "But I must confess, society is at a loss without your presence. You always add a special spark everywhere you go."

"How sweet of you," Sara blushed.

Such a flirtatious comment to a married woman – from a married man, no less. But Mr. Rives had a special place in her heart, generated by their encounter last year; she'd grown ill at the news of her friend, Elizabeth's, impending divorce. George had proven to be her hero, coming to her rescue when she'd fainted on the street. He'd taken her to his suite where she'd recovered from her distress. Sara fought the remembrance of his kiss, and the fondness it had established between them – a fondness she kept well hidden.

Alva entered the ballroom, taking her place at the main table in the front of the room, her sister-in-law at her side. William joined them as the orchestra started a snappy polka, the party now in full swing.

Sara turned back to George with a shy smile. He met her eye, surveying her. "If you think for a moment I believed your story about Oliver being away on business, you are quite mistaken," he said quietly. "I've been around him enough to know that he doesn't stay with anything for long. I'd sincerely hoped, for your sake, those tendencies did not include his wife."

Sara stared at the marble floor below the skirt of her geisha costume. "Why ever would you say such a thing?" she asked, keeping her voice calm. "You're much too suspicious, George."

He continued looking at her with a skeptical eye. "Are you sure you don't want to tell me the truth, Sara? I thought we were friends."

"Of course we're friends," she answered quickly.

"Then why isn't your new husband escorting you tonight?" He narrowed his eyes, giving her a direct look. "It's a simple question – and don't tell me he's on a business trip. Oliver hasn't worked a day in his life, if he can avoid it. With his penchant for partying, it's uncharacteristic of him to miss such a highly touted event."

"George, do stop interrogating me," Sara begged. The noise and heat of the room suddenly overpowered her, causing the champagne to sour in her stomach in a most undesirable way. Perspiration beaded on her forehead, and she grew woozy, reaching to steady herself on a nearby chair.

"Are you all right?" George moved to her side with concern. "You've gotten as pale as a sheet. Sit down. Let me get you some water."

"I think what I really need," Sara said, sliding into the empty chair, "is some fresh air." He poured her a goblet of water from a pitcher on the table and handed her the glass. The sounds in the room began to sway and fade, resembling a carnival funhouse. Sara's hand trembled as she sipped from the goblet.

George noticed a French door leading to the gardens. "Let me help you outside." He reached for her arm, discreetly guiding her out to the porch. The two escaped unnoticed from the surrounding festivities.

With George leading her, Sara walked to an ornate garden bench and sat down, gulping in the fresh air. The fragrance of the earth and dew refreshed her senses, and she relaxed in the night air.

"Thank you George," she said, relaxing. "I don't know what came over me. I'm suddenly not feeling well. Once again you've come to my aid."

"If you keep fainting every time we meet, you'll have me thinking I'm the cause of your distress."

"Don't be silly."

"Sara, you've been pushing yourself too hard," he suggested. "All the excitement and travel with your wedding and now you're back in New York..."

"I feel better, already," Sara said, tugging at her wig. "This costume is so heavy and warm. I must be a little more tired than I realized."

George looked at her with open scrutiny. He tilted his head, assessing her, while a cool breeze blew across the lawn. "You still haven't told me where Oliver is."

"Can we not talk about him right now?" Sara asked. He caught her eye, and a moment of understanding passed between them.

"Just as I thought," George quietly seethed, "The scoundrel's left you, hasn't he?"

"Please, George, I don't want to discuss this now."

Quiet fell between them, the wind rustling the branches of nearby trees. Sounds of laughter echoed over the lawn, melding with the music from the orchestra.

The fresh air calmed Sara's queasiness and she started to feel better.

"Thank you for coming to my rescue. You're very gallant." She fought against lightheadedness, while viewing George in his costume, quietly deciding he made a very handsome prince. "Go back to the party. I'm certain your wife will be looking for you," she urged. "I'm feeling much better. I'm just going to sit here a bit more, then I'll be right in."

"I'm not going anywhere until you're strong enough to return with me," he insisted. "I simply refuse to leave you out here alone at night."

Sara smiled weakly, her stomach swirling again with a nauseous feeling. Too bad Oliver isn't this attentive to my needs, she thought.

"If you insist," she acquiesced. "But let's not start any rumors, shall we?" she said, hinting at the incident in his hotel suite.

Sara worked to recoup her strength, knowing it was improper to stay alone on the porch with George for too long. Summoning all her energy, she stood up, ignoring her queasy stomach.

"Mr. Rives, shall we return to the party? I can hear the orchestra starting a new dance."

George quickly moved to her side, and taking an arm to assist her, he led her toward the French door.

As they reached the entrance the door swung open, and William stepped out on to the patio. "Well, well, well… what have we here?" William's tone dripped with insinuation. "Two married people alone on the terrace?"

"Sara's not feeling well," George told him. "She was overcome by the heat of the room."

"Is that so…" William gave her a look of concern. "Should I call a doctor?"

"No, no," Sara insisted. "I feel much better," she steadied herself. "I just needed to cool off. My costume is so hot, and it must weight fifty pounds." She gave the men a reassuring smile. "The fresh air helped immensely." The last thing I want to do is create a scene, she thought, and headed toward the door with a smile on her face. "Gentlemen, shall we return to the party?"

"Of course," George answered, unconvinced of her recovery.

They followed her back inside where Sara found the nearest chair. Settling into it as gracefully as possible, she raised her fan to cool herself, and focused on the performance of the Mother Goose quadrille.

SARA SWAN WHITING BELMONT
VANDERBILT FANCY BALL 1883

GEORGE L. RIVES
VANDERBILT FANCY BALL 1883

CHAPTER NINE

Ten days later
April 5, 1883
Paris, France

HER ARM WRAPPED FIRMLY AROUND Sara's waist, Bridget assisted her mistress to the door of the Whiting's Paris apartment. Not wishing to alarm the family, the maid had waited until they'd arrived in France to send a note informing Mrs. Whiting of Sara's ill health. Finally reaching the suite, Bridget grabbed for the door, when it swung open. Mrs. Whiting and her French housekeeper, Élise, were waiting for them, their faces tense with concern.

"Quickly, get her to her room," Mrs. Whiting instructed.

"I am not an invalid," Sara complained. "I can get there fine, just let me lean on you a bit."

Mrs. Whiting helped her daughter move down the hallway to her room. Sara gingerly shimmied onto the bed, pulling the blankets around her shoulders.

"The doctor has been called. He'll be here shortly." Mrs. Whiting shook her head and demanded, "What on earth has you so ill, Sara?"

"Nothing Mother, I assure you," Sara leaned against the pillows. "I just haven't been feeling well for the last week or so. I seem to tire easily and my stomach keeps churning." Sara was careful not to discuss any ocean voyages.

"Be certain to tell the doctor everything," her mother commanded. "Just relax and try to rest until he gets here. I'm sure it's nothing serious, dear."

"Would you like some peppermint tea?" Élise asked sympathetically. "It will soothe your stomach."

"Yes, please. That would be lovely." Sara gave the housekeeper a weak smile. Her attention shifted to her maid. "Bridget, we're home now. Why don't you get settled, and relax a bit after our journey."

"If you're certain miss," Bridget's face was cloaked with worry, her devotion most evident. Sara knew she'd been very upset at her terrible case of seasickness on the homeward voyage. The maid could be trusted with their secret destination, but Bridget was weary and Sara didn't want her mother grueling her with questions at a time when she might crack.

"Yes, I am most certain," Sara insisted. "Take a hot bath and a nap. There'll be plenty of time to unpack and talk about our trip." She finished the last sentence with a frown directed at her mother to drive the point home.

"If you're certain…" Bridget gave Mrs. Whiting a sheepish glance. Mrs. Whiting nodded her permission, while moving to sit in the bedside chair. The maid escaped the room just as Élise returned with the tea tray clanging with silver and china.

"Set the tray down on the side table," Mrs. Whiting ordered. "I'll stay with Sara. You wait by the front door for the doctor to arrive."

"Yes, ma'am," Élise replied. She set the tray where instructed and left the chamber on a hasty step.

Mrs. Whiting busied herself, pouring tea and adding sugar. She handed the saucer and cup to her daughter, tucking a tiny piece of shortbread on the dish.

Sipping the hot tea, Sara leaned her head back on the pillow, and let out a long sigh. "Oh my goodness… I can't remember when I've felt this terrible." She worked to get comfortable, but it seemed an impossible task. Giving the shortbread some consideration, her stomach heaved at the prospect and she decided against eating.

A commotion at the bedroom door sent her mother in that direction as Élise led the doctor into the chamber.

"Hello young lady," Doctor Nichols greeted, entering the room. "Mrs. Whiting," he added with a nod. "Perhaps you should leave Sara and I alone for a few moments, if you don't mind."

"Of course, doctor," Mrs. Whiting acquiesced, ushering Élise out of the room in front of her. "Please let us know if you need anything – anything at all."

Sara heard the latch as her mother closed the door behind herself, leaving Sara alone with the physician. She broke into a light sweat, shifting upright on the bed. Suddenly she was frightened to hear her prognosis, and her stomach flipped again in objection.

Pulling a stethoscope from his black bag Dr. Nichols moved to the bedside. "Now, let's have a look shall we?"

The same day
New York, New York

"So, you're on a break from Congress?" August Belmont glanced at his oldest son relaxing on the library sofa.

"Yes, I've got a few weeks before we reconvene," Perry answered. "I must admit, I was glad for a chance to get out of Washington and visit with you and Mamma."

"Your visit is well-timed, with Auggie and Bessie here, too. What do you think of Auggie's young son? Your nephew has grown quite a bit already."

"Yes, the little man is a healthy young Belmont, that's for sure," Perry chuckled. "August Belmont the third – he has quite a legacy to live up to." He smiled fondly at his father. "It seems he's the only person in New York who didn't attend the Vanderbilt Fancy Ball. That was one party that won't soon be forgotten."

"Yes. It was quite an event," August agreed a bit grudgingly. "There was a time when your mother could throw a party like that. Now it looks as though Mrs. Astor has a bit of competition in creating entertainment for society's party-goers."

"Indeed. I saw Sara there. She came as a geisha," Perry mentioned, his tone casual. "I'm surprised she came without Oliver – especially in light of the recent problems on their honeymoon. Did you and Mamma have a chance to speak with her?"

"You must be mistaken," August frowned. "Your mother just received a letter from Sara and she's still in Paris with her family."

"Paris?" A puzzled look crossed Perry's face. "I'm certain she was in New York. In fact, I spoke with her."

"You actually spoke with her?" August asked, surprised. "Neither your mother nor I noticed her there. Are you absolutely sure it was Sara? It *was* a masquerade party."

"It was Sara, alright. I'm certain of it. And apparently, she was alone," Perry assured him. "The photographer took her picture." After a moment he continued, cautious, "Have you received any word from Oliver? Do you know what's going on between the two of them?"

"I really don't know what to tell you where Oliver is concerned," August said dismally. "I cannot fathom how he could walk out on his wife like that, even if Mrs. Whiting was annoying him. You simply don't walk out on your wife, especially on your honeymoon."

"It's a horrible affair. And it certainly doesn't shine a favorable light on him," Perry agreed. "Why he's acting this way is a mystery to me, especially since a marriage to Miss Whiting was all he clamored about for months on end. He seemed to desperately want it. There must be something more to this than we're aware of." He looked to his father for an answer.

"I'm past trying to figure out Oliver's conduct – or meddling in my children's lives," August asserted. "Frankly, I don't know any more than Mamma has told me. And she only knows what she is told through the letters she's received from Spain. Hopefully Oliver will return to Paris and make amends before he casts the family into a scandal."

Perry sighed, shaking his head. "Let's hope it's a simple lover's quarrel and that they'll work things out favorably for all concerned." He sported an optimistic smile, "Shall we change the subject and talk about something more pleasant? How about politics?"

August laughed, "Politics is always a good topic of conversation, especially when my son is a congressman." He got up from his desk and poured them both a glass of whiskey. Settling on the easy chair next to Perry he asked, "What's the latest news from Capitol Hill?"

Three weeks later
April 29, 1883
Tangiers, Morocco

Fighting the trembling in his hands, Oliver scanned Mrs. Whiting's letter again, though he knew he'd read it correctly the first time.

Sara was pregnant.

It was that simple – and that difficult.

Apparently his Mamma knew about the pregnancy as well, writing him an urgent letter demanding he return to Paris immediately and try to make amends for his absence.

"When will Mamma stop with these letters filled with useless advice?" he whispered. Oliver crumbled the note, angry and exasperated. The tone of reprimand resounded through his brain, though he tried hotly to discount it.

Unsure of his next move, he focused on Mrs. Whiting's note, "Sara has forgotten nothing of what happened to her…" [28] And neither had he, Oliver fumed! If her meddling mother and sisters had just gotten their own suite, none of this would have happened! He took a long, deep drink from his glass of absinthe.

Both letters were filled with a sharp sentiment of reproach. "You must take into consideration that women are subject to serious misgivings in the most unaccountable ways. The fear of the unknown and possibly terrible results of a first confinement preys upon the mind. A husband's gentle treatment and devoted attention is put to the test, and above all things helps to alleviate a wife's restlessness, to give her the peace of mind necessary to the proper development of her child and its safe delivery. You would never forgive yourself," Mrs. Belmont added, "if you were to do anything in ignorance which could cause your wife or child's ruin." [29]

"Why such a sour mood?" The nameless woman rolled over on the mattress, her eyes blurred with sleep. "Is the party over already?"

"Yes, my dear." Oliver tried to muster a friendly tone. "I'm afraid I'm going to have to leave Morocco as soon as possible." He'd been successful in putting Sara and their wedding far out of his mind while in this exotic place. But now, the realities of his marriage were creeping into his holiday. He couldn't avoid his vows any longer. "Do you mind getting your things together? I'm going to be leaving in a bit…"

"Don't worry. I get the message loud and clear." The woman sat up in bed, pulling the sheet around her naked body. "I'll disappear like a ghost."

"Thank you." Tossing some cash on the bed he offered an apathetic smile. Grabbing his suitcase and traveling papers, he headed out to book a train ticket to Paris. There was no way to avoid this conflict, Oliver thought glumly, exiting the suite.

"Sara is pregnant," he repeated softly, walking on a leaden step down the hotel hallway. Pondering this new development, he tried desperately to come to grips with the news.

A son?

A daughter?

A son would be preferable as a rival to Auggie's new family addition. Oliver wished he didn't feel such competition with his older brother, but it really did appear to him that his parents weren't being fair, showing distinct favoritism toward his older brother.

Perhaps a child could patch things up between he and Sara. Perhaps finally he would get some respect from his parents. He reached the hotel lobby and stepped out into the exotic Tangier morning, troubled and uncertain about his future.

CHAPTER TEN

Six days later
May 5, 1883
Paris, France

"MRS. BELMONT MUST NOT HAVE all the facts correct if she thinks you're to blame for this tribulation!" Mrs. Whiting huffed. "No man should drink himself stupid and then treat his wife with such brute violence. The nerve of that young man, leaving you alone while he gallivants in foreign countries." She bit her tongue from adding 'in the company of *dancers*', deciding to spare her daughter the shame of Oliver's activities.

Sitting in a chair by the window Sara watched her mother and Bridget pack their trunks. "Mrs. Belmont claims, 'I must do all that a loving wife and true woman can do to guard against calamity.'" [30] Sara looked up from the note. "I'm telling you Mother, it sounds as though she truly does blame me for Oliver's actions."

"We shall see about that!" Mrs. Whiting clenched her lips in fury. "I witnessed his violent moods myself. It's clear Oliver learned to drink spirits very well while in Bremen. The fault of that cannot be placed upon you my dear, so chase the thought from your mind."

"That's the last of it ma'am," Bridget announced.

"Just in time. Call the bellman and tell him to come and get our bags," Mrs. Whiting ordered the maid. "We're leaving for London immediately."

The same day
New York, New York

Bright sunshine and blue sky brought no solace to the mood in the magnificent carriage moving at a regal pace down New York's Fifth Avenue toward the Belmont home.

"What if it's true?" Mrs. Belmont pressed her husband. "What if Oliver has taken to strong drink since living in Bremen?"

"I truly hope that's not the case, Mamma." August tried to allay her fears while rubbing his temple, brooding. "I had the best intentions for Oliver to learn a respectable trade. I thought time away from the set would discourage him from marrying Miss Whiting. Drinking spirits in excess was not part of the plan."

"I know August, I know." Caroline patted his arm. "But what if our best efforts have failed? I hate to say it, but what if he has become an alcoholic?" She thought back to the scribbled letters she'd received from her son while in Germany, silently renewing her worst fears.

"Now, let's not jump to any conclusions." He took her hand, holding it tenderly. "Have you received a letter from him recently?"

"Yes," she nodded. "He's on his way back to Paris as we speak." A heavy sigh escaped Caroline. "I only hope it's not too late."

Two days later
May 7, 1883
London, England

The sight of breakfast made Sara's stomach gurgle in a most unpleasant way. Preoccupied with the mess of her marriage, her emotions ran rampant between relief and terror at the thought of going back to New York – without her husband. The only consolation was their plan to move on to the comfort and safety of Swanhurst.

She had departed Newport a bride in a wedding carriage bound for a new life. I never in my wildest dreams imagined I'd be returning again to my family home, she thought sadly, especially so soon after my marriage. Fighting back anguished tears she gingerly pushed away the food.

"What if this situation turns up in the newspaper?" Sara looked to her mother, speaking the fears she'd been afraid to voice.

"Just don't you worry about any of that in your condition," Mrs. Whiting told her sternly. "We'll take matters into our own hands if we have to."

Reviewing the steamer tickets, Mrs. Whiting contemplated how to deal with this very problem. She planned to rescue her daughter's reputation if it took her dying breath to pull it off. The thought occurred to her that actually going to the newspapers with the story might generate public sympathy for Sara. But right now, the most important thing was to get Sara back to Newport at once.

"What's that supposed to mean?" Sara watched her mother closely. Waving the question away, she released a sigh of weariness. "Forget I asked... I'm not sure I want to know what you've got up your sleeve."

Bridget closed up a small satchel and set it by the door with the other luggage. "I've finished packing the bags, ma'am."

"Where are Milly and Jane?" Sara asked. She suspected her mother had spoken to them about being kind to her, in light of her pregnancy. If the truth be told, she was relieved they weren't around at the present moment.

"They're already downstairs, waiting for us." A loud knock interrupted Mrs. Whiting.

Bridget opened the door to a bellman dressed in uniform. "I've come for your bags," he announced. "A load of luggage is departing for the ship in fifteen minutes and I need to get them downstairs right away."

Mrs. Whiting pointed to their trunks. "Over there," she said. "We'll be leaving momentarily, as well."

The women watched silently as he loaded their bags onto the cart. Mrs. Whiting tipped him a coin, and he left, pushing the baggage down the long hallway.

Turning to Sara, she asked simply, "Are you ready?"

Rising from her chair Sara wrapped a light shawl around her shoulders. "As ready as I'll ever be."

The three women vacated the suite without a backward glance, almost as if they believed the past could be wiped away if one simply ignored it. Taking the stairs they descended into the lobby, bustling with travelers on holiday in London. Weaving their way through clusters of families and couples making hotel arrangements, Sara followed her mother, as Bridget dutifully trailed both women.

"There are your sisters." Mrs. Whiting waved them over.

"The ship is scheduled to depart on time," Jane informed them, walking up. "I just spoke with the liaison at the concierge desk."

"Well, at least something is going as planned," Mrs. Whiting sighed. "Let me go to the front desk and check out, then we'll grab a taxi to the port."

Spotting a chair away from the clamor, Sara sought its momentary comfort. Mrs. Whiting headed across the lobby toward the front desk. A distinct sense of urgency pulsed through everything that was happening, as if an impending typhoon approached that would not be ignored. Settling into the lounger, Sara fiddled with her gloves, working to stay calm, grateful for her mother's experience and assistance.

Approaching the clerk Mrs. Whiting informed him they were checking out of the hotel.

"Very well ma'am," he said, handing her an invoice for their room.

Signing the paper with a quick hand, she authorized payment for the suite. Setting the pen on the counter, she turned to go, when the clerk called after her.

"Mrs. Whiting," he motioned, "a cable has come for you." The clerk handed her the small paper from the telegraph company. With a quick glance she saw it was from Oliver – and intended for Sara. The message was sent from Paris, short and succinct:

"Leave for London tonight." [31]

She glanced at Sara resting in the chair. *I don't want to upset her with this,* Mrs. Whiting deliberated, contemplating the chance of a public confrontation with Oliver. Disgust and concern clouded her thoughts, and Mrs. Whiting became more determined on a swift escape from England. *Isn't that just like him, to come running back now,* she seethed. *He's most probably been reprimanded by his father and ordered to make things right.* Her mind raced, evaluating her options. After a moment's consideration she waved down the clerk, "I'd like to send a telegram at once."

"Of course ma'am," he said, reaching for a telegraph form. He slid the paper across the desk.

Taking it from the clerk she decided to answer for her daughter. *It's my duty as a mother to protect her, especially in her present condition,* she reassured herself. Lifting the pen, she wrote a quick response, impersonating Sara.

"Do not come for the present. Cannot see you now. Will write." [32]

Mrs. Whiting handed the message back to the clerk, "It's very important this telegram go out immediately."

The clerk nodded his understanding. "We have our own telegraph office on the premises," he informed her. "I'll have it sent at once."

"Thank you." She paid him for the service and left the hotel desk.

Fresh anger coursed though Mrs. Whiting as she contemplated Oliver's latest move. Marching across the large lobby to rejoin her family, her thoughts were colored by her recollections. Could she really trust this man with her daughter after the way he'd threatened her? Was there any hope at all of him giving up his crazy, alcoholic lifestyle and being a good husband – or a good father to her unborn grandchild? The answer suddenly became clear. She stopped mid-step in the center of the lobby, spun around and walked back to the clerk.

"I'd like to make a change to the telegram," she told him.

"I've already sent the message to the telegraph office," the clerk informed her. "You said it was urgent so I ordered a bellman to take it immediately."

"Then I will write another," she told him firmly.

Once again he handed Mrs. Whiting a message form and she wrote to Oliver again, simply saying:

"Everything at an end." [33]

No _____ Mots _____
Date _____ Heure _____

Indications
spéciales : _____

Taxe _____

Transmis à _____
Fil n° _____
Heure _____
L'Employé : _____

Adresse de l'Expéditeur : _____

5 mol.

Mrs Salmons Claridges hotel London

leave for London tonight 7am long
do you intend being in London Queens
hotel Bath

Oliver

Certifié conforme
L'Employé

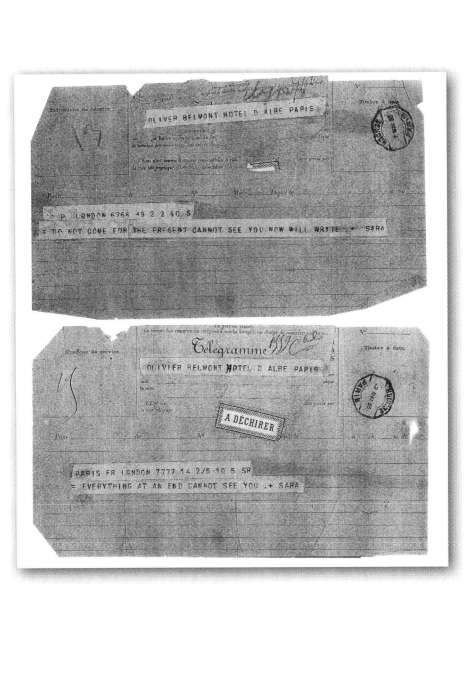

CHAPTER ELEVEN

One week later
May 14, 1883
Atlantic Ocean

THE JOURNEY ACROSS THE ATLANTIC was a bit easier on Sara than the trip at the end of March had been. Perhaps due to the summer weather, the seas were smoother for their journey home. Grateful for some relief from her symptoms Sara rarely left the stateroom, preferring to be away from the gaiety of other travelers. Sheltered in the cabin she read books and magazines to pass the time. Struggling to resist the grief and embarrassment of her predicament was a task much easier said than done. In spite of her best effort to stay optimistic, a deep melancholy permeated Sara's mood. Heartache caused by Oliver's abandonment clouded her outlook on life, the future an unknown, black void.

Except for this baby, she thought, gingerly rubbing her belly.

A baby. Not any baby, but a Belmont baby. And she, Sara Swan Whiting Belmont, was going to be a mother. So much had happened since Oliver had walked out on her. Now on the journey back to New York she could finally catch her breath, and contemplate the new life growing inside her.

An earlier conversation with her mother had revealed Mrs. Whiting's opinion. I know my mother wants me to get a legal separation, Sara thought glumly. Possibly even a divorce! But Oliver *is* the father of my child, she thought, and my child deserves a father.

The memory of being slammed against the apartment wall in Paris brought a shudder. Was I pregnant then, she wondered? He could have hurt the baby! Sara tried not to worry, but she was concerned for her unborn child's health. The realization hit her that if Oliver had treated her that way once, he was prone to do it again.

Unless he stopped drinking absinthe. Would he? Or perhaps the question was could he? Sara's mind spun in circles with questions that eluded answers.

Writing letters became another pastime during the long hours of the trip. Sara had written to Frederika, Oliver's sister, for some understanding. The two ladies had become friends after the marriage, but now Sara wondered if she would lose that friendship in the wake of her husband's misconduct.

She also wrote again to her mother-in-law, no longer addressing her as 'My dearest petite-mere', but in the more formal greeting of 'Mrs. Belmont'. Sara had known the greatest happiness in the first month of her marriage. Nostalgia for those few fleeting weeks trailed through her mind, making her yearn for their return. Although she was clear in her language to her mother-in-law that a separation seemed imminent, she could not help but tell Mrs. Belmont "I can never forget how sweet you have been to me." [34] Sara groaned, unable to understand how her life had become a shambles so quickly.

Looking up as the door opened, she saw her mother quietly enter the cabin.

"You're awake," Mrs. Whiting said. "I thought you might be napping."

"I was." Sara mustered a wan smile.

"We'll arrive in New York harbor tomorrow morning."

"And not a moment too soon," Sara grumbled, leaning back in the soft chair. "Are we staying at the house in New York?"

"No. Tomorrow night we have rooms at the Hotel Brunswick. I don't want to bother opening the house. I think the Belmonts are in New York, so we're going to Newport right away. I want to make every effort to avoid a confrontation with them."

Mrs. Whiting didn't speak of her decision to go to the newspapers with word of Oliver's escapades. She wanted to keep this news from Sara in an effort not to worry her. It was clear at this point that a scandal would be unavoidable. And if anyone was going to feel the brunt of the disgrace it should be the Belmonts, *not* the Whitings – and certainly not Sara.

She assessed her daughter's strength. The color seemed to be coming back to her cheeks, although her sadness was another matter. Thankfully the weather was warmer now that spring was shifting to summer. Perhaps the sunshine would cheer her up a bit.

"Are you hungry? Do you want to go up to the dining room and get something to eat? You've been holed up in this room for days. Why not step out for some fresh air?"

Considering her offer, Sara shrugged, "That might be a good idea." She gave her mother a feeble smile. "I think I'm craving chicken soup."

Relief swept over Mrs. Whiting at this news. Sara had eaten very little and she seemed to sleep much too much, even for a pregnant woman. It was obvious her daughter was depressed and humiliated by Oliver's absence. Mrs. Whiting hoped and prayed it wouldn't take a heavy toll on her usual gay mood. It wouldn't be healthy for her – or for the baby.

"Come on then. Maybe a short walk on the promenade deck as well." Mrs. Whiting gave a hand to steady Sara out of her chair. "Some exercise will be good for you."

Grateful for her mother's kindness, she followed her obediently out of the cabin.

The next day
May 15, 1883
New York, New York

Disembarking the carriage, Mrs. Belmont hurried up the porch steps. The butler opened the front door while a maid took her cloak and hat.

"Where is Mr. Belmont?" she asked Jacob.

"In the study ma'am."

Patting a crochet handkerchief on her forehead, she sought to wipe away the worry breaking on her brow as she rushed down the hallway in search of her husband.

"There you are," she said, finding him relaxing in his chair, puffing on a fragrant cigar. "We must speak at once!"

"What has you so distressed?" he frowned. "Or do I need to ask?"

"I'm sure you don't," Caroline grimaced. "But we'll have the discussion anyway." She sat down in the chair nearest him.

"Oliver?"

"I just came from *Sherry's*," she explained. "I was having lunch with the Endicotts and Mrs. Tiffany."

Eyeing her, August took a long draw on his cigar.

"It seems that the Whitings have been spotted in New York," she blurted out. "Well, Mrs. Whiting anyway," Caroline was quick to add. "No one has seen Sara, but I feel certain she's with her mother."

"Do you think they returned from Paris without Oliver?" August leveled his eyes on his wife, while contending with his temper.

"They must have," Caroline wrung her hands. "The last letter I received from Oliver said he was on his way to Paris."

"Are you certain Oliver isn't traveling with them?" August pressed his wife for information. "Maybe he caught up with them in London."

"Then why would Sara be in hiding?" she countered. "If they'd patched things up I'm sure they would make a public appearance – together – if only for the sake of quieting the gossip. Besides, he would certainly have let us know he was here, if only to beg for forgiveness for the mess he's made of things – again."

"And for assistance," August added, "as is his usual *modus operandi*."

"What do you think we should do?" Mrs. Belmont implored her husband, unsure of their course of action.

Staring at the burning ember of his cigar, August grew quiet contemplating the question. Taking a last drag, he reached over and calmly snuffed it out in the ashtray.

He met Caroline's concerned eyes. "Nothing," he answered in a calm voice. "We will do absolutely nothing."

"Oh August, I don't know if that's the right way to handle this," Caroline argued. "Perhaps we should pay the Whitings a visit and try to talk this through."

"And say what?" he demanded. "So sorry our son deserted your daughter while on honeymoon. And oh, by the way, maybe this wouldn't have happened if you'd have left the newlyweds alone in their suite?"

He scoffed at his own statement – and the outrageousness of the circumstances.

Covering her face with a hand, Caroline shook her head, pained at the position in which they found themselves. "Maybe you're right," she conceded. "I wish I felt more confident about staying silent. But perhaps it would be best to wait for Mrs. Whiting to contact us."

"And we can still hope that Oliver will make an appearance – and soon! Even though there's talk of a separation – or divorce, God forbid, no one has filed any legal documents. There may still be time for Oliver to salvage his marriage amicably, especially since there's a baby on the way."

August got up and went to the bar where he poured himself a glass of whiskey. "Let's give it a day or two Mamma before we make any decisions, or take any action."

Saying that, he drained his glass dry

Later that day
New York, New York

After looking quickly at the message, Mrs. Whiting's eyes darted around the room as she weighed her options. She'd sent a telegram from the ship to Newport giving word to open Swanhurst immediately as the family would be returning home as soon as possible. She'd gotten a reply from their houseman, Owen. Mary was preparing for their arrival but unfortunately, Swanhurst would not be ready for at least a week. Owen informed her that a rental was available on Catherine Street and could be retained immediately if she so advised. [35]

"What's wrong Mother?" Sara asked, watching her pace the hotel room.

"Nothing dear. Nothing at all."

"You're not being truthful with me," Sara pressed. "Is it the Belmonts? Are they still in New York? Do they know we're here?"

"Slow down, Sara." Mrs. Whiting kept her voice breezy, "One question at a time, dear."

Wearing an expectant look, Sara waited for an explanation. Her mother seemed at a loss for words, which rarely happened. Sara would have thought it almost comical watching her mother struggle, if the situation had not been so dire.

"To answer your first question, yes, the Belmonts are in New York. But to your second question; do they know we're here?" She paused with a sigh, "Well... I wish I knew the answer to that one."

Glancing at Owen's telegram Mrs. Whiting continued. "One thing I know for certain, we must get to Newport right away. The less time we're in New York, the less chance there is of starting a scandal before we can manage to get home."

In that quick moment Mrs. Whiting made up her mind to take the rental on Catherine Street. Desperate times called for desperate action.

Grabbing her pocketbook, Mrs. Whiting headed for the hotel door. "I'm going out to send a telegram. Bridget, make sure everything is ready to go. We're leaving for Rhode Island early in the morning," she announced. "And you..." she looked at Sara. "Try to get some rest and let me handle things."

The door swung shut in her mother's wake, leaving Sara and Bridget in silence. A dark foreboding encroached on Sara's emotions, and once again she wished that she could live the last few years of her life over again. An image of Mr. Waterbury proposing marriage ran through her mind...

But there was no going back in time. Gathering all the courage she could rally, Sara summoned her strength to face the scandal she knew was headed straight for her.

The next day
May 16, 1883
Newport Rhode, Island

Mary bustled around the rented house ordering the linens to be changed and the windows opened to let the ocean breeze freshen the home. Owen had gotten word that the Whitings were returning to Newport immediately.

Something was wrong – she could feel it in her bones. The family had planned to stay in Paris for the summer season. As a result, Mary had not opened Swanhurst this year. There was no way she could have the house ready in a few days, so Mrs. Whiting sent word to rent the Catherine Street house for a week or two until Swanhurst could be cleaned and organized for the season.

Owen told her Miss Sara was returning with the family. "My goodness…" Mary wondered aloud, "what could have happened for that to occur?" Sara was a married woman now and should be taking up housekeeping with her husband.

A smile touched her lips thinking back to Sara's wedding day. Her young mistress had been so happy. Watching the girl grow from a child to a woman, Mary had felt her own sense of pride and happiness at the nuptials.

Perhaps Oliver had stayed in Europe on business, she considered. His father does have a lot of associates in Germany. Somehow though, Mary could not shake a nagging feeling of apprehension. Why were the Whitings in such a rush to return home? Maybe there had been an accident, she thought with horror. No. Someone would have sent word. Maybe someone fell ill while traveling? That sort of thing happens. She certainly hoped that wasn't the case. Mrs. Whiting was in good health, she reflected. Jane and Milly also both had strong constitutions.

Her speculation focused on Sara. She was young and beautiful – and married. Mary tried to imagine why she was returning with the family instead of heading to the Belmont home where she should now live as the newest Mrs. Belmont.

Walking into the kitchen Mary spotted Owen entering from the porch carrying a box full of groceries.

"Where do you want these supplies?" he asked, glancing around the room.

"Here on the counter top," Mary directed.

Owen put the box on the counter where Mary indicated. He took off his cap, running his hand through a crop of sandy blond hair. Replacing the hat on his head, he jerked at the suspender strap of his faded blue jeans.

"There's more on the wagon," he said. "I stopped at the dairy and got the milk, cheese and eggs you asked for, too."

"Thank you, Owen. Do you know when the family will arrive?"

"I just got another cable telling me to pick them up from the four o'clock ferry." He gave her a quick look as if waiting for instructions. Getting none, he went back outside to get the rest of the groceries.

Mary looked at the clock over the kitchen mantle. Almost noon, she thought, hurrying to stock the cabinets and ice box with fresh food. That would give cook just enough time to get dinner ready.

CHAPTER TWELVE

The next day
May 17, 1883
Newport, Rhode Island

THE SWEET SINGING OF A songbird emanated from a tree outside her bedroom window. Sara tossed, waking from a restless sleep. *Morning is always a time filled with promise,* she thought glumly. Rolling over with a sad laugh, she pulled the blankets tight. *Be that as it may,* she pouted, *I don't want to get out of bed.*

The family had arrived in Newport late yesterday afternoon, and although she wasn't back home at Swanhurst, at least she was back in her City-by-the-Sea. Admittedly, that brought some comfort. But what would happen next was anyone's guess.

With the summer season underway the town was alive with parties and balls, all of which she could not attend in her pregnant condition. Wishing for the simplicity of her débutante days, she surrendered to the fact that her summer would be spent in confinement, hidden away from the season's merriment.

Her thoughts drifted to the first kiss she'd shared with Oliver on the lawn at Elizabeth's wedding. It seemed like a lifetime ago. The moment so tender, his kiss so sweet. She gently touched her lips with a fingertip. How she longed for that Oliver to return, sweep her off her feet and make this nightmare disappear. She groaned, and covered her head with a pillow trying to push away her thoughts.

If Sara was perfectly honest with herself, divorce was not what she wanted – far from it. Things were happening too fast for her to think clearly, she silently admitted. *I think I can find forgiveness for Oliver's* outbursts and desertion, Sara thought, especially if he apologizes and tries to make amends – at the least give up the absinthe. She hadn't heard from him since leaving Paris. Did he love her enough to make the effort to salvage their marriage? If only it were true. Sara wished it was, and fervently hoped they could avoid all this ugly scandal nonsense and enjoy the summer, awaiting the birth of their child together.

The horrible memories returned… Oliver drunk in the night, smashing bottles and throwing obscenities around the room like daggers. The sound of him yelling *she was not his wife* echoed in her ears. She remembered the pain and shock of her head slamming against the wall from blows delivered by Oliver in a fit of his inebriated rage.

She realized how lucky she and her baby had been to escape injury. Her mother was pushing for divorce, even suggesting she see a lawyer. Sara appreciated the help, but felt her mother was being a little overbearing in her opinions. After all it was her life, her marriage and her decision if there was to be a divorce.

Unless of course, Oliver made the decision first and started proceedings against her, although Sara couldn't fathom what grounds he could use to file a complaint. She had a much better case against him for abuse and abandonment.

Oh, how she hated her thoughts! What an absolutely preposterous situation! I've only been married a few months and already I'm considering a divorce, she brooded. This was even worse than Elizabeth's marriage, which at least lasted a year. I'm so ashamed mine's endured mere months, she thought sadly.

Such a cruel twist of fate.

"There's no avoiding it," she whispered, throwing the pillow on the floor. "Sara Swan Belmont you are caught in the web of scandal and there is simply no way to avoid it." She sat up on the bed catching her reflection in the bureau mirror. Her long brunette hair fell across her creamy shoulders in a sleepy tousle, but it was no distraction from the dark circles of worry under her eyes.

For a moment she contemplated lounging in her room all day long. "I'll just ignore everyone today," she whispered. A minute later she reconsidered, throwing her legs over the side of the bed in a huff. "No, I can be strong…" she affirmed, walking to the washstand.

Pouring water from the pitcher she gave her face a splash, rubbing the sleep from her eyes. "Staying in bed is the most boring thing I can think of to do," she murmured. Sara peered at her face in the mirror. "And being in confinement for the summer season is a close second."

With a heavy heart she pulled on a mint-green muslin day dress and headed for the dining room, focused on a cup of strong tea.

I wonder if Mother has any news from Oliver, she thought, leaving her room. It was certain to be an eventful day, but how those events would unfold she was not so certain.

Uncertainty had apparently become her specialty.

The same day
New York, New York

Leaning his crutches against the wall, Oliver dutifully sat down at his father's insistence. His mother glared at him — a stern and silent look. He'd sprained his ankle in London rushing around after Sara, and hobbled like an invalid from the pain. He'd hoped it would bring him a little sympathy, but the mood in the room was anything but compassionate.

"What on earth possessed you to leave your wife in Paris?" August demanded. "You can't seem to commit to a vocation and apparently you cannot even commit to your marriage!" He fought to contain his anger. "A marriage that you insisted on — against our wishes, I might add!"

"And now your wife is pregnant," his mother took up, as if he needed reminding.

"I offered to get her family their own apartment," Oliver began in his own defense. "Sara was more loyal to them than she was to me. After a while I could stomach no more of her mother and sisters. I had to get out of there — they were driving me insane."

"Stop being so dramatic," his father barked. "It's not as if you didn't know Mrs. Whiting had made plans to stay with you." He paused, shaking his head. "Regardless, there were much better ways to deal with the matter than walking out and taking off for Spain!"

"And what about these rumors of you drinking in excess and spending time with dancers!" his mother asked angrily. "Didn't you bring enough scandal upon this family by leaving your wife? To be spotted publicly in the company of that type of a woman is a double insult, not only to us, but to your wife waiting in Paris for your return."

Rubbing his face with his hands he grimaced, trying to block out the verbal lashing. Confrontation had never been one of his favorite pastimes. "What do you want me to say to you?" he asked in resignation. "I acted impulsively, but once I left, I admit my pride would not allow me to return."

"Your pride!" his father bellowed. "What about your honor? What about the family's honor? Did those things ever cross your mind Oliver, or were you more intent on having a fun time traveling with your French dancer?" He drove the last words home with vehemence.

"And now Sara is with child," his mother repeated. "There is no undoing that fact. As a gentleman you are forced to conduct yourself in a responsible fashion toward your wife and your unborn baby." She scowled at him, hoping the truth of her words would sink into his philandering faculties. "You must put away your wild ways and think about the repercussions of your conduct," she commanded.

Studying the parquet floor Oliver said nothing, avoiding his parents' eyes. How could they possibly know what it had been like living with the Whitings in Paris? They could yell and scream all they wanted, but he knew he'd done what he needed to by escaping France.

After a moment his Papa spoke, "I'm giving you Oakland as a marriage gift. The two of you can take up housekeeping and prepare for the child." He kept his tone even. "But you're not to follow Sara back to Newport straight away – is that clear? It could be seen as an admission of your guilt. You'll remain here for at least a week," he ordered. "In the meantime we must somehow sway public opinion to see Sara as a straying wife by returning to the States without your consent.[37] We must maintain your innocence at all costs as there is certain to be a scandal."

The dispensation continued from his Mamma, "I'll help you draft a letter to your wife," she said flatly. "This must be handled with finesse. You must insist that things cannot and must not remain as they are now and an early solution is demanded by every law of decency and propriety."

"Tell her to meet you at Oakland where you'll live as husband and wife and prepare for your child's delivery," August added. "Explain you'll be delayed because you've injured your ankle and cannot travel at the present time."

"What kind of excuse is that?" Oliver objected. "I just crossed the Atlantic Ocean on a steamship and my condition had no consequence to my traveling."

"It is an excuse that we must use to buy us some time," August dictated.

"You must express surprise to Sara," his mother added, "and deep regret that she should have come to America with her family in your absence and without your knowledge. Tell her you're willing to do whatever you can to save you both from a scandal that will affect you the rest of your lives!" [38]

So this is what is meant by wedded bliss, Oliver thought with contempt. He let his thoughts drift back to the first time he saw Sara at Mrs. Stevens' ball swirling in her gold gown like a princess. Sara, so beautiful on their wedding day, her veil lifted to him, revealing her innocent face at the altar. Marriage had been his escape plan from his father's control. Now, here he sat, being berated like a child.

His plan had backfired.

Their first weeks in Paris had been so wonderful. Oliver really did love her – although not so much her family. He began to consider that his parents might be right with their advice on how to resolve the fiasco. Maybe he and Sara could recapture their nuptial happiness and find a way to start their marriage fresh at Oakland. Maybe once settled in their own home they could begin anew on a more positive note. He looked up at his parents staring at him with open disappointment.

"As you wish," he capitulated.

The next day
May 18, 1883
Newport, Rhode Island

"Try to eat some toast," Mary said, placing a dish in front of her. "Your mother gave me strict orders that I should get you to eat something. I'm going to make you some coddled eggs."

"Where did Mother go this morning?" Sara asked. "It's unusual for her to leave so early. She didn't mention any appointments."

"I'm not sure miss, but she said she'd be back before noon."

Taking a tiny sip of tea, Sara watched the housekeeper return to the kitchen for her breakfast. Placing the cup back in the saucer she heard the front door slam and looked up to see her mother stroll into the dining room.

"You're up," Mrs. Whiting said. "How are you feeling this morning?"

"As well as can be expected, I suppose. Although, I must admit I'm happy to be back in Newport. I'll be even happier when I'm back in my own bed at Swanhurst."

"It'll only be a few days," Mrs. Whiting assured her with a comforting smile.

"Where did you go to so early this morning? Did you meet someone for breakfast?"

Hesitating, Mrs. Whiting sat down at the dining room table. "Nowhere special," she waved away the inquiry.

An air of deception hovered over the room.

"Mother... what have you done?" Sara was almost afraid of the answer.

Mary emerged from the kitchen with a silver teapot. "I thought I heard the front door. Would you like some breakfast, ma'am?"

Thankful for the interruption Mrs. Whiting smiled, "That sounds wonderful." Fiddling with her napkin, she measured her words carefully, loathe to share her whereabouts with Sara.

Once Mary left the room, Sara gave Mrs. Whiting an expectant look.

"I have a sneaky suspicion there's something you need to tell me."

"Sara, you're right," she admitted. "I did do something. Something to protect your reputation, as well as the Whiting family's."

"Oh no, Mother. What did you do?"

Mrs. Whiting looked up from her teacup, pausing… "I went to the newspapers with your story."

"The newspapers!" Sara's eyes were wide with horror, "That's exactly what we're trying to avoid!"

"The *New York World* to be exact," Mrs. Whiting added, unfazed by her daughter's response. [39] "I decided it was best to try to sway public opinion in our favor as soon as possible. And I thought the easiest way to avoid the unfavorable gossip was to go straight to the papers with the truth: Oliver deserted you to go cavorting around Spain with dancers. No decent man would do such a thing to his new wife – and no one in society will approve of his conduct."

"Oh, no…" Sara moaned, rubbing the bridge of her nose. "I'd really hoped to avoid going public with this embarrassing affair." She leaned back in the chair shaking her head with aversion. "Now that you've gone to the newspaper there is most definitely going to be a public scandal."

"I only have your best interests in mind," Mrs. Whiting insisted. "In light of your pregnancy we must do everything in our power to protect your reputation."

"But Mother, haven't you considered the option of Oliver and I working things out – what then? How will we explain the appearance of a newspaper article?"

"Work things out!" her mother nearly shouted. "How can you even dream of working things out with him when no one even knows where Oliver is? Besides, if he were to return this very moment, as your mother I don't know if I would trust him alone with you. Remember young lady – I was there when he struck you. I know the depths of his anger and his lack of self-control. When Oliver drinks he turns into a violent monster. I cannot risk him hurting you – or my grandchild!"

"But he is my husband," Sara countered, her voice harsh, "and the father of my child. In spite of his conduct, I still love him. Alcoholism is a disease – the doctor told me so. I might be able to get him to quit drinking now that there's a baby in the picture. Perhaps his duties as a father will motivate him to straighten out his bad habits."

"You're lost in a fantasy, child!" Her mother slammed her hand on the table. "A man like Oliver thinks of no one but himself. If – or when – he does return, I assure you the Belmonts are going to try to hang the blame of this situation on *you*. Do you understand me? As long as I'm alive I will not let them do that!"

Confusion clashed with anger as Sara bit away her tears. She tried to speak but couldn't find the words. What was left to say?

They both grew quiet.

"Good," her mother said evenly. "I'm glad you see things my way. Divorce is your only recourse."

CHAPTER THIRTEEN

The next day
May 19, 1883
New York, New York

LEANING HEAVILY ON HIS CANE August walked slowly down the city sidewalk. The sky was overcast, threatening rain, but he'd decided to walk to Delmonico's anyway for a quick lunch. The weather was causing his leg to ache, making his limp more pronounced.

He'd sustained the wound in a duel back in 1841 when he was yet an unmarried man. The conflict had been necessary to protect his honor against malicious rumors of illicit favors from a married lady. Although dueling had been recently outlawed, August felt the insults left him no recourse but to challenge the accuser to a shoot-off in an effort to save face.

The *New York Herald* had a field day with the story, and gossip about the duel moved through society like wildfire. It took August nearly a year to recuperate, physically and professionally. He nearly lost the backing of the Rothschilds over the affair. Afterward, it became clear he was destined to live out the remainder of his days with an evident limp. "Better than death I suppose," he consoled himself.

Reflecting on this foolish event August considered that perhaps Oliver had inherited a bit of his impetuous spirit. I certainly had my fun as a young, wealthy man, he admitted silently, and I was the brunt of many false rumors and public hearsay, as well.

But August had never brought dishonor to his family or to his wife, as Oliver had done to Sara. Still, heading down Wall Street to his office, the ache in his leg reminded August of his own foolhardy actions as a young man.

Returning from lunch, he walked past a newsstand and stopped to pick up a few papers – *The New York Times* and the *New York World*. He tossed the newsboy a few pennies for the papers and continued down the street, tucking them under his arm. Finishing the short walk, he entered his office and hung his coat on the rack near the door.

His secretary Jonathan Walker handed him several telegrams from the Rothschilds, along with the latest stock reports. Reviewing the cables, August set them in a corner of his workspace and settled back in his cushioned chair for a quick read of the newspaper. Opening the *World* for a brief update he saw the article glaring at him in bold print.

"A Social Sensation"
"Society Marriage Dangles in Discord"

"The circus has arrived in town," August whispered with resignation. Scanning the words with trepidation, he noted that the tone of the prose showed definite sympathy for Sara. There in black and white was the whole lurid tale of Oliver leaving his wife in Paris and cavorting in Spain with dancers. "I hope Caroline hasn't seen this," he murmured, knowing it was useless to try and keep this new development from his wife. She'd most certainly be inundated with questions due to the article. August threw the newspaper against the desk, frustrated, the pages scattering on the floor in a rustle of paper.

It took him only a moment to gauge the situation. Obviously the article had been planted. August had employed the *World* for his own uses in the matters of propaganda, and apparently someone else had done the same in this instance.[40] He searched through his mind for a list of probable suspects.

"Mrs. Whiting," he said simply. She's clearly trying to protect her daughter's reputation. Silly old woman. Didn't she realize that by going to the press she'd started publicizing a private situation that'd be seized upon by the gossipmongers? They'll feed on this like ravenous wolves, he thought with chagrin – and spit her daughter out like gristle.

It was too late to undo this latest move by the opposition. And that's what the Whitings had become: the opposition. August knew an angry mamma lion was as dangerous a foe to deal with as any he'd confronted in business. But if the Whitings wanted a propaganda war he was up to the challenge – and certainly more experienced at the task. They'd met their match when it came to his skills in dealing with the press. He called Walker in to his office.

"Yes, sir." The young man appeared at August's summons.

"I'd like you to set up a meeting with *The Times*," he said flatly. "And I need you to help me draft a press release immediately."

"Yes, sir." Walker scribbled notes on his pad as his employer spoke.

He who laughs last, laughs best, August chuckled. And I will not be undone by the Whiting women. In an authoritative voice he began his dictation.

Nine days later
May 27,1883
Newport, Rhode Island

Rocking gently in the wicker chair a breeze cooled Sara, relaxing on the Swanhurst piazza. Reading the last page of the letter from Oliver's mother, she grew agitated. The words brought up anger and hope, creating a stew of emotions that churned in her mind.

On the one hand, Mrs. Belmont's note had a ring of reproach, implying that Sara was the cause of Oliver's violent behavior by holding the well-being of her mother and sisters over that of Oliver's wishes for a separate apartment. On the other hand, she encouraged them to work things out, get a place of their own, and raise their child.

"Have patience and forbearance with my poor boy, when he should be at fault. He is your loving husband and the father of your unborn child, and he ought to be nearer and dearer to you than all the world." [41] Mrs. Belmont wrote, "Young people always get along best alone when they have their own snug home." She suggested that Sara and Oliver have a fresh try at marriage, and get a small cottage in the country. [42]

Mrs. Whiting on the other hand, believed Oliver's behavior toward Sara was unforgivable. Mrs. Belmont had written that Oliver had never before shown any signs of an ugly temper and if he had 'sadly changed' it must be the result of something that happened after the wedding.[43] That statement really made Sara fume. In her mind no gentleman would treat a lady with such brutishness, no matter what the impetus or circumstance.

But her real melancholy began to set in when Mrs. Belmont wrote, "My misgivings at your engagement and marriage have given way to sincere affection for you. Both Mr. Belmont and I are ready to love and cherish you as one of our own children. The news of your marital difficulties almost breaks my heart. What is to become of you, when on the very threshold of your wedded life, such things can happen?" [44]

The baby was growing bigger every day and Sara was averse to the idea of raising the child without a father. The doctor said the baby was due in September, and it was already nearly June. Sara let herself daydream about a new life with Oliver. Yet, her mother refused to stop with her insistence on a divorce.

The screen door slammed as Sara slipped the letter back in its envelope.

"How are you feeling, miss?" Bridget, always close, kept a watchful eye on her mistress. "I must say you've got that beautiful baby-glow about you today."

Smiling, Sara brushed the wind-blown hair from her eyes. "I feel good now that we're back home at Swanhurst. But I do seem to tire easily. And I suddenly want to eat all the food in the kitchen." She smiled at the thought of her seemingly insatiable appetite.

"Well, that's a good thing. You're eating for two now," Bridget reminded her with a pat on the shoulder. "Is there anything you need right now? Would you like some lemonade?"

"Oooh, that sounds delicious," Sara's eyes sparkled. "And a few of cook's snicker-doodles, too?" She'd developed a new fondness for the cinnamon cookies. "Although I had better be careful not to eat too many or I may need to buy an entire wardrobe."

They laughed together at the picture of Sara fat and round.

"Don't you worry about that miss," Bridget chuckled. "As far as I'm concerned, you'll always be the loveliest lady in Newport."

"Such a sweet thing to say," Sara smiled, gently rubbing her baby belly. "Although I must confess I already feel as big as a house. I'll be enormous by the time the baby arrives!"

"You just stop fretting. Now's the time to focus on your health, not your figure," Bridget admonished, opening the screen door. "The most important thing is for you and the baby to thrive." She winked, stepping into the house, "I'll grab you a few cookies."

Looking back at the letter from her mother-in-law, Sara grew indignant. The time had come for her to speak her mind about a few things. She needed to defend herself against Mrs. Belmont's accusations and bias concerning Oliver. Lord only knows what he's told them, and in his often-drunken condition, Sara felt sure it was inaccurate.

Reaching for her stationery box on the side table, Sara decided it best to show her regret regarding the article in the *New York World*, not wanting her mother-in-law to suspect the Whitings had planted the article. Although Sara was disappointed her mother had divulged the story to the newspaper, it was a done deal. The rumors and gossip had already started. There was no backing out now. The only direction to move, was forward.

With one hand on her belly-bump Sara began writing in a flourished hand. Looking up, she saw the postman strolling toward the house, a leather sack of mail hanging from his shoulder.

"Good morning, Mrs. Belmont," he greeted her in a jovial tone, handing her a fistful of envelopes.

"Good morning," Sara smiled, taking the letters.

With a wave the postman moved on to the next house. Sara gave him a polite wave in return. Shuffling through the notes, her heart skipped a beat when she saw a letter addressed to her.

From Oliver.

A confrontation seems impossible to avoid, Sara thought, slowly opening the envelope. "How can I feel such excitement and dread at the same time?" she murmured, as her eyes scanned the note.

The next day
May 28, 1883
Newport, Rhode Island

"Thank you so much for putting this party together," Mrs. Whiting said quietly to her friend. "I've been doing my best to shine a favorable light on Sara's circumstances."

"I'm happy to help however I can," Mrs. Wilson smiled. "Throwing a ladies' luncheon gives us a chance to talk to them about what they've read in the newspaper. I hope it will help build support for Sara, especially in her condition."

"So far, everyone seems to be very sympathetic to her plight," Mrs. Whiting nodded. "The way I see it Oliver doesn't have a leg to stand on. The facts speak for themselves and the fact is, he left his wife to go frolicking around Europe with tramps." She finished in a whisper as they joined the others at the table.

"I must tell you," Mrs. Endicott said to the group, "I heard Oliver married a French girl when he was in the navy a few years back." [45]

A gasp escaped Mrs. Whiting. "Wherever did you hear such nonsense?" she asked flabbergasted. "That is preposterous!"

"Margaret Woodruff had a son in the navy with Oliver at the time." She raised her chin authoritatively. "Bobby said it was common knowledge Oliver had married – and he swears it's true."

"Don't you think Caroline Belmont would have made an announcement if it really were true?" Mrs. Parker joined the conversation.

"Absolutely not! Especially not if the Belmonts had it annulled." Mrs. Endicott delighted in their proper shock, lackadaisically sipping her iced tea. "I'm certain the affair would have been kept under wraps."

Still in shock from the revelation, Mrs. Whiting could only listen to the gossip drifting around the table.

"Any way you look at it, Oliver has conducted himself in a most ungentlemanly fashion," Mrs. Wilson stated crisply. "As women, we must do all we can to support Sara."

"I completely agree," Mrs. Parker rallied. "I grow weary of men making the rules of propriety – rules they apparently feel are suited only for women's etiquette. We must show solidarity in defending Sara's reputation against her reckless young husband."

Relieved to hear the ladies' conversation sway in Sara's favor, Mrs. Whiting relaxed. Her plan was working just as she'd hoped.

"How is she holding up under all these rumors?" Mrs. Endicott asked politely.

"She's doing as well as can be expected. But I'm sure you can imagine, she's a little despondent." Mrs. Whiting made an effort to sound upbeat. "We're all looking after her to make sure she follows the doctor's advice. Everything seems to be fine right now, and we're hoping to keep her calm through the summer."

"She must be disappointed at having to spend the season in confinement," Mrs. Parker commiserated. "Many years ago, I was pregnant through summer and it made me a bit melancholy."

"I must admit, it's very unfortunate," Mrs. Whiting confided. "But there's simply nothing that can be done about it."

"What if Oliver were to return and try to make things up to her?" Mrs. Parker offered. "Do you think there's any chance of that?"

"I don't think I would be happy with that outcome." Mrs. Whiting shook her head, "Oliver was drinking like a fish and prone to violent rages, the likes of which I'd never seen."

"There's a lot of that absinthe liquor in Germany and France," Mrs. Endicott interjected. "But it was mostly with the Bohemian types. Certainly not a pastime that should be enjoyed by a young man in Oliver's position."

"Nevertheless, he has become quite fond of it," Mrs. Whiting assured them. "And it causes the most unpredictable behavior."

"You just let us know if there is anything we can do to help you and Sara," Mrs. Wilson offered graciously. "Grace and I are more than willing to be of service," she added, referring to her own daughter.

"Yes, indeed," Mrs. Endicott nodded, "in any way possible."

"Thank you so much," Mrs. Whiting replied, relieved by their support. "We truly appreciate your assistance." She stood, lifting her purse from the chair, "I really must be getting home now. Ladies, it was lovely seeing you again."

The women said their 'good-byes' to Mrs. Whiting, and she headed for the carriage in the driveway. So far, my strategy is going just as planned, she thought, with a growing sense of victory.

Four days later
June 1, 1883
Newport, R.I.

Pouring the tea with an expert hand, the maid set the cups in front of Mrs. Belmont and her guest. Giving a curtsey she left the room quietly.

"It's all a terrible business," Mrs. Belmont gave her friend a troubled smile. "We're doing our best to get through it, but Oliver has put us in a very uncertain situation."

"I've seen the papers," Mrs. Cushing said with a tight smile. "I'm sure you know that everyone in the set is talking about what happened in Paris, some to the point of debate."

"I haven't been out much," Mrs. Belmont quietly confessed,

"Are you getting your rest, Caroline?" Mrs. Cushing surveyed her friend with concern. "I know you're worried, but making yourself sick over this isn't going to help anyone."

"Of course, you're right. But with this matter hanging over the family, resting is easier said than done."

Setting her teacup on the table Mrs. Cushing turned in her seat. "Tell me what I can do to help."

Growing thoughtful Mrs. Belmont gazed at the Persian rug, considering her options. "You were in Barcelona at the same time as Oliver?"

"Yes. Mr. Cushing bumped into him."

"Perhaps you can write me a letter?"

"What would you have me say in this letter?"

"Maybe you could say something to the effect that Mr. Cushing personally witnessed Oliver hard at work in Spain, toiling from morning until night. Write something – anything, to discount the rumors of dancers and previous marriages and all that nonsense."

"That's a simple enough request," Mrs. Cushing nodded her agreement. "I'd be happy to supply you with such a letter. Anything to help."

"I'm not sure how much good it will do, but at least it will be a firsthand account. Something real and tangible, instead of hearsay and rumors."

"Consider it done." Mrs. Cushing rose from her seat with a glance at the wall clock. "I'd stay longer, but I have a previous appointment. Let me know if there's anything more I can do." Turning to Mrs. Belmont she added, "...and Caroline, please try to get some sleep. These things have a way of blowing over."

CHAPTER FOURTEEN

Three days later
June 4, 1883
Newport, Rhode Island

SCANNING THE LETTER FOR A second time, Carrie blinked her eyes in disbelief. Each word from Sara shrouded her heart in sadness. She had tried to warn her friend against pursuing a courtship with Oliver, but to no avail.

"She was blinded by love and ignored my misgivings..." Carrie whispered.

With her relationship to Marshall growing increasingly serious, she had the highest hopes for a happy union, just as Sara had had. Carrie struggled to understand the circumstances of her friend's dilemma, praying her courtship with Marshall would bring only joy.

What in the world had happened while they were in Paris? No woman expects to be dealing with loneliness or a wayward husband while on her honeymoon. Carrie gazed into space, pondering the story Sara shared in her note.

Stepping into the room Mrs. Astor caught her daughter lost in thought.

"Ah, I see you've gotten a letter from Sara as well," Mrs. Astor lowered her eyes. "A very unfortunate situation to be sure."

"I'm having a hard time accepting that Oliver would do this to her – abandon her on their honeymoon! For heaven's sake, this is absurd!"

"Well, I know for a fact it's all true," Mrs. Astor said tersely. "I was worried about Sara marrying that young man in the first place. Oliver didn't have a stellar record when it came to his responsibilities. She insisted they were in love and things would be peachy. Now she's in the throes of a horrible scandal."

"I know you had your misgivings, and admittedly, I had my own. But the two did seem to share a special relationship."

Her mother sat down beside her, "You're old enough now to know that it takes much more than love to make a marriage work. Large dowries don't make love any easier." Mrs. Astor let out a sigh, "I've always been so fond of Sara. It upsets me to hear this sordid tale. I've had my suspicions all along that Oliver had ulterior motives. I believe much of his matrimonial efforts were an attempt to get his father to resign from further action in regards to his future occupation. Anyone can see Oliver has an aversion to exerting himself."

"You can't be serious!" Carrie objected. "What man would go to such lengths and break a lady's heart to escape working? Not to mention the scandal. I have to believe that Oliver loves Sara – or at least he did." She glanced at the note in her hands, "Sara thinks we should keep our distance. She doesn't want her problems affecting me. She's asked for my understanding."

"Unfortunately, Sara has an awful mess to clean up." Mrs. Astor surveyed her daughter with an air of wisdom. Carrie was still so naïve in the selfish ways of men. "There's nothing we can do about it other than show our support."

A glum mood filled the sunny parlor. Carrie glanced at her mother, who was studying her with concern.

"Let's not dwell on this any more, shall we?" Mrs. Astor suggested. "We've got a garden party coming up at the end of next month. There's still a lot of planning to do, and time has a way of getting away from us. The event planner is coming in a few days for a meeting."

Leaning forward in her seat, Carrie set the note on the coffee table. "Yes, there are a lot of arrangements that need to be taken care of, but my heart isn't in it." She glanced at her mother, "Everything feels so different. With Sara married and pregnant, everything has shifted – irrevocably changed. I hardly think life will ever be the same." She took a sip from a goblet of water. "I rarely see her anymore. I thought, perhaps, she was avoiding me, and her letter confirms my suspicions. I'm sure she's humiliated over the state of her marriage. But we're close friends…"

"Most certainly Sara is feeling disgraced by Oliver's escapades," Mrs. Astor conceded. "And if you take into consideration her pregnancy, she's sure to be going through a rough patch." She met her daughter's glance, "But Sara is clearly aware of the controversy brewing around her. She has enough sophistication not to drag you into this nasty scandal. I suggest you take a cue from her and keep a wide distance from all the controversy for the time being."

"This is horrible," Carrie moaned. "I truly hate Oliver Belmont. How could he do this to Sara? Why didn't his parents raise him to be more honorable, especially in regard to the treatment of his wife? Now he's destroying our friendship as well!"

The women grew quiet, each lost in their deliberations over Oliver's exploits, and Sara's pregnancy. It seemed a hopeless affair.

"Isn't there anything you can do, Mother?" Carrie implored her with urgency. "Perhaps you can sway the gossip in Sara's favor."

"I'm doing what I can to gain support for her plight, but for the most part, the matter is in the hands of the set. Stop getting worked up over this Carrie," Mrs. Astor advised. "Be thankful your name hasn't been mixed up in this mess. I'd advise you to steer clear of things until this blows over, especially if it culminates in a divorce – which I staunchly disapprove of. But, as I said, we won't know the outcome for many months. In fact, it may well be next year before this situation is resolved."

"What are you saying Mother?" Carrie frowned. "It almost sounds as if you don't want me associating with Sara."

"Not at all. I'm only suggesting you be prudent where Sara is concerned."

"How can I do that?" Carrie wailed. "We've been friends forever. And I'm excited to see her baby when it's born. I can't simply pretend that I don't know her."

"Of course not, Carrie. But I think you should spend more time with your unmarried friends," Mrs. Astor instructed, "at least for the summer."

"I don't know if I can just desert Sara in her hour of need." Carrie thought back to Sara's loyalty when they'd gotten word of Elizabeth's divorce. Never in her wildest dreams did she think that a similar calamity would befall Sara. What was the world coming to?

"Unless you'd like to be outcast from social circles along with her, you'll do as I say," Mrs. Astor insisted. "Rumors grow old and are replaced with new gossip. These things have a way of sorting themselves out with time." The older woman grew sympathetic watching her daughter come to grips with the harsh reality of society.

"Come now, Carrie," she said in a gentler tone. "You know how fond I am of Sara. Believe me, I'm gathering a lot of support to help her and the Whitings get through this predicament. So, at the very least, my dear, please keep your distance from the Belmonts."

"That will be easy enough," Carrie grimaced, showing her disgust. "But, I wish there was something more I could do…" she said softly.

Moving to the writing desk, Mrs. Astor pulled her quill and stationery from a drawer. "Let's forget about this for now, shall we? As I said, we've got important plans to make for our garden party. That's where our attention should be focused." Changing the subject, she asked, "Have you given any consideration to what type of flowers we should use? I think tea roses would be lovely… pink or red. White is too plain."

Two days later
June 6, 1883
New York, New York

Wandering into the library with his coffee mug, Oliver rubbed his eyes, groggy from sleeping late. His life certainly wasn't going the way he would have liked, but at least he was back in New York. His father had released him from his commitment in Bremen and there'd been no mention of putting him to work at the firm. *I can deal with scandal as long as I do it at my own pace,* he thought. He sat down in a satin club chair and leafed through the newspaper, searching for a particular article in today's publication.

His father had arranged an interview with a reporter from the Associated Press early yesterday. The Belmonts were confident the effort would counter the previous story regarding his trip to Spain, obviously circulated by the Whitings. Then he spotted it:

AN UNFOUNDED REPORT
AFFECTING THE FAMILY RELATIONS OF OLIVER BELMONT

A story put in circulation in New York from Newport to the effect that Mr. Oliver Belmont, a younger brother of Congressman Perry Belmont, has been separated in Paris from his wife, formerly Miss Whiting, is absolutely untrue. Mr. Oliver Belmont arrived in New York to-day, his wife and her mother having preceded him about a week ago, and he will rejoin them in Newport.

Feeling like a voyeur, Oliver couldn't stop himself, curious to read the blurb. Finishing the short article, he closed the newspaper, folding it tightly.[46] It was a simple retraction, but effective. Oliver decided his parents were right in handling things with a counter-attack. He puffed up like a barnyard cock, filled with a smug sense of vindication. Sometimes it wasn't so bad to be the son of August Belmont!

And Oakland isn't such a bad wedding gift, he decided. Either way, things were turning in his favor.

"There you are." His mother stood in the doorway, a cold demeanor evident in her posture. "I see you've read the newspaper."

"Yes," Oliver nodded. "I think it accomplished what we set out to undo."

"The newspaper is just the first step in saving our name from discredit," she chided. "There's something you should know. We're having a dinner party tomorrow night and you're going to preside over the event.[47] We've invited the Howlands, the Posts and the Bayards – and a few other influential families from the set. Unfortunately, Mrs. Astor has declined. As you know, she's always favored Sara. She could prove to be a powerful foe in our efforts."

The thought of Mrs. Astor didn't trouble him one bit, but a boring and extravagant dinner for the purpose of stimulating positive propaganda did. He'd have to cancel his plans for poker. Clearly, his mother was in no mood for dissension. He should be grateful that his parents knew best how to counter the bad press, but he hated being under their thumb again.

Obviously, he would be taking directions from them for the foreseeable future.

"If you think it will help," he acquiesced. "I'll be happy to preside over dinner."

"Good," she said, a razor edge in her tone. "Your father and I have also written letters to our friends and acquaintances in an effort to gain a sympathetic inclination to your plight. I suggest you do the same."

"Certainly. If that's what you wish," he complied. She was in no mood for an argument.

"We can only hope that it sways loyalty in your direction," she continued. "Papa has decided you and I should leave for Newport in a week and continue our efforts during the summer season at Bythesea. If there's any business that needs your attention in New York, other than poker," she snapped, "now would be the time to take care of it. Furthermore, until this unfortunate affair blows over, try not to draw attention to yourself. And please stay away from strong drink, especially in public. It'll only negate the positive opinion we're trying to secure."

She disappeared down the hallway, leaving a chill in her wake. Oliver leaned back in the seat, surrendering to the dictates of his parents.

An image of Sara popped into his mind, laughing with him on the rocks at Easton Beach. It had been so perfect at first, he reminisced. Maybe he should reach out and talk with her – alone. Dare he think they could work this mess out? Perhaps it would be an exercise in futility. He weighed the idea, uncertain of the outcome from such an effort. Getting up, he gave a cursory glance at the newspaper, and quietly left the library.

Four days later
June 10, 1883
Newport, Rhode Island

Relaxing in an easy chair, Mrs. Whiting perused the society pages, sincerely hoping the Whiting family had not made the newspaper. Barging in on her quiet time, Sara stomped across the room throwing a letter on the table with a smack.

"Do you mind explaining this to me!" she demanded, her voice laced with anger.

Looking at the envelope Mrs. Whiting could see it was from Oliver, addressed to her daughter.

"I haven't seen this letter."

"No. Because I got it directly from the postman," Sara said dryly. "Oliver asked me why I didn't wait for him in London. He also asks why I sent a telegram stating that 'Everything is at an end.'" Sara let her words sink in, glaring at her mother. "We both know that I did *not* receive a telegram from Oliver while in London, nor did I send a telegram declaring all was at an end."

Biting her tongue, Mrs. Whiting flushed, feigning a look of innocence. Clearly, her little ploy had been discovered. She wasn't prepared for the level of anger her daughter displayed at the news.

"But you did receive his telegram, didn't you Mother!" Sara accused. "It's obvious, you pretended to be me and took delivery of a telegram that was intended for me! I cannot tell you how angry this has made me. I know you have my best interests in mind but this just crosses the line of good conduct."

"I wanted to spare you any hardship, especially as you were feeling so ill during our travels. I was afraid of a confrontation with Oliver in your tender condition."

"Why must you always assume the worst? Perhaps a meeting with Oliver would have been advisable. There's a chance we could have avoided this entire scandal we now find ourselves muddled in."

"Don't tell me you're still considering a reconciliation with him. I warn you young lady, if you do, you're asking for more trouble."

"How dare you make my decisions for me, Mother!" Sara spat. "Oliver is the father of my child. I must do what I think is right for myself and my baby, not what you think is right for us."

"And what exactly do you think is right for you?" Her mother's tone grew sarcastic, the cadence rising in anger. "Marrying Oliver has produced the opposite results you intended. Instead of joyfully starting your married life surrounded by high society, you're embroiled in disrepute from *his* actions. It's possible with a divorce you'll retain the Belmont name and perhaps a monetary settlement. I'm older and wiser in how best to deal with the rules of conduct, and I suggest you follow my advice." Looking at the letter, she asked blithely, "What new promises has Oliver made to you?"

"He wants us to start again at Oakland. His father has given him the estate as a wedding gift and he wants me to join him there in a few weeks."

"Surely you're not seriously considering his offer!" Mrs. Whiting grabbed the letter to read it for herself. Scanning the contents, she threw it back on the table. "You must know this is a ploy on the part of his parents to save their family's reputation," Mrs. Whiting seethed. "Let's say that you do decide to move in with Oliver – who will be there to protect you from a future outburst? Need I remind you if he's acted violently toward you once, he'll most certainly do it again. You must put the well being of your baby before your own feelings, Sara. Even you must recognize that fact."

"Whatever I decide to do Mother, it will be *my* decision," Sara insisted. "Have you seen today's paper? The Belmonts are claiming it is you who's at fault for our marital problems. They're saying none of this would have happened if you and my sisters had remained here in Newport while we were on honeymoon."

"You should be grateful we were there to help you, considering the way events transpired," Mrs. Whiting shot back. "Oliver's drinking had nothing to do with our visit, and *his drinking* is the cause of your marital problems. You need to stop reading the Belmonts' propaganda."

"Regardless, Mother," Sara's voice was firm. "You will cease and desist from intercepting my mail. And you most certainly will not send any letters or telegrams masquerading as me! This stops and it stops now! Do you understand me?" Sara grew faint from the fury coursing through her veins. Impulsively, she grabbed Oliver's letter.

Mrs. Whiting heard the front door slam as her daughter left the house for the piazza.

CHAPTER FIFTEEN

Five days later
June 15, 1883
Newport, Rhode Island

STANDING UNDER THE SHADOW OF a tree, Oliver watched dusk fall around him. The sun had disappeared over the horizon, and a few bright stars made an appearance, twinkling dimly in the indigo-blue sky. He'd returned to Newport five days ago escorted by his Mamma in a public show of solidarity. Both families were surrounded by rumors and gossip, mostly in favor of Sara, although the tide seemed to be shifting a little his way.

I haven't had a drink in almost a week, he boasted to himself. Once the fog had lifted and his mind cleared, he began to really miss Sara. Sick and tired of defending himself, he'd decided on his own plan of action and sent a note to Swanhurst asking Sara to meet with him. Maybe they could sort this mess out. He really wanted this conflict to go away. His mother was annoying him with her sharp attitude and his father was constantly griping at him. Besides, he hadn't meant for things to get so out of hand when he'd left Paris – and that included his indulgence in absinthe. He'd only planned to leave for a few days to make his point, but had gotten caught up in the fun and adventure.

He waited at the top of Memorial Avenue near Cliffwalk. The path led along the Atlantic behind the cottages on Bellevue Avenue. Secluded, he thought it was a good place to meet without being noticed. "I'm not sure what I thought would happen when I left Paris," he murmured, staring down at the ocean crashing against the cliff. Night quickly descended on Newport, a cool breeze giving him a chill. Pulling the pocket watch from his trousers, he checked the time. Sara was nearly an hour late.

Maybe she changed her mind and decided not to come, he mulled, a hollow feeling churning in his gut – although she'd written back, agreeing to meet him there. I'll wait a little longer, he decided, noticing the sky now glittered with a multitude of stars.

The moments passed, his thoughts drifting in echoes of their courtship. Sara's laughter came alive in his memory, and as the clock ticked away the minutes, he yearned for her more and more. Keeping his eyes glued on the sidewalk he watched anxiously for Sara to appear.

"How did things get so complicated? I never meant for any of this to happen."

He sighed, sending a wish to the brightest star.

The same evening
Newport, Rhode Island

Noiselessly tiptoeing through the kitchen, Sara moved toward the back door. Without a lamp, she relied on her familiarity with the room to navigate her way, as her eyes adjusted to the growing darkness.

Oliver had sent a note begging her to meet with him – in secret. He expressed his remorse for leaving her alone in Paris, and asked for a chance to talk things over. Oliver mentioned that he'd quit drinking, and that gave her some peace. But even if it wasn't true, Sara was large, and obviously pregnant. No man, no matter how drunk, would harm a woman with child. At least she prayed as much.

Luckily, his note was delivered while her mother was in town – Mrs. Whiting knew nothing about the correspondence, and Sara planned to keep it that way. After contemplating the request she decided to give Oliver the benefit of the doubt, and sent a note agreeing to the meeting. The two arranged a rendezvous that very evening near Cliffwalk.

There was no question she was still furious with him – not to mention embarrassed and humiliated by the gossip. But he was her first love, and retained a special place in her heart. Absinthe was the root of the problem, and if that wasn't an issue any longer, they still had a chance with their marriage. In so many ways, Sara was taking a risk meeting with him, but her mind was made up.

The kitchen floor creaked under her weight as she moved the lock, unlatching the door to the back porch.

"What are you doing slinking by the door like a thief?" Jane asked.

Sara jumped out of her skin. "What are you doing sneaking up behind me, scaring the bejesus out of me! I was just going out for some fresh air," she stammered, trying to look casual.

"With your hat on?"

"What concern is it of yours anyway?"

Mrs. Whiting appeared behind Jane, a nightcap covering her hair.

"Sara says she's going out."

"At this time of night? Alone?" Her mother held a candlestick high against the darkness, illuminating Sara in her hat. "Get back in this house. It's too late for you to be going out anywhere, even if you had a mind to."

"I was just going to sit on the porch for a bit. It's stuffy in my room. I need some fresh air." Sara stood tall against her mother, her voice calm and cool.

Squinting at her daughter, now suspicious, Mrs. Whiting's jaw clenched. "You expect me to believe that? It almost looks as if you have a rendezvous…" Her voice faded, a streak of realization dawning in her eyes.

"Please don't tell me you were going out to meet with Oliver!"

"Of course not," Sara replied weakly. "I just wanted some fresh air."

"Do you think I was born yesterday?" Turning to Jane she said, "Would you excuse us please?"

"Not another conflict," Jane scowled, leaving the kitchen in a snit.

"Come over here," Mrs. Whiting ordered, "Sit down at the table."

Furious with herself for getting caught, Sara did as she was told.

Studying her daughter, Mrs. Whiting spied a letter stuffed in Sara's dress pocket. In a quick move, she snatched the note. Too late, Sara noticed what was happening, reaching to retrieve the envelope from her mother's hand.

Waving it in front of her face, Mrs. Whiting shook the envelope. "I feel certain I don't have to read this to know what it says." Her voice was hot with reproach. "Admit it. You were going to meet with Oliver – without telling anyone, no less. Have you lost your senses?"

"Need I remind you he is my husband?" Sara snapped back. "I don't have to check with you if I want to see my husband."

"Under normal circumstances, certainly not, but there's nothing normal about these circumstances. What if he's been drinking, for God's sake! Have you considered that?"

"Oliver assured me he hasn't touched any spirits." Sara held her chin high, "I felt it only fair to give him a chance to explain himself. Face to face, Mother. No intercepted letters. No miscommunication – but an honest to goodness, face to face conversation."

"Here we go again." Mrs. Whiting shook her finger in Sara's face, "You've got to give up these false hopes, Sara! I can't stand to see you hurt any more than you've already been. If you go back to Oliver you only ensure yourself a life of misery, not only for yourself but for your baby, too. It's best to sever ties now. What do I have to do to convince you of that?"

Pressing a hand to her temple, Sara's head pounded – just as the baby turned over. It was as if the little one knew its father was the subject of the conversation. Suddenly too weary to go anywhere or discuss anything with anyone, Sara stood. "I'm going to bed."

"I hope you won't try anything this foolish again," Mrs. Whiting warned. "I'm not in the habit of watching my grown daughter try to sneak out of the house like a child." Her mother stared at her with a stern eye. "By the way, you should know, I found you a lawyer."

"A lawyer!"

"Yes. The sooner this divorce is taken care of, the less messy it will be. Ideally before the baby is born."

"*Before* the baby is born!"

"There is the matter of custody, Sara. You're pregnant with a Belmont child. By rights Oliver could fight you for paternal custody if he decides to – or if his parents plant the thought in his mind. Things could get very, very nasty."

"Enough Mother! Apparently you have my entire future mapped out for me!" Sara waved her hand dismissively. "I'm going to bed. I have a headache and I can't deal with you for one more minute."

The yellow light of the candle shrouded Sara as she got up from the table. Defeat and sadness were companions she felt helpless to disperse as she left the room.

Checking the lock on the kitchen door, Mrs. Whiting snapped it shut, and followed her daughter with an uncompromising step.

Six days later
June 21, 1883
Newport, Rhode Island

"George, this is a nice surprise!" Sara entered the parlor, moving to greet her friend with an extended hand. Curious at his appearance at Swanhurst, she wondered what had prompted his visit. Then again, considering all the rumors, he probably was there to validate the gossip.

Removing his hat, he took her hand in greeting. "I hope you don't mind my showing up without first sending a note. I suppose I acted spontaneously. I've been in Washington working with the Secretary of State on national business. I just got back yesterday morning, and felt I had to see you right away." He paused, his eyes dark. "I was terribly upset when I heard the scuttlebutt around town concerning you and Oliver. Good God, please tell me it's not true! A separation? Already?"

The comfort of the brocade settee beckoned her, and Sara carefully sat by the bay window, her pregnant condition quite obvious. She waved him toward a chair, but he declined with a brusque shake of his head.

"I see Oliver has wasted no time in securing a Belmont heir."

Sitting tall, a contrite expression crossed her face. "I'm not sure what you've heard…" She touched the bump under the pink linen dress.

"I've heard a lot of things. Most of which I hope are untrue." He watched her fidget. "The word is Oliver left you in Paris and took off for

Spain or Morocco or God-knows-where." George paced in front of the windows, waving his hand as he talked. "There are some things I heard that I cannot bear to repeat for fear of upsetting you."

A resigned chuckle escaped her, "Don't worry about that – I've heard it all. Or read it in the newspaper. French dancers, annulled marriages..." her voice faded. "It seems my life has become more scandalous than the latest novel."

"I had my suspicions when I saw you at the Vanderbilt's ball, but this is worse than I imagined. Tell me it isn't true – tell me Oliver did not leave you alone in Paris, pregnant."

"Well, I wasn't exactly alone, but he did leave..." Sara lamented. "It's true George. But I was glad he left – at first, anyway. He was drinking a lot and became quite unpredictable, at times rude, even violent."

"He didn't strike you, of course. No gentleman would treat his new bride in such a barbaric manner."

Sara met his eye, but did not speak. Embarrassed as she was by Oliver's thrashing – it suddenly seemed too horrific to discuss.

"You must be joking!" he growled, crimson with anger. "That over-privileged little runt! No gentleman strikes a lady. I have half a mind to take him to task at this news." George took up his pacing again, then stopped abruptly, aware he might upset her.

"He didn't know I was pregnant at the time. None of us did."

"As if that should matter! Was all of this going on when you came to New York? I had a feeling there was more happening than you were telling me. It was obvious you weren't well. I was suspicious about the reason for your ill-health, but I had no idea things were so complicated."

"I'm afraid the situation is very complicated. And I'm confused as to the best course of action. Oliver arrived in Newport this week and sent a note for me to meet with him. My mother forbids it. She's insistent that I keep my distance and file for divorce immediately. I have an appointment with a lawyer next week, but I'm not sure I'm doing the right thing..."

"I agree with your mother completely. You can't possibly be considering returning to that scoundrel." He paused, his face softening, "Sara you deserve much better – more than Oliver can ever give you, in spite of his family's wealth. How can you entertain thoughts of a reconciliation?"

"I'm pregnant with his child. I don't want my baby to grow up without a father. Surely you can understand my quandary? Fortunately, our friends have been very forgiving – so far. There were several parties held in my honor and everyone is quite sympathetic – at least to my face. I made the requisite appearances, but other than that, I'm confined to my home. No matter – I'm tired of the questions and whispered looks. Especially now, knowing the Belmonts are in Newport assembling their troops. Apparently Oliver is moving into Oakland up in Portsmouth. There's been some talk of him wanting me to join him and silence the rumors once and for all."

"Sympathy is on your side Sara, I assure you," George said. "Oliver's lack of vocation and his public escapades are well known among the set. You must stay strong to protect yourself and your unborn child from all this sensationalism. Hold your head up high and move on. Get rid of him while compassion is in your favor."

"I have been strong, George. As I said, I was on several outings before my pregnancy was too far along. I made myself very visible at Mother's insistence. Everyone's been kind enough, although I can only imagine what they're saying behind my back." Staring out the window, she continued, "The memories of my wedding day are still fresh in my mind. They aren't so easily dismissed. Is it so hard to understand my desire to find a peaceful reconciliation?"

"I do understand Sara, but not at the cost of making a fool of yourself." He vacillated, choosing his words carefully, "I shouldn't tell you this…"

Her eyes reflected apprehension, "What now – what don't I know?"

"I saw Oliver at the Casino last night. It was late. He was cavorting with the gentlemen as usual. I saw him leave with a young débutante – unchaperoned, I might add. I don't think anyone noticed, but I couldn't help but keep my eye on him because of the fondness I feel for you. Tell me, why would he be entertaining a young lady if he were committed to repairing his relationship with you? He's no more than a puppet for his parents' propaganda. I assure you they're more concerned about the family's reputation than your well-being."

Oliver with a débutante? She fought the tears that brimmed her eyes. Why was she surprised? Digesting this new information, her sadness slowly turned bitter. Folding her hands in her lap, she remained silent. George was right, she'd been a fool to want to meet with Oliver. Clearly he had no consideration for her plight, or for his unborn child. They were just a complication to his easy lifestyle.

"I'm sorry," George said, suddenly penitent for causing her anguish. "Perhaps I shouldn't have told you. But I simply can't stand by and watch him dupe you into thinking he's suddenly become a gentleman." Walking to the settee he sat down beside her, taking her hand. Lifting her chin with a gentle touch, George met her eye. "Sara, you simply must put Oliver and that farce of a marriage behind you. He can only make a fool out of you if you allow him to."

Hesitating, he studied her face. "Your mother is right. You must see a divorce lawyer and do the right thing for your child. If you don't, I fear your life will be fraught with scandal and heartache as long as Oliver is a part of it. I can't bear to see you in such a predicament."

"I promise to consider your opinion," she said rising from the seat. "And I appreciate your candor."

"I hope my visit hasn't upset you too much." George rose, reaching for his hat on the coffee table. "I can see you're tired. I'll be on my way, but please think about what I've said. And if there's any way I can possibly assist you, don't hesitate to send for me."

His voice grew tender. "I mean what I said Sara."

Turning, he left the room and disappeared into the foyer.

CHAPTER SIXTEEN

Five days later
June 26, 1883
Portsmouth, Rhode Island

THERE WAS A SUPERCILIOUS LIGHTNESS in his step as Oliver sauntered around the cottage, enjoying the pride of new ownership.

Oakland.

This was his new home – with or without Sara. Master of his domain, he fully planned to establish a new life here. His father had purchased the place many years ago, although his parents had never actually lived on the property. Oliver suspected it was bought in an effort to keep up with the Vanderbilts who'd taken to gentleman farming at a place down the road in Middleton.

Oakland was a large and fancy farm, in fact, one of the best on the entire island; perhaps even in all of Rhode Island, he boasted to himself. The house was fully furnished and ready to occupy, aside from the need of a good cleaning, which had been underway by his mother's order before they'd even arrived in town. He wasn't particularly fond of some of the furnishings, but it would be fun to decorate it more to his own tastes in the coming months, especially with his new increase in allowance – a wedding gift from his Papa. Although Oakland stood five miles outside of Newport, Oliver knew he was within easy traveling distance of the Casino and other entertainments of the summer season.

"This is working out better than I'd imagined."

His eyes flashed with a cunning glint. It occurred to him the land would be well-suited to raising horses, a hobby William and his Papa enjoyed, avid patrons of the sport. Perhaps he would pursue the pastime, as well.

"Sir, the trunks have been unpacked and the servants are waiting for your instruction."

"Thank you Bailey," Oliver nodded. He liked the way this felt. He was the boss now, the king of his castle. Walking over to the sideboard he picked up an envelope. "Have this delivered to the Whiting home on Bellevue Avenue immediately."

"Of course, sir. Right away." Bailey took the letter, excusing himself with a bow.

Sara will have to do my bidding now, he thought arrogantly; I'm her legal husband, this is our home, and she will obey my wishes and return at once.

The letter had been drafted with the help of his mother, who was much better at writing. The message was clear... "save us both from scandal and from steps which will affect us all our lives. As your husband, by all the ties that bind us I must demand that you return to me at once." [48]

Oliver wasn't really worried about all the bad press printed about him, although his parents didn't share his indifference. He knew after a while the rumors and rumblings would go away and life would go on as it did before. Money had a way of doing that. The way I figure it, he surmised, Sara is the one who should be worried. Women bear the burden and difficulty of keeping up their reputations, as their decorum weighs so perilously with the pompous members of the set. Even though she was a favorite among society, Sara, divorced and left with a child, would end up worse than a widow. No man would give her a second thought.

His heart softened while he considered the events of the past few years. The navy, Bremen, the wedding... Sara drifted through his memory – like a summer wind, her carefree spirit wisped through his mind.

Oliver wondered how long she'd continue this ridiculous show of independence. She was a fool if she went through with the divorce. And what of the child? He knew the baby was his, but wasn't so sure he was ready to assume the responsibilities of fatherhood. He was young, and had lots of energy left to sow his wild oats. I guess I should have thought about that before I married, he shrugged. But he couldn't resist the opportunity to get out of Bremen. I did love Sara once, and I suppose I could adjust to having her around the house, Oliver decided, thinking himself quite generous.

Walking outside he stood on the veranda, viewing the panorama of land. Acres and acres that were now his. Entitlement, and the wealth of his birthright colored his observations. He walked back in the house, deciding if Sara was a smart lady she would return to him immediately.

The next day
July 27, 1883
Newport, Rhode Island

"Oliver has sent for me," Sara looked up from the letter.

"I suspected as much. Does he really think he can just demand your return?" Mrs. Whiting scoffed. She'd anticipated this move after an article appeared in the Newport paper announcing his arrival at Oakland.

"Apparently so."

Hurt and angry over George's revelation of Oliver's philandering conduct at the Casino last week, Sara had succumbed to the reality of divorce. She was done being deluded by that man. Dancers and débutantes, indeed! She planned to keep her appointment with the attorney, Mr. William Sheffield, arranged for Thursday. At the very least, affidavits could be written for a legal separation. The pregnancy was advancing, and she felt protective of her child, making her more certain of her decision to divorce Oliver.

"I'll write to him at once," Sara said. "Apparently he is feeling more arrogant than I thought possible in the face of this disaster."

"You just stand strong, Sara. Public opinion is in your favor," her mother encouraged. "Before you know it, this will all pass."

"Oh, how I hope that you're right." Sara got up and went to the desk where she pulled out a piece of her stationery embossed with the name: *Mrs. O. H. P. Belmont.* How much longer will I be 'Mrs. Belmont', she wondered absently, writing a message on the paper.

The following day
June 28, 1883
Portsmouth, Rhode Island

"If that's the way she wants it, then so be it!" Anger erupted from him in a furious volcano of emotion. Holding the letter, Oliver regretted the day he met Sara.

"I was compelled to leave Paris upon your continued and prolonged absence. In my present condition, if you had continued your conduct it would have been almost certain death for me. I need scarcely add that it was by the doctor's advice that I sailed for home, and you know that this is all true." [49] *"I will not comply to your demands and you should know that I am commencing divorce proceedings immediately. In the interim, you are not welcome to call at Swanhurst, as the doctor has advised against any excitement or agitation. Please cease writing unless it is of a business nature."*

"Well, I suppose things have really come to an end, particularly if she's meeting with a lawyer," he proclaimed loudly, though there was no one around to hear. Most certainly his parents would be displeased. What could he do? No need to worry about this anymore, he thought, ringing for the butler.

"Yes, sir."

"Bring me a bucket of ice, will you Bailey," Oliver ordered. He walked to the liquor cabinet and removed a sealed bottle of absinthe.

Later that day
Newport, Rhode Island

Familiar with the location of the Audrian building on Bellevue Avenue, Sara had never before had a reason to enter. Unfortunately, now she did. Embarrassed at the prospect of being seen at the lawyer's office she had worn a plain, dark dress and a veiled hat to hide her face, praying she wouldn't see anyone she knew en route.

Double checking the suite address on the notecard, she entered the building and headed to the second floor in search of Mr. Sheffield's office. Her mind raced with the details and facts of the honeymoon confrontation, causing her much anxiety and agitation. Sara trembled and worked to control her emotions, willing her dread to transform into courage.

Moving down the hallway, she noted the names etched on glass doors. Finally, she found the lawyer's office, frosted glass blaring ATTORNEY AT LAW. Pausing to gather her wits, Sara entered the suite, a bell jangling her arrival. The sitting room greeted her, professional and formally furnished. A young man shuffled through papers at his desk, glancing up as she entered.

"Mrs. Belmont?" he asked politely.

"Yes."

"Mr. Sheffield is expecting you. Please have a seat while he finishes a meeting. I'm sure it will only be a few more minutes."

"Of course."

Sara clutched her purse as she sat down in the nearest chair, her pride battling with the humiliation of her failed marriage. She riffled through some magazines sitting on the table, deciding on a copy of *Tribune and Farmer*. It had a woman's column that Anita and Edith had both said was enjoyable. Leafing through the pages, she distracted herself, trying to ignore the men's voices seeping through the open door of the adjoining office.

"Yes, of course," an unknown man said. "We'll make a public announcement in today's newspaper for interested artists to send in their sketches and proposals."

"I'm certain there will be a lot of excitement for the assignment," a deep voice replied. "The paper may even want to do an article on the statue."

"I agree, especially in light of the fifteen thousand dollars Mrs. Belmont has donated for the commission. It's quite a generous budget."

The first man chuckled. "Commodore Oliver Hazard Perry memorialized in bronze. It will make a nice addition to Touro Park or Washington Square. We can decide which park will be the most suitable location at a future meeting."

"That sounds agreeable. In the meantime, as members of the executive committee assigned to fulfill Mrs. Belmont's wishes, we must make every effort to insure that the money is used wisely. Only the best possible design will be selected, and the vote must be unanimous." The sound of chairs scraping the tile floor preceded four men, emerging from the inner office.

"Thank you, Mr. Sheffield." A gray-haired gentleman extended his hand.

"We'll be in touch," said another, tipping his hat.

They exchanged farewells and filed into the hallway, their footsteps fading in the distance.

A distinguished man in a well-tailored suit turned his attention to Sara, eyeing her from behind a monocle.

"Mrs. Belmont," he said. "I apologize for the delay. Our meeting went longer than planned, as can sometimes happen. Your mother-in-law has commissioned me to oversee the committee erecting a statue of Commodore Perry for our local park. It should be quite spectacular, she's sparing no expense to honor a Newport citizen, and one of our country's great war heroes." [50]

Nodding, Sara hid her discomfort. Mr. Sheffield had only confirmed her suspicions as to the nature of the meeting. What kind of cruel joke of fate was this? Arriving just as the committee adjourned – just as *she* arrived to divorce the Commodore's namesake: Oliver Hazard Perry Belmont.

"I'm sorry for your recent problems, Mrs. Belmont," Mr. Sheffield began, waving her into his office. "I've read some accounts in the newspaper, but it's hard to know what's true and what's gossip." He closed the door behind them, pointing to a chair in front of the desk.

"Well," Sara began, taking a seat, "I suppose that depends on which newspaper you're reading." She blushed, ashamed, and affected a meager smile. Organizing her thoughts, she began her story, giving the lawyer a full account of events since her honeymoon in January.

"So you see," she finished, "with Oliver's behavior so unpredictable and often violent – especially when he drinks, I simply cannot risk my safety or the well-being of my child. Aside from the fact the he deserted me, I must admit, I'm in perfect terror of what he may do." [51] She finished, resignation emanating from her words, "I've decided not to reconcile our marriage. Not now and not ever."

His crystal eyes drilled her, as if searching out any falsehoods or loopholes. Mr. Sheffield knew Oliver, and he'd heard about his failure in the navy, but never any tales of abuse. He seemed a good-natured young man, although a bit irresponsible. Hardly a crime.

"I can see you've made up your mind."

"Yes sir, I have."

"Do you have any requests as to a monetary settlement?"

"I wouldn't know where to begin in such matters. I prefer to leave that to your discretion. The one thing I do insist, is that I retain custody of my child, and that Oliver – Mr. Belmont, is never allowed to see the baby."

"That may be a little difficult to prevent." Mr. Sheffield glanced at her through his monocle. "After all, he is the father. Besides, your child is a Belmont and would be entitled to child support, possibly a family inheritance by its own rights. Do you really want to deny your child its lineage?"

"My concerns are more for our personal well-being and safety than for wealth. My father has left me a considerable dowry. I don't want my child exposed to Oliver's temper or his unpredictable moods."

Tapping a pencil, he surveyed his client. "Well, in light of the physical violence you claim and his use of spirits, I think I may be able to sway the judge in your favor."

Sara visibly relaxed, allowing herself to breathe a little lighter.

"As you know," he continued, "Rhode Island's laws are some of the easiest in the country for securing a speedy divorce. We're only behind Illinois at present, with our divorce statutes. I'm glad you didn't delay with legal proceedings, as there's word the legislature is going to try to reform the marriage laws when they reconvene in January. As they stand at present, I think we'll be able to get your divorce decree without complication."

"It will be a great relief to me," Sara confided. "And of course I'd like to keep this out of the newspapers at all cost. I'm sure you can imagine the shame this situation has brought me."

"I'll be as discreet as possible. But you must understand that legal proceedings are of a public nature, although the specifics can be kept private.

Once divorce papers are filed, the press will have access to them at the courthouse, but the details of your grievance will be revealed to no one outside of this office. I can assure you, your case will be handled with the utmost attention and privacy."

"Thank you."

"Also, I'm required to advise you to remain in the state until this is over. Hopefully it will be within six months, as long as Mr. Belmont doesn't file a counter suit against you." He offered her a soothing smile, "I'll have the papers drawn up immediately. Once I have the documents finished I'll need to see you again, to make sure they meet your approval." He set the pencil on the desk, concluding their appointment. "Then all I'll need is your signature to file with the court."

"Of course," Sara stood, and shook his hand. "I'll expect to hear from you."

"Good day, Mrs. Belmont."

"Good day."

CHAPTER SEVENTEEN

One month later
July 28, 1883
Newport, Rhode Island

HEAVY GRAY CLOUDS PROMISED THE cool blessing of rain, yet were unsuccessful in blocking the steaming summer sun from the sky. Shaded by the leafy branches of the copper beech tree, a small circle of well-known ladies of society gathered around Swanhurst's piazza table, seeking shelter from the heat.

Listening to the conversation, Mrs. Whiting smiled in gratitude. It's good to know we still have the backing of these women, she thought. She glanced at Sara in the rocking chair, pumping her fan against her face in a meager effort to create a breeze – but the thick air allowed little relief.

It was very clever of me to host a small luncheon here at Swanhurst, Mrs. Whiting acknowledged to herself. With Sara unable to socialize at this late stage of her pregnancy, this was an ingenious way for her to enjoy some companionship – a small diversion from her confinement.

After days roaming the rooms of the manor, boredom had become Sara's métier, and with only books and letters to occupy her mind, Mrs. Whiting worried she was growing melancholy. Munching on a light menu of crepes, finger sandwiches, and fruit salad, the women were happy to visit, well aware of the detrimental effects monotony could bear on the mind of a confined woman.

"The city is quite full of visitors for the season," Mrs. King said. "The town caterers and florists are booked well into autumn. I'm arranging a dinner party for August and I had a terrible time finding a proper chef. I have to bring one in from New York."

"Yes, it seems there are more events this year than last, and last year was very busy," Mrs. Endicott chimed in. "All topped off with another visit by President Arthur in September."

"We'll be taking the carriage up to Dead Head Hill to watch the polo match tomorrow," Mrs. King chimed in from her cushioned bamboo chair. "Is your son going to play in the games?" she asked Mrs. Whiting.

"I suspect as much. He enjoys polo and the fox hunt. Gus loves his horses, and he's accomplished at both sports." Mrs. Whiting sipped her iced tea, the glass frosted from humidity. "There are so many matches and hunts planned this summer, a person could drop from exhaustion with all the hustle and bustle! I'm afraid I'm getting too old to keep up."

Laughing along with the ladies, Sara smiled congenially. Mrs. Havemeyer, newly arrived to the luncheon, took a seat around the large table. Drinking iced tea, lemonade and mint juleps, the circle of friends comprised the set's most influential wives, all married to powerful men. Sitting together under the tall potted palms on the veranda, Sara watched them in admiration. They seemed so smart, albeit opinionated, exuding a self-confidence she sought to emulate in her own mannerisms.

"My daughter is competing in the fox hunts and doing very well," Mrs. Havemeyer commented. "My Abby, Miss Turure and several other young women certainly give the men something to admire besides their beauty." Her mouth tilted in a befuddled frown. "Why she enjoys such a wild sport is beyond me, but I suspect it's her love of horses." The older woman paused, then turned her attention to Sara. "How are you feeling dear? It must be difficult in this heat."

"I'm doing well. Just wishing for a stronger breeze to blow off the ocean," Sara laughed, and took a sip from her icy lemonade. She had long ago resigned herself to missing the season due to her present condition. But today she felt chipper, donning her prettiest flowered sundress. "I'm so glad for your company," she said. "I was beginning to go a bit stir crazy. Your visit affords me a brief escape from my solitude."

"Well, be mindful to take good care of yourself. We're all shocked by the lack of maturity Oliver exhibited in Paris."

"Simply dreadful," Mrs. King shook her head, tsking. "But certainly not surprising if you consider his tenure in the navy, as well as his lack of success in banking. But that's no excuse for the way he treated you."

"Especially not in your condition!" Mrs. Weaver added. "We'll help you get through this nasty affair dear, don't you worry. Of course you're aware that the Belmonts have been wining and dining everyone in society in an effort to woo them into forgetting about their son's lack of scruples. But in spite of their best efforts, few in the set are quick to forgive him."

"Certainly not," Mrs. King scoffed. "You're one of our favorites, dear! It was awful of him to drag you into this mess. I hope you don't mind us talking about it."

"It has made for a hard time." Sara ignored the question. "And I truly appreciate all of you being my advocates. It means the world to me."

"Indeed," Mrs. Whiting echoed. "Thankfully, the set is familiar with the reckless way the younger Belmont sons have conducted themselves."

"I hear they're having trouble with Raymond now." Mrs. Havemeyer sipped her mint cocktail. "I assure you Sara, no one holds you at fault for your present problems."

"That's nice to know...." Sara ran a finger over the fogged glass, droplets running down the side.

"We're glad to visit and do what we can to help," Mrs. King assured her. "Besides, your cook makes the most fabulous crepes I've tasted outside of France."

"I couldn't agree more," Mrs. Endicott nodded, as a trill of laughter swirled around the table.

"Anyone going to the Vanderbilts tonight for the dinner party?" Mrs. Havemeyer asked the circle of friends, while glancing up from her plate.

"Is Alva having a party, too?" Mrs. Weaver replied. "We're invited to Sidney Webster's tonight. He's entertaining Senator Bayard. I find politics dreadfully boring, but my husband is continually preoccupied by it. In any event, I'm compelled to attend."

"The summer season in Newport," Mrs. Whiting chuckled. "A lady needs a personal secretary just to keep up!"

Sara spotted Carrie and her mother, the two sauntering down the stone walkway toward the house. "Excuse me a moment," she said easing from the chair. "I see the Astors have arrived."

She left the women chatting amongst themselves, and found her way on slow feet. It felt good to stretch, in spite of the fact that her body was so heavy with child. Reaching the edge of the piazza she waved, catching Carrie's eye.

"Sara, how nice to see you!" Mrs. Astor smiled, walking toward her.

"Hi Sara!" Carrie gave her friend a light hug. "I've missed you. How are you feeling?" The three meandered to the table to join the other ladies. "It looks like the baby might be arriving any day now."

"A few more months... I suppose I'll spend most of the summer warding off the heat, waiting for the baby's appearance."

"Well, the baby will be here before you know it," Mrs. Astor encouraged. "Hello everyone," she greeted, settling into a wicker chair at the table with the older women. Sara and Carrie walked to the side of the porch and sat on the glider.

"How nice to see you Mrs. Astor," Mrs. King welcomed brightly.

"Lovely indeed," Mrs. Whiting nodded, waving to Mary to serve Mrs. Astor and Carrie.

"How are you Lina?" Mrs. Havemeyer asked.

"Very well, thank you," Mrs. Astor said. "Although, I would be grateful for a cool breeze. I'm ready to hire new servants just to wave fans."

Everyone laughed, while seriously considering the merit of the idea. Mary set a cocktail in front of Mrs. Astor, as well as a plate and silver service so she could enjoy the appetizers arranged on the table. Moving to the side porch she also handed Carrie a drink, while putting a dish and silverware within easy reach on the end table.

"Thank you, Mary," Carrie said, taking a sip of the cool beverage. "This is just what I need to fight against this heat. You could cut the humidity with a knife."

"My pleasure," The housekeeper curtseyed and excused herself, heading for the kitchen to refill the plate of fresh blueberry crepes.

"Yes, the mugginess is unrelenting," Mrs. Weaver commented.

"I'm trying not to let it bother me," Mrs. Endicott interjected. "Summer is my favorite season and before you know it, autumn will be here. And you know what follows autumn…"

The conversation drifted on the air of the lazy afternoon while the women relaxed against the sweltering heat, tête-à-tête in private discussions.

"How is your summer going?" Sara turned to Carrie. "I heard your garden party was lovely. Everyone was talking about it."

"It was a nice afternoon," Carrie nodded, "but I miss you and our fun times together." She tilted her head ruefully. "I received your letter explaining your avoidance of my company. I simply can't tell you how upset I've been. This is all quite disturbing to me."

"It is upsetting, but things will be better this way."

"This entire situation is absolutely absurd! Why Oliver's conduct should interfere with our friendship is beyond my comprehension."

Touched by her friend's show of loyalty, Sara patted her arm, "I know, Carrie. We've always been there for each other, but this scandal between Oliver and I has changed things. I would never forgive myself if it had unfavorable repercussions on your social standing."

"Sara…" Carrie's dismay ruined her smile, "I wish there was a way around this, but Mother has endorsed your decision. I must say you've garnered new favor with her, although I'm completely distressed by the turn of events."

"Your mother and I have always been close." A lump grew in Sara's throat. "I'm very grateful I haven't been blacklisted from her good graces."

"Of course not!" Carrie blurted. "Mother is very fond of you, Sara, and she's doing all she can to sway opinion in your favor." She reached for her cocktail and took a sip, replacing the glass on the table. "How I wish things were different," Carrie moaned, "but Mother does detest rumors and wants to avoid them at all costs." The two exchanged a glance of unspoken understanding.

"Carrie, please don't give it a second thought," Sara leaned back in her chair, disguising her dejection. "I completely understand your mother's perspective. As long as I can still count you among my friends, things will be fine."

"I'm truly sympathetic to your plight. I can't imagine the hardship you've had to deal with. I don't think I'd have the strength for it."

"I won't pretend it hasn't been very challenging," Sara confided. "Which is why it's best if I keep my distance – for now, anyway."

Sitting on the porch, the conversation forged a deep camaraderie between the two young women negotiating the parameters of their friendship.

"Enough of this gloom," Sara brushed away their discussion. "I insist we dwell on happier events." She nodded at the fresh crepes. "You really must taste these treats."

Three weeks later
August 17, 1883
Newport, Rhode Island

A cluster of carriages delivered exuberant visitors, convening in the farm fields just outside of town for the red fox hunt. There had been large hunts in the past, but Oliver couldn't remember such a huge crowd gathered for the event. The road appeared to be completely blocked, police whistles blowing shrill directions at the drivers. The newspapers announced that Royals visiting from Europe were among the spectators, as well as society people on holiday from around the country.

"This is going to be more fun than I'd imagined," Auggie said to his brothers. "You, me and Raymond, all riding in the same event. It adds an extra measure of competition."

"Don't forget about the rest of your rivals." Center Hitchcock approached, chuckling. "Everyone's here today: Morgan, Keene, Weaver... The Belmont brothers have some stiff competition. They don't call Keene 'Foxy' for nothing," he teased. "Regardless, I feel lucky today and I intend to get the fox first!"

"There are other kinds of foxes to be had." Raymond eyed a young débutante strolling by twirling her parasol.

"Keep your mind on the hunt or the women just might outdo you," Oliver joked.

"Indeed," Hitch added. "There are some talented ladies riding today."

"Like who?" Auggie asked. "Miss Havemeyer?"

"She's the best," Hitch nodded. "But Mrs. Smythe and Miss Prince are equally skilled at the sport. In any event, it'll be pleasant to watch them try for the fox."

Bugles sounded across the field summoning the riders to gather at the starting point of the course. Oliver and his brothers moved toward the stable, mounting their horses to join the other riders on the knoll of the hill.

It took no effort at all for Oliver to forget about Sara in confinement while surrounded by such a thrilling atmosphere. Why should I sit out the summer, he thought, because she's being stubborn, refusing a reconciliation? Oliver had every intention of continuing his life as before, and to that end, enjoying the afternoon chase.

The summer sun beat hot and bright on the throng. Excitement rippled through the crowd on a current of energy from spectators impatient for the riders to start the competition. Caged hounds barked incessantly from their pens, eager to be unleashed on the field. Without delay, the riders organized their horses, and the hunt was started by the blare of the bugle. Cheering rose from the bystanders, a jubilant roar for the riders, hungry to view the competition.

In a flash the hounds took off, veering decisively in the direction of the reservoir. Oliver charged his horse ahead with the others, shifting, unsettled in his saddle. Nearing the first wall, he erred on the side of caution, deciding against the risk, as did his fellow riders. Knowing they could go around by way of the road and avoid the peril of the jump, they deviated, aware they'd still maintain their glory. Three riders tore up a growing cornfield in their pursuit and Oliver felt certain there'd be trouble from the landowner. Adding to the mayhem a herd of cattle joined the hunters as they crossed two fields. If that wasn't enough, pigs started running with the fox before the finish, confused by the pandemonium.

Keene, riding a polo pony, easily handled all obstructions and in the end was awarded the trophy for the kill. Miss Havemeyer was the only lady to reach the end. Raymond was thrown but not injured, as were several other hunters. Out of thirty riders only fifteen saw the hunt to the end. [52]

Leading his horse back to the stable, Oliver met up with Raymond, his riding gear dirty, his face sheepish, embarrassed from the fall.

"I'm sure the newspapers will tell everyone I lost my mount."

Oliver patted him on the back. "Not to worry. A change of clothes and a good dinner party will take your mind off the fall."

Two days later
August 19, 1883
Newport, Rhode Island

Popping her parasol open, Mrs. Whiting climbed down from the carriage. Jane and Milly disembarked the ride in her wake. "Take Sara back to Swanhurst, Owen," Mrs. Whiting ordered. "You can come back for us in a few hours."

"Yes ma'am. I'll park right here when I return and wait for you."

"Now, don't overexert yourself," Mrs. Whiting cautioned Sara. "I'm not so sure letting you rumble around in the coach is such a good idea. But I suppose there's no harm in a short ride. I'm sorry you have to miss the yacht race tomorrow, but your health is more important."

"I feel fine, Mother. I'm going stir crazy sitting around the house all day. The walls are closing in on me."

"You're a stubborn one," Mrs. Whiting frowned, sizing up her youngest daughter.

The day was fraught with the thick air of late summer, hanging over the city like a cloud. Sara was thankful for the occasional sea breeze blowing through the open carriage window, as she watched her family stroll down the Newport sidewalk.

"Owen, please let's just sit here a while," Sara implored the whip. "A few more minutes won't make a difference."

"I have my orders, miss."

"Please Owen ..."

The driver gave her a sympathetic look, then relented, shrugging his shoulders. "I suppose a few minutes, but then it's back to the manor with you."

Keeping her weariness at bay, Sara glanced at the harbor, viewing the sailboats anchored in Newport for tomorrow's yacht competition. The Goelet Cup would race from here to the Vineyards, and sailboats had been arriving in Newport all week. Gaily decorated with colorful flags and bunting, the vessels dispatched a festive air, dotting the harbor like an impressionist's painting where they moored.

With her due date quickly approaching Sara felt as big as a barn. Bored and listless, she yearned for the excitement of the season. The doctor advised fresh air and exercise as long as she didn't overdo it. Overexertion had a lot more to do with her emotions these days, than any physical activity, and Sara relished the thought of a short excursion to see the boats. It took some finagling to win the argument with her mother to ride along, but it was worth the effort to have a change of scenery, no matter how short-lived.

Gazing out the open coach window, her thoughts meandered to Oliver. He had sent for her yet again, insistent she join him at Oakland. Once more she'd refused. Their separation was now a public affair, with articles printed weekly in the papers about the demise of their marriage. The propaganda and hearsay was hard to swallow, but in spite of the Belmont's campaign it seemed the majority of public sympathy remained sided with her.

Each day Sara vacillated less, growing more certain of her choice to divorce Oliver. But it was a heavy decision, imposing a constant effort to stay cheerful. She hoped with time she'd adjust to the idea of being a single mother, but as the summer hinted at autumn, she found her insecurities mounting. Certainly money would not be an issue. She received her allowance now from her father's inheritance, but she was wise enough to know it took more than money to raise a child in the modern world.

Lethargic from the heat, Sara watched her sisters prattle in the distance, her mother pausing occasionally to chat with a friend. Pushing her worries to the corner of her mind, she sat in the coach, distracting herself by critiquing the stylish summer dresses and hats displayed in the shop windows across the sidewalk. None were meant for a pregnant woman, and her interest quickly waned. She sighed in resignation, wondering if she'd ever fit into those tiny dresses again.

The townsfolk promenaded on the sidewalk, some throwing a glance her way. She smiled through the window, thankful her girth was out of their view. They'll think what they will anyway, Sara thought, knowing it was unusual for an expectant mother to be out of the house.

Listening to the chitchat, it was apparent that the yacht festivities were the main topic of conversation. The Goelet Cup was a high point of the season and seemed to be on everyone's mind. Growing weary, her spirits sank with her energy. Sara found it arduous to join in the happy mood. All she could think about was the baby growing inside her, soon to appear in the world. A child that would be born to a soon-to-be divorced mother and an absentee father. She felt caged and powerless to do anything about it.

"Mrs. Belmont. What a pleasant surprise, seeing you out of the house."

Sara glanced over at William sauntering up the sidewalk toward the carriage window.

"Hello Mr. Vanderbilt." She mustered a courteous voice. He always seemed to appear when she felt her worst, but polite conversation was a respite from her loneliness. If Sara turned a blind eye to his curt attitude, she could find him a happy distraction from her present concerns.

"How are you dealing with the heat?"

"I'm doing as well as can be expected."

They passed a moment in silence. Sara gave a glance to Owen standing near the coach, and fanned herself while noticing her family far down the thoroughfare.

"I heard the President's daughter, Nellie, is in town with her aunt and cousins," William shifted the conversation. "Word is he's coming to Newport to join them. The town has a full schedule of activities arranged for his visit – and I'm sure a bit of political courtship. I think he's coming in early September. That's right around the time your baby is due, isn't it?"

"The doctor said it could be any time in September. I'm sure you understand the President's visit is the last thing on my mind right now." How tactless to remind her of the gay times she'd miss due to her pregnancy.

"I read in the papers you've met with a lawyer. I suppose that means you and Oliver haven't been able to resolve your problems."

"You know Oliver. He's running about town carrying on in an ungentlemanly fashion. He leaves me no alternative if I'm to raise my child with some semblance of propriety. In spite of his position in society, he's dreadfully lacking in the maturity this situation demands. I think in the end we'll be better off without him creating problems in our lives."

"I'm terribly sorry to hear it. Although in Oliver's defense, he's always had to deal with his parent's expectations and demands. The best I can figure, it all got to him in Paris and he snapped for one reason or another." William offered her a contrite look, "For what it's worth, I think he's a fool for throwing everything out the window. A marriage to a beautiful débutante and his new child to boot."

"I can't tell if you're defending him, or standing up for me."

"I think I'll remain neutral, if you don't mind. But I want you to know that in spite of everything, I'm very sorry to see things end so badly for you. If you do go through with the divorce, remarriage is unlikely with a child in tow. Most men prefer to start from scratch, shying away from a ready-made family."

"You needn't remind me of the reality of my unfortunate predicament, but thank you for your opinion, Mr. Vanderbilt. I'll keep it in mind."

Sara caught Owen's eye as he climbed onto the box with the reins in hand. "Well, I must return home..."

William tipped his hat cordially, "Take good care of yourself and let us know when the baby arrives."

Sara nodded from the seat, watching through the window as William crossed the street to join a circle of giggling young débutantes out for an evening stroll.

CHAPTER EIGHTEEN

Three weeks later
September 5, 1883
Newport, Rhode Island

SETTING THE COPY OF *LADIES Home Journal and Practical Housekeeping* on the tea table, Sara gripped her belly. The pain was sharp, demanding her attention over that of the magazine. She breathed, willing the ache to subside. It's too soon for the baby, she thought, concerned for its well-being. She gingerly rose from the chair, the worst having passed, and started for the bedroom door. A fresh spear of pain moved through her and she reeled, leaning against the chamber wall. Perspiration beaded on her forehead; her mouth was parched and dry. Relief was slow to come, and much too brief. The raw pain seared her again, and she moaned in spite of herself. Before she could regain her strength, Bridget was at her side, yelling for Mrs. Whiting.

"Come over to the bed, miss." Bridget threw Sara's arm over her shoulder, helping her walk.

Her body felt like a vise, wrenching without mercy. Sara could only whimper, moving as instructed. Her mind raced, intimidated by the fear that overpowered her. She had known this day would arrive, but now that it was here, she doubted her courage to face the lying-in.

"What's happening?" Sara barely heard her mother's voice over the roar in her ears.

"It's the baby," Bridget exclaimed in a low voice. "I think it's time."

"It's too early for the baby." Mrs. Whiting took Bridget's place, helping Sara to the bed. "Send for the doctor at once. And have Mary come up here right away."

"Yes ma'am," Bridget ran quickly from the room.

Stuffing a pillow behind her back, Mrs. Whiting's hand caressed her forehead, helping Sara get comfortable.

"Shhh now… It'll be okay, daughter. Just stay calm. Everything will be fine."

Sara tried to focus on her mother's words, but pain demanded her attention, overpowering her attempt at fortitude. All she could do was grip her mother's hand for strength.

The New York Times
Polo, Receptions, Germans, and other Entertainments.

Newport, R.I., Sept. 5, - Mrs. Oliver Hazard Perry Belmont, the daughter of Mrs. S.S. Whiting, of New-York, has just given birth to a daughter. [53]

At present, although the mother is seeking divorce from Oliver H. P. Belmont, she and the child will retain the Belmont surname.

The next day
September 6, 1883
Newport, Rhode Island

Oliver sat alone in the darkness, ice clinking inside the glass of double malt scotch.

He was a father.

He struggled to embrace the idea – he had a daughter. He tried not to be disappointed that it wasn't a son. A male heir could carry the Belmont name into the future, rivaling Auggie's son for dominance. But no matter. A little girl was sweet and wonderful, too.

Late last night his mother sent a note bearing news of the birth, instructing her footman to deliver the letter to him at Oakland. He'd gone immediately to Swanhurst to see the child, but Mrs. Whiting had blocked his entry, shouting threats about restraining orders. He'd argued with her, filled with regret, desperately wanting to see the baby. But she fought back, calling for the servants to fetch the police. Rather than create a public scene he'd returned to Oakland, dismally unhappy, yearning to lay eyes on his daughter.

A daughter.

Natica Caroline Belmont.

His daughter. He softened while sipping his cocktail. I'm surprised how fond I am of the idea now that she's actually arrived, he thought. How he wished he could see her, if only briefly. His paternal instincts turned protective as he considered her future and the wonderful life he could give her. But not if the Whitings refused him visitation. And by what right could they prevent him time with his own flesh and blood? There were laws about such things.

The urge to know his baby occupied his thoughts and he considered his options to gain access to her. In the end, he surmised, it would all come down to a judge and the courts. But he was not without recourse. If the Whitings refused to allow him to act as the child's father, then he'd refuse to recognize her as his child. She wouldn't be a Belmont heir or entitled to any of the family ancestry – or treasury.

Let's just see how they like that, Oliver thought.

He took another sip of his drink and set the empty glass on the table, engulfed by the darkness of night.

CHAPTER NINETEEN

One week later
September 12, 1883
Newport, Rhode Island

LAYING THE BABY IN THE bassinet, Sara felt her heart bloom with a love deeper than any she'd ever known. She lingered, gazing at the tiny sleeping face bundled tight in a soft, flannel receiving blanket. Her precious daughter was beautiful perfect in every way. Sara inspected each teeny feature with wonder, realizing the miracle of life.

She'd heard women talk about the marvel of birth, but for the first time she truly understood what they meant! Her heart was smitten at the first glimpse of her baby, and motherhood delivered a joy unlike any she'd known.

She'd named her Natica, after her friend Lady Lister-Kaye. For a middle name Sara had decided on Caroline – not after Mrs. Belmont, but as an homage to Mrs. Astor, her staunch defender. In her mind she was already planning for the baby's christening. Sara intended to ask Carrie to be Natica's godmother, along with the baby's namesake, Lady Lister-Kaye. Two godmothers would give the child an advantage, she chuckled. A soft knock interrupted her reverie. Bridget tiptoed into the room, joining her beside the cradle.

"She's precious and beautiful, miss. I'm so delighted for you."

"She does make the pregnancy forgettable," Sara smiled.

"More gifts and flowers have arrived. We haven't had this many visits from the florist since your début. Why don't you take a break? I'll sit with the baby for a bit."

"I think I'd like that. She was a little fussy last night and wore me out, the little dear." Sara sighed, tired but content. "I just fed her, so she should sleep for you. Let me know if she wakes and I'll come up right away."

Knowing she sounded like a nervous mother, Sara's maternal instincts had their own needs since the baby's arrival. She'd earned the right to be vigilant, so why fight it? Her strength was quick to return; she was hopelessly bored from laying in bed all day, even though the doctor insisted on it. But each new morning she felt more like her old self. Finally, today, the doctor had given his okay for her to get up if she wanted to – and she certainly did.

"I've got everything under control. I'll just sit right here in this rocking chair until you come back." Bridget sat down next to the bassinet, cooing at the baby asleep in the cradle.

Quietly leaving the nursery Sara smiled at Bridget, confident her daughter was in good hands. Padding down the hall on slippered feet, she moved past the adjacent bedroom. Sara had insisted the baby sleep in her chambers until she was older. Mrs. Whiting suggested they put a second cradle in the adjoining room, declaring it the nursery. This way, the other ladies could help care for the baby when necessary, and Sara could rest and recuperate in her own bedroom. The arrangement seemed to work out well for everyone.

Descending the staircase with a slow careful step, Sara's nose was treated to the sweet scent of roses and lilies wafting up to greet her. Reaching the foyer she realized Bridget hadn't been exaggerating about the deliveries. Her face lit up like morning sunshine at the sight of the vases and floral arrangements adorning every empty space in the parlor. She moved to the nearest table, laden with an enormous vase of pink stargazer lilies, and slipped the card from its envelope.

"Congratulations on your baby girl," it read, from Edith and the Jones family. A second was from the Wilsons and a third from Alva and William Vanderbilt. She continued reading the notes of congratulation, while admiring the flowers. Entering the sitting room, she discovered even more blooms adorning the tables and shelves.

And if that wasn't enough, the drum table was stacked with gift boxes and packages wrapped in every shade of pink paper and fabric, tied with matching satin ribbons. Viewing the gifts awaiting her attention, Sara chuckled at the literal meaning of 'birthday presents'. Lifting the lid off the nearest box, she pushed aside the tissue paper to discover a pink silk crib quilt with exquisite lace trim. The card was signed by Carrie, promising to visit as soon as Sara was up to receiving guests. Grateful for their strong friendship and the support of Mrs. Astor, Sara's hands lingered on the cozy quilt.

"Well, look who's up and about. How are you feeling?"

Sara turned, startled by her mother who was toting a small crystal vase filled with dainty pink tea roses toward the sideboard.

"I'm a little tired but other than that, I'm feeling much better. The baby is sleeping. Bridget is with her, so I thought I'd come downstairs for a while."

"I'm relieved to see the color coming back to your cheeks. I can't tell you how happy I am that all went well, considering your little daughter's decision to make an early appearance into the world."

"She's a bit tiny. But, thankfully, Dr. Turner says she's strong and healthy."

Wading through the gift cards, Sara opened packages while they chatted. "Nothing from Oliver or Mrs. Belmont?" Paper rustled as she sorted through the gifts.

"No dear. No word from the Belmonts. But I'm pleased to say we've heard from all of the Whiting and Swan families, not to mention our friends in town. There was a birth announcement in *The New York Times*. Everyone has expressed delight over your new daughter."

"She's so beautiful," Sara breathed. "I thought the Belmonts would acknowledge her arrival and send flowers, or a card at the very least."

"Just don't you worry yourself about the Belmonts. If they want to behave badly that's their business. Take a look around this house." Mrs. Whiting waved her hand at the flowers and gifts. "You have one lucky little girl to create such excitement in Newport."

"You're absolutely right," Sara agreed, examining a silver rattle from Tiffany's. "Oh look..." she pointed. "It's engraved with roses."

Leaning over for a better view Mrs. Whiting spotted the petals etched into the silver handle. "Who's that from?"

"Mrs. Havemeyer. This will make a wonderful heirloom one day."

"That it will."

Replacing the rattle in the box Sara set it back on the table with the other gifts. Honestly, she thought, I'm disappointed the Belmonts haven't sent a card. She didn't know what she expected, considering the feud they'd been raging against each other for months now. But childbirth is a major milestone in anyone's life, and she was Oliver's daughter and his parents' granddaughter. She'd hoped to hear some type of congratulations.

"I think I'm going to lay down for a while. It seems I still tire easily. Do you mind helping Bridget with the baby? I'm suddenly too weary to keep my eyes open."

"Of course I don't mind. You go and take a nap," her mother urged, shooing her upstairs. "We'll watch over little Natica for as long as you need."

"Thank you." Sara moved toward the staircase with the fatigue of a new mother.

The next day
September 13, 1883
Newport, Rhode Island

"Good afternoon, Mr. Belmont. Your mother is in the parlor."

Oliver handed his hat to the servant. "Thank you," he replied off-handedly. He felt certain he'd been summoned to Bythesea to discuss the birth of his daughter. His father was in New York working, but Oliver knew his parents had conferred since Natica had arrived last week. He moved down the hall to find his mother sitting in the parlor, sorting through dinner invitations.

"Hello Mamma, how are you? Have you heard from Papa?"

"Hello Oliver." She looked up with a sidelong glance. "Yes. I sent him a telegram last Thursday. He's in the middle of important business with Mr. Morgan and can't leave the city for at least another week."

Oliver sat in a chair beside the desk. "The Whitings won't let me visit Swanhurst. They've prohibited me from seeing my baby," he complained. "They've completely barred me from the premises."

Raising an eye, Mrs. Belmont frowned. "I received your note. Neither your father nor I are quite sure how to handle this development. Sara seems bent on divorcing you, and as far as I can tell, her mother is encouraging her."

"This is exasperating!" Oliver bellowed. "Sara won't even meet with me to discuss the divorce proceedings. Is that so much to ask? I feel like I've hit a brick wall. Any attempts of mine to reconcile are met with refusal. Now this – with the baby. I'm beginning to lose my patience over the entire mess."

"Again, I must ask you," Mrs. Belmont needled. "What did you think would happen when you walked out on Sara during your honeymoon? Did you even stop for one second to consider the consequences of your actions? How are we to counter her claims of physical and verbal violence in light of your carousing? There were witnesses. From what our attorneys says Sara is well within her rights to divorce you."

"Well, I have rights too and I intend to exercise them. My case is just as strong against her for leaving Paris before I could return."

Lips sealed by pessimism, Caroline shook her head, dismayed. "Your rights can't force her to repair your marriage. At best, you can only counter sue for divorce. Although your father and I agree, if the Whitings won't let you be a parent to the child, then you don't have to acknowledge her as your own – or as a Belmont. The decision is yours. You won't have to pay any child support, but the baby will appear illegitimate. I don't think the Whitings will be too happy about that."

"The thought crossed my mind as well," Oliver frowned. "It seems dreadfully unfair that my daughter is caught in the crossfire of this battle, and branded as a bastard." He gave her a haggard smile. "I must admit, I do want to see the baby, Mamma. I can't help wondering what she looks like…" After a moment he added, "I could sue for paternal custody."

His mother scoffed openly, while he struggled with his instincts. "You couldn't even stay with your wife through the difficulties in Paris. What makes you think you can raise a child on your own? The baby would be raised by nannies and as distressed as I am about the situation, I do believe a child is best off with its own mother – and I'm certain any court will rule in favor of the mother for custody." Turning gentle, she smiled, "I understand your frustration, but I don't think suing for custody is the answer. Yet, I do wish Sara wouldn't take such a strong stand against your visitation. If she wants to get divorced, fine. But why she insists on dragging your child through the mud I can't understand."

"Maybe it's a misguided effort to protect the baby from these trumped up accusations she's made against me," Oliver offered. "I confess I have no idea what's going on in her mind. But I do know that if Sara won't allow me to visit Swanhurst to see my own baby, then I must seriously consider refusing to recognize the child as my daughter. No one can prove she's mine anyway."

"What if she looks like you?"

"How can we know, if we've never been allowed to see her!" Oliver fumed. "Ah! This situation is intolerable."

"I couldn't agree more, but throwing a tantrum won't do any good."

He grimaced, then walked to the sideboard for a drink.

Watching from her seat, Mrs. Belmont remained calm. "I haven't sent a card or a gift. I really wasn't sure what would be proper considering the circumstances. Although the child is legally a Belmont, as is Sara…"

"I think we should ignore the entire birth," Oliver cut her off, his voice empty and cold. "I've made my decision. From this point forward I refuse to recognize the child as a Belmont – or as my own!" He spun around, "And I'd appreciate it if you and the rest of the family would do the same." [54]

Nodding, Mrs. Belmont agreed. "If that's your wish, for now at least, we'll remain quiet about the baby. But Oliver, a child has a way of growing up, and it may not be as easy as you think to deny your paternity."

He walked back to his seat carrying the glass. "I disagree with you Mother," he countered. "It's as easy as saying, 'she's not my daughter.'" Lifting the glass to his lips, he drank it dry.

CHAPTER TWENTY

Seven weeks later
October 31, 1883
Newport, Rhode Island

PUSHING THE PRAM DOWN BELLEVUE Avenue, Sara strolled on a light step, Bridget at her side. The October afternoon was breezy, scattering aromatic autumn leaves across their path. A warm wave of late fall weather had made for a beautiful Indian summer day, and Sara had decided a short walk with the baby would be good for both of them.

"Little Natica seems to be enjoying the day," Bridget cooed at the smiling infant bundled in her carriage.

"I don't want to keep her out long," Sara said. "But tonight is Halloween and I always loved the holiday. Pumpkins, gourds and the smell of autumn leaves always puts me in good spirits. Since Mr. Sheffield has insisted I stay in Rhode Island until the divorce is final, I figure I might as well make the most of it and enjoy the fine weather."

Reflecting on a similar walk the year before, her optimism wavered. She'd been so happy that day, returning to Swanhurst with Bridget from an afternoon with Carrie planning her Christmas wedding. So much had happened in one short year, but nothing had turned out like her daydreams.

More like her worst nightmare.

Again Sara wished she could rewind the hands of time and do things differently, but that was never going to happen. All she could do was move forward, much wiser than she'd been, albeit more bitter.

"The christening will be a beautiful affair," Bridget sighed. "It's so wonderful of Miss Astor to accept your invitation to be Natica's godmother. Lady Lister-Kaye as well. What a lucky little girl to have two godmothers."

"I am very grateful to Carrie and Mrs. Astor. Lady Lister-Kaye is most flattered that I named Natica after her," Sara's voice bubbled with appreciation. "If anyone can help me save our position in society, it's the Astors and the ladies of the set. There are very few people who would oppose Mrs. Astor in any manner, except perhaps the Belmonts. I know Carrie had her misgivings about Oliver courting me. She advised against it from the beginning. But she's clearly demonstrated her support by agreeing to be the baby's godmother. [55] Hopefully this will quiet the gossip and help us retain our place among the set, in spite of the scandal."

"It certainly is auspicious," Bridget agreed. "And the most wonderful gift the Astors could possibly have given the little one."

A fresh breeze blew down the avenue sending autumn leaves cascading from the treetops. They scampered through the piles, continuing their stroll toward downtown.

"Most everyone's gone back to New York to prepare for the holidays. Spending the winter here will keep me out of the loop for yet another season."

"There'll be time enough for all that miss," Bridget consoled her. "You're still young and very beautiful – and don't you ever forget it."

A chuckle escaped Sara. Her maid was so loyal. "I suppose you're right. Besides my life is different now that I have Natica." Sara smiled at the baby in the pram. "She's brought me so much joy. I shouldn't care about missing a few parties when I've got this little angel to occupy my time."

The autumn wind rustled bronze leaves over the sidewalk, swirling around the ladies as they pushed the stroller. "The wind seems to be picking up. Maybe we should head back." Bridget glanced at the sky. "Your mother will pitch a fit if we keep the baby out too long."

"You're right." Sara turned the carriage around toward Swanhurst without breaking her stride.

"Mrs. Belmont?" A gentleman wearing horn-rimmed glasses approached them from the direction of the cafe.

"Have we met?" Sara asked cautiously.

"A. J. Roland," he extended his hand. "I'm with *The New York Times*. Do you have a brief moment to talk? I'd like to ask you a few questions."

The newspapers were still trying to dig up as much dirt as they could about her and Oliver. So far, her family had been able to orchestrate what was printed from their side of the scandal, and Sara wanted to keep it that way.

She kept her hands firmly on the carriage. "I'm sorry Mr. Roland, I don't have time. I must get the baby home." She refused to be ambushed on the street. Was it too much to ask for a simple stroll in peace?

"I won't keep you long, I promise," he cajoled. "It's just so unusual for one of society's favorites to stay in Newport past the summer season. I should think the cold northern climate might make for a hard first winter for the baby. Might I ask why you're remaining in Rhode Island?"

Ignoring his question, Sara continued walking toward home. "I'm sorry, Mr. Roland. Now isn't a good time." Firmness edged her voice.

Undeterred, he pursued the women. "Isn't it true the only reason a lady of your position would remain in Newport would be if the rumors are true, that you intend to divorce your husband? It's common knowledge that Rhode Island court proceedings are some of the quickest and easiest in the country. But the law demands you be a residing state resident – why else would you remain here?" [56]

Bridget moved between Sara and the reporter. "Sir, you're being most rude with your questions. I should politely ask you to leave our company and take your conjecture elsewhere."

The maid blocked his path, barricading Sara and the baby. At first he acted to press the issue, but with a clever smile he backed down, pushing his glasses up on his nose.

"As you wish," he complied. "I'm fairly certain I've gotten my answer. Good day."

Perturbed, Bridget threw him a nasty look. "I shouldn't be printing rumors if I were you, sir," she called after him.

He tipped his hat, unfettered by her warning, and walked toward town.

Bridget turned to Sara, clearly peeved. "The nerve of that man!"

"He has certainly taken rudeness to new heights," Sara glowered, picking up the pace. "And there'll probably be something printed in tomorrow's news about my winter stay in Newport. It's just as well. Maybe then Oliver will get the message that I'm serious about this divorce."

"Let them say what they will, miss," Bridget bristled. "There'll always be gossipmongers lurking in the shadows. The important thing is that you do what needs to be done so you and the baby can move on with your life. Sooner or later this will have to blow over."

Nodding her head, Sara agreed. "Sooner or later it is bound to pass. I must admit, I can't wait for that day to arrive! Until then, I'm staying here in Newport to see this through to the end. And no rogue reporter is going to ruin my stroll!"

The next day
November 1, 1883
Newport, Rhode Island

"I thought I'd stop by and cheer you on a bit, Oliver." Perry smiled sympathetically at his younger brother. "Mamma says you intend to stay here at Oakland through the winter."

"Yes. I'm going to show a fight," Oliver replied. "What else can I do under the circumstances? I refuse to let that woman make me look like a deserting husband."

"I think you're doing the right thing," his brother nodded. "If you stay on in Newport then at least it gives the appearance that you're trying to reconcile your marriage."

Sounding more determined than he felt, Oliver agreed. "I think it's the best plan of action. But if Sara is bent on getting the divorce, it should be final by springtime regardless of whether I'm here or in New York."

The room fell quiet as Perry searched for some way to relieve the heavy gloominess. He'd had a hard time understanding Oliver's devotion to Sara until he'd met Marion Langdon, a woman in the New York set. There was something wonderful about the way she made Perry feel and he found he'd totally lost his composure to flirtation whenever she was near.

"Women certainly have a way of complicating our lives, don't you think?" Perry asked. "Too bad we can't just keep our minds focused on politics and business."

Chuckling, Oliver threw him a curious look. "Is there a special woman in your life I should know about?"

"No," he answered quickly, "not yet, anyway."

"Well, before you do anything impulsive I hope you'll learn a few lessons from my tribulations. In the end marriage is more trouble than it's worth."

"I hope you don't mean that, Oliver," Perry balked. "You're just going through a rough patch. Besides the alternative is to spend days and nights alone without the warm company of a woman. And what about an heir? I should think life would seem most dull without a family to enjoy it with."

"Right about now I would enjoy a little dullness. All this prattle in the papers is taking my constant attention. Now Sara's announced she is remaining in Newport. I suppose I should make a statement as well."

"Would you like me to contact the newspapers for you? I've got a friend who's a reporter with *The World*. I can let him know you won't be in New York this winter." [57]

Considering the offer, Oliver nodded in agreement, "That might be a good idea. It wouldn't seem like a rebuttal to her article if it comes from someone other than me. Do you mind?"

"Not at all," Perry smiled. "I'm on my way to New York tomorrow. I'll arrange to meet my friend and make sure he knows why you're spending winter in Newport."

"Thank you. I appreciate your help."

"Then I'm going back down to Washington. I'm considering trying for another term in Congress. Have you ever thought about going into politics?" Perry asked him. "Something tells me it would suit you."

"You must be joking," Oliver laughed. "This situation with Sara and her family is about all the politics I can handle right now."

"Well, maybe after this scandal's died down you can give it some consideration." Perry picked up his hat. "I've got to go or I'll miss the ferry. You can count on me to get word into the newspaper within the next couple of days. In the meantime, try to cheer up. Get a hobby or something to occupy your time. Winter nights can be quite long."

Oliver walked him to the door, "I'll try to take your advice. And you take mine about courting Miss Langdon. Things always seem to start off with chocolates and roses and then…"

He drew his finger across his neck like a guillotine.

Perry laughed and said good-bye. Oliver watched from the doorway wishing he were riding in the carriage with his brother, headed back to New York.

One month later
December 1, 1883
Newport, Rhode Island

Taking her coat from the butler, Sara followed her mother and sisters through the home's foyer. Several other guests were taking their leave as well, and the group loitered under the massive crystal chandelier, chatting as they waited for the coaches to arrive under the porte-cochère.

"Thank you again for a lovely evening," Mrs. Whiting said to Mrs. Endicott. "Your dinner party was wonderful."

"I'm very glad you could join us," their hostess smiled, bidding farewell to her guests.

Susan Matsey sauntered into the foyer, giggling with her friends, Lena and Lydia. The cousins were visiting from Wilkes-Barre for the holiday season. Sara turned, and caught Susan's eye. The débutante smiled politely over an expression of clear disdain, and moved past Sara toward the entrance. Whispers emanated from the three as Susan threw Sara a haughty look. Laughter erupted from the cousins, and Susan joined in with a lilt of ridicule.

"This is our coach," Mrs. Whiting ushered the family toward the door, giving a wave to Mrs. Endicott. If she'd noticed the undercurrent of criticism coming from the débutantes, she didn't let on.

Jane stepped after Milly and Mrs. Whiting, with Sara following behind. As she passed Susan she couldn't help but overhear the conversation.

"Mrs. Cushing is having a *huge* Christmas Eve ball," Susan told Lena. "Everyone who is anyone will be there. I received my invitation today. We will have the most fun!"

"What a wonderful way to celebrate the holiday!" Lena smiled. "And I have the perfect dress."

"I can hardly wait!" Lydia agreed.

The butler closed the door to the house behind Sara, silencing the discussion. She took the footman's hand and climbed into the carriage, settling into the seat beside her mother. The coach creaked into motion, headed for the comfort of Swanhurst where Bridget was watching over the baby.

A light conversation moved around the coach as Mrs. Whiting and her sisters chatted about the party. But Sara was lost in thought, feeling like she'd just been smacked.

This was her first party since the baby's birth. Sara knew she'd be faced with some disapproval, considering all the reports of her life in the newspapers, but the evening was harder than she'd imagined it would be. The denunciations were secret and covert, a quiet assault on her character. Her mother and her mother's friends offered a cushion of support, yet it had been hard to keep a brave face through the evening considering her own personal shame at her short-lived marriage.

Didn't everyone realize that she was not to blame? Oliver had abandoned *her*, she lamented, not the other way around.

Yet, Oliver carried on as if nothing had happened. His life and social standing were mostly unaffected by the scandal. But she faced whispers and gossip, feeling shamed and tainted. Men certainly got away with more than a woman ever could, she sighed.

Thinking about the conversation she'd overheard, Sara's spirits ebbed even lower. She had not received an invitation to any Christmas Eve ball – and she knew that she would not be getting one any time soon.

Mrs. Cushing was a friend of Mrs. Belmont. The two women had clearly been conspiring against the Whitings to deliver the blame of the divorce squarely on Sara's shoulders, while striving to retain Oliver's good standing among the set. I wonder if the ball is being held for my benefit, Sara thought glumly. A hurtful way to drive home the point that I'm not welcome at their society party.

The coach arrived at Swanhurst and Owen expertly guided the horses down the driveway to the front door. Climbing out of the carriage, Sara suddenly felt too weary for words. Walking into the manor she headed for the stairs.

"I'm going to turn in," Sara said, as she removed her gloves.

"It's been a long night. You must be tired," Mrs. Whiting replied.

Watching her daughter climb to the second floor Mrs. Whiting knew it had been a challenging evening for Sara. Other than rally her friends in support, there really wasn't much more she could do. She quietly hoped it would get easier for Sara – and soon.

"Good night," Mrs. Whiting called. "Get some rest."

CHAPTER TWENTY-ONE

Two weeks later
December 15, 1883
New York, New York

FOLLOWING THE BUTLER INTO THE parlor where drinks were being served before dinner, the servant announced their entrance in a resounding voice.

"Mrs. Astor and Mr. McAllister."

The butler took his leave as Mrs. Wilson, the hostess for the evening, walked toward the new arrivals.

"Mrs. Astor," Mrs. Wilson greeted them with a wide smile. "How lovely of you to join us. Mr. McAllister," she nodded, "Please, let's get you a cocktail, or some wine."

"Thank you." Mrs. Astor glanced around the room where a small group of about twenty visitors mingled in conversation, enjoying canapés as they chatted.

Mrs. Wilson signaled to a footman to attend to her guests. "How have you been?" she asked. "Marshall and Carrie seem to be quite the couple. As you can imagine, we're all very happy that they've found favor with each other."

"Yes," Mrs. Astor gave a courteous nod to the hostess. "I suppose we'll have to wait and let nature take its course. Perhaps one day soon we'll be planning a celebration."

"Wouldn't that be lovely," Mrs. Wilson smiled.

Joining the conversation, Mr. Wilson shook Mr. McAllister's hand. "We're so glad you could make our dinner party."

"Thank you." Mr. McAllister offered an aloof smile, his arrogance creating a discernible aura of haughtiness around him.

The butler returned, proclaiming dinner was being served in the dining room, and the group politely followed their hostess to the adjacent room.

Turning, Mrs. Astor noticed August Belmont and his wife Caroline among the guests. Their eyes met, and a wave of displeasure swept over Mrs. Astor's good mood.

She raised her chin, "I believe my evening has just been ruined," she spoke directly to August. "I certainly hope your cad of a son, Oliver, isn't here as well."

"Pardon me?" August's eyes drilled into the woman. "I truly hope you're not addressing me."

Looking from side to side in a mock search, she noted, "All the others have adjourned to the dining room. Clearly, I *was* addressing you, Mr. Belmont." Boldly, she continued, "We are all very aware of the offensive treatment your son delivered to his new wife. I should think you would have the decency to keep out of sight after creating such a harsh scandal for the young woman."

"What do you know of the matter, anyway?" August snapped. Mrs. Belmont stood quietly at his side, watching in dismay as her husband's temper gave way.

"As my daughter is a close friend of Sara's, not to mention one of the godmothers of the child, I should say I know quite a lot. Enough to know that Oliver deserted not only the mother, but the infant as well, disowning his very own flesh and blood. Sophistication is sadly lacking in the young man's scruples."

"How dare you speak to me in such a manner!" August retorted, his face scarlet red. "The girl is the one who left Paris without her husband."

A shrill laugh escaped Mrs. Astor, "I'm sure that's what you're trying to convince the set, but everyone knows how irresponsible Oliver is. Not to mention running around Europe with a French *fille de joie,* and God only knows what other Bohemians." The social queen tsked with displeasure, glaring at Mr. Belmont. "The least he could do is show some respect for his own child. I can't imagine where he learned such shabby conduct."

Mrs. Wilson, returning from the dining room in search of her guests, interceded. "Oh dear," she fretted. "I'd hoped to avoid such a confrontation."

"Then I suppose you should have been more selective in your guest list." Mrs. Astor turned a cold shoulder to the Belmonts.

"I am an esteemed member of society," August barked, "and no woman will speak to me with such disrespect."

"Now, now…" Mrs. Wilson worked to calm the argument.

Slamming his cane on the carpeted floor, Mr. Belmont ordered, "Keep your distance Mrs. Astor. In the future, consider yourself cut from my circle of friends."

"The pleasure is mine," Mrs. Astor retorted. Turning her back to the Belmonts she walked into the dining room with her head held high. Mr. McAllister, his brows lifted in snobbish judgment, threw the Belmonts a withering look of disdain, and followed her out of the parlor. [58]

Ten days later
December 24, 1883
Newport, Rhode Island

The late afternoon light settled into dusk, as Swanhurst assumed the festive glow of Christmas Eve. Mary moved through the room lighting candles on the pine tree and in the windows, while Owen, outside, lit the luminaries in the driveway. A gentle snow was falling, large flakes covering the brown grass with patches of frosty white. Sara watched through the sitting room window, gently patting the baby's back, working to keep her own spirits high.

"How's the baby?" Mrs. Whiting joined her at the window. "Oh, my sweet little granddaughter," she cooed, tickling Natica, who burped in her mother's arms.

"I'm just trying to work the bubbles out so she sleeps well. She's been restless the past few nights. Maybe she knows it's Christmas and is waiting for Saint Nicholas."

Jane and Milly entered the parlor carrying several gaily wrapped presents. "I'm putting my gifts under the tree now," Jane announced. "I can't wait for you to see what I got for the baby."

"Something wonderful?" Sara's eyes brightened at the thought.

"You'll have to wait till morning to see," Jane smiled with good humor.

"I will not be outdone," Milly interjected. "We plan on spoiling little Natica since this is her very first Christmas. It's an aunt's job you know, and one Jane and I take very seriously."

"Yes, we do," Jane agreed, placing the gifts under the evergreen tree, decorated with strings of popcorn and delicate glass ornaments. She joined them by the window, making goo-goo sounds at Natica while Sara gently rocked the baby against her shoulder.

"Do you want to hold her for a while?" Sara offered to Jane.

"Of course," she said. Easing the little one from her mother's arms, Jane carried the baby over to the chair where she gently bounced the infant on her lap.

"I'm going to run upstairs and change into my dinner dress. Do you mind?"

"Go ahead," Milly waved. "We'll see if we can get her to sleep in spite of all the excitement."

"That would be wonderful. Maybe I'll get a good night's rest myself, for once."

Leaving Natica in their doting care, Sara headed upstairs to her bedroom. Her chamber was filled with the soft yellow glow of the gas lamp, casting cozy shadows around the room. Bridget had set out her red satin gown, and it waited for Sara from a hanger on the chifforobe.

As she changed, Sara couldn't help but note that her wedding anniversary was only a few days away. Melancholy descended over her like the cold snow blanketing the town, and she fought against its power to consume her thoughts.

In spite of her best efforts, Sara succumbed to the memories of her wedding with mounting nostalgia. She recalled dressing in her wedding gown and veil, and adorning herself with the plethora of diamonds she'd received as gifts. The ceremony and reception had been everything she'd dreamed it would be. It was hard to believe that a year ago all of society's influential families had graced the halls of Swanhurst to witness the nuptials.

"How did I get in this situation?" Sara murmured, dwelling on her disastrous marriage. How did things go so terribly wrong? Instead of living with her new husband and celebrating the holidays in her own home with their new baby, she was fighting for her reputation and place in the social ranks – through no fault of her own!

I've done everything I was supposed to do, Sara thought. She had courted appropriately, endured Oliver's assignment in Germany, finally had a proper engagement and wedding, then delivered a child to the Belmont dynasty. All Oliver had done was carouse his way around Europe complaining about his life. How could he have delivered Sara and their baby to such unhappiness and ruin?

Many had warned her about pursuing a courtship with Oliver, but her attraction to him had been so strong, Sara doubted she could've resisted his overtures even if she'd tried to do so. Now in the wake of his selfish actions, she wished she'd taken the advice to heart and tried to find another suitor. One that truly loved her – and could commit to marriage and family.

"Too late to be prudent now," she mumbled.

The sound of sleigh bells echoed from the avenue and Sara glanced out the window. Several gaily garlanded coaches rolled down Bellevue under the light of the street lamps. She remembered overhearing Susan Matsey and her friends commenting about the Christmas Eve ball hosted at the Cushing's home tonight, and her spirits plummeted even lower.

I'm not on the guest list, she frowned, shaking her head in sadness. Sara knew the Cushings were close friends of the Belmonts, but being left out of the festivities still brought a sharp ache to her heart. As Oliver's wife, she should be there.

She felt so hollow. So empty. Thanks to Oliver she was now a social pariah. And only time would tell how the scandal would affect their daughter.

"What's to become of me?"

A knock on the chamber door roused her from her thoughts and she quickly wiped a tear from her eye. "Who is it?"

"It's me, miss," Bridget called. "I've come to see if you need help dressing."

"Come in, Bridget."

The maid entered the room, closing the door behind herself. "How are you doing?" Bridget asked softly, assessing Sara with a concerned eye.

"Oh Bridget," Sara smiled weakly. "I'm trying very hard to be fine."

"Well now… Chin up. After all it's Christmas Eve."

"Honestly, I'm trying to keep a happy face. I don't want to ruin everyone's celebration," Sara confided, "but my wedding anniversary is in a few days…"

"I know miss," Bridget tried to console her as she buttoned the back of Sara's dress. "But you've got to try and look on the bright side." She smoothed the fabric as she tied the bow in place. Moving to face Sara, she met her eye. "The baby is healthy. You're healthy. I know things have gone badly, but try to look at the big picture."

"I know, I know…"

"This dispute is bound to blow over. By springtime you'll be the belle of the ball again."

"I'm afraid those days are gone forever – and I'm only twenty-two," Sara's voice grew soft. She glanced at Bridget, "But I appreciate your optimism."

Sleigh bells jingled again as another carriage moved down Bellevue on its way to the party. Bridget glanced at the window, then back to her mistress. "I know it's hard right now, but remember, you've got Mrs. Astor on your side. If anyone can make the situation right, it's Mrs. Astor." Bridget opened the door to the hallway, "Soon enough you'll be on everyone's invitation list again."

"I'm sure you're right," Sara nodded, trying to rise to the occasion.

"I'll be downstairs. Let me know if you need anything else."

"Thank you."

Bridget pulled the door closed behind her, leaving Sara alone again with her thoughts. She walked to the vanity to tidy her hair in the mirror. A small glass snow globe sat on the dressing table, glittering in the flaming light of a candle. It had been a Christmas present from her grandfather many years ago, when she was still a small child. All these years later it remained a treasured gift.

Absently, Sara picked it up, shaking the snow over the Christmas scene. The snowflakes swirled inside the globe, bringing thoughts of the New Year, a year that would escort her divorce decree into reality. Already feeling like an outcast, it was hard for Sara not to wonder how she'd be received in society once her marital status was legally declared.

She faltered, and the snow globe slipped from her fingers, falling fast to the floor. Watching in horror, Sara saw it smash into bits of glass and water on the hard wood.

Frozen and forlorn, Sara just stared at it, unable to react to the mess. She could only think how her own life had become like the shattered snow globe. One big broken wreck. Fresh tears burned her eyes and she made new battle against her melancholy.

Christmas is a joyous time, she sniffed, and I'll find happiness if it kills me. She refused to let Oliver steal her joy – or their daughter's! She summoned her determination with a heartfelt pledge.

I'll rise stronger from this scandal, I swear it, she silently vowed. She'd grown wise in the ways of the world, and would persevere if it took her dying breath. Sara made a covenant with herself, "My position in society will not be denied! And I'll make certain Natica's future is secure in society as well!"

But her emotions did not match the challenge and confidence of her thoughts. "Who do I think I'm fooling?" Sara wondered. Releasing a cheerless laugh, she reached for a towel and carelessly threw it onto the broken snow globe.

A glint of light reflected off a phial of laudanum sitting on the dressing table amidst a cluster of medicine bottles, capturing her attention. The doctor had given her the opiate after childbirth to ease any lingering pain. Lifting it from the dresser, she slowly turned the amber bottle in her hands.

Divorce will most certainly taint my reputation, she thought. With or without Mrs. Astor's help, she would never be able to put the stain of scandal behind her. It was sure to follow her the rest of her days. Sara had a hard road to climb, one she felt much too weary to face.

She recalled William's comment to her in the harbor… *"Remarriage is unlikely with a child in tow. Most men shy away from a ready-made family…"*

An idea for escape occurred to her fatigued mind as she glanced down at the brown bottle, a skull and crossbones glaring its warning. If she drank the contents, all her problems would go away – forever. Sara clenched the phial tightly, giving serious consideration to the option. Peace and quiet held a strong allure. A very long nap from which she would never awake…

"Natica would be well cared for by my family," she realized, with despondent deliberation. "Maybe she'd even be better off without me… No one will miss me – not really. They've already moved on with their lives without a worry for me. Except maybe Carrie and Edith…"

Eyeing the warning label on the bottle again, she sighed, "I'm starting to sound like a tragic character from one of Edith's novels…"

Yet, Sara's eyes remained fixated on the laudanum as she rotated the bottle in front of the gas lamp.

"It would be so easy…" she whispered, unscrewing the cap.

The story of the Belmont-Whiting Scandal continues

AMERICAN GILT

SCANDAL
BOOK III

"SCANDAL" THE FINAL BOOK OF the American Gilt TRILOGY continues in 1884 as Sara Swan Whiting, once a popular débutante, finds herself disgraced by divorce, and left with a child to raise alone. Previously an admired member of the social set, she is now shunned, and becomes the target of judgment and criticism by her contemporaries. Sara has a friend in Mrs. Astor, the queen of the Four Hundred, but will Mrs. Astor support Sara now that she is divorced?

Sara's daughter, Natica, born of the ill-fated marriage, is denied paternity by her father, Oliver Belmont, and subsequently the lineage of the powerful Belmont family. Sara never speaks of the divorce, keeping the circumstances of Natica's birth a secret from her daughter. Years pass – Natica grows into a lovely young woman following in the débutante footsteps of her mother. Now a society favorite, Natica is spunky and beautiful, with a striking resemblance to her father.

While Natica charms society, her father regrets their estrangement, and watches her grow up from a distance. Anxious to know his only child, Oliver approaches Natica, but his efforts are thwarted by Sara, who forbids him visitation in retribution to his denial of paternity. As Natica comes of legal age she grows curious, and secretly sets off to find the facts behind her ancestry. Natica discovers the truth of her birth father's abandonment and abuse of her mother. Oliver attempts a reconciliation with his daughter, but fate steps in when tragedy strikes.

AMERICAN GILT

Scandal

J.D. PETERSON

BASED ON THE TRUE STORY OF THE BELMONT-WHITING SCANDAL

In the exciting finale to the AMERICAN GILT TRILOGY, readers are again transported through time to the wealth and confines of elite society during America's Gilded Age. With information gathered from family letters, historical newspapers, books and personal interviews, J. D. Peterson dramatically concludes the tale based on the true account of the Belmont-Whiting Scandal of 1883.

Dear Mrs Belmont,

Sara tells me
that Oliver is thinking
of returning in ...
and I feel ...
... you a ...
... object which ...

on ... Paris ...
my having
than I
... which was
... but which
... idea You would

Jan 22,

My dear Papa
I am really
to write and task ...
forgive me for my ...
silence and can ...
what gives the ...
gratitude and ...
... ... I ...
though I have ...
... ...
... ... the Br...
the back
... little ...
We have ...
... together ...
all engaged ...
... writing and ...
... time that ...
be left as ...
... best, until ...
... ... I ...
letter when ...
... ... for

Bremen
May 26/82

My dear Papa
I started to answer
... ... letter immediately
... ... finished.
... seen
... ... of my
... was very little
... she avoided
... not wishing

Paris — Hotel Westminster
April 30th —

My dear August.
I have received
your letter, with one enclosed
Oliver. I am sorry that
... did not settle
... ...

Sept 24"

copy

Dear Mrs Whiting
I have received
your letter of yesterday
& appreciate fully
your feelings as a
mother, but I regret
that I cannot give
...

Newport
Sea.

My dear Mrs Belmont
You don't know how
happy I am to ...
...

The Direct United States Cable Company,
Principal Office, 82 OLD BROAD ST., LONDON, EN
New York Offices, 16 BROAD STREET AND 444 BROOME STREET
No. ... The following CABLEGRAM was received
No. of Words 6 at 6 10 M 6 16 Bremen
From Brindisi To Venice
en route Venice

THE BELMONT FAMILY PAPERS 1799-1930

Author's Note

ON THE FOLLOWING PAGES I have transcribed some of the Belmont letters, part of a collection from the Belmont family papers, 1799-1930. These personal letters, written by members of the Belmont family, their friends and associates, are the property of the **Columbia University Rare Books and Manuscript Library, New York, N.Y.**

We all owe a great debt of gratitude to our historical societies, libraries, and in this case, to the Columbia University R.B.M.L. for their contributions to preserving these, and other archives.

The letters were handwritten in the style of the times; the writing contains many flourishes and is sometimes illegible. When I could not decipher a word or name, I inserted brackets [X] to demonstrate there may be missing text. Occasionally I attempted to decipher but wasn't certain I was correct, and there the word is present in the brackets, i.e. [Tom]. Miss Sara Swan Whiting was known to friends as 'Sallie', and she is addressed as such in some of the letters. I have made note of this in the same manner: Sara [Sallie]. In addition, I have arranged the letters in chronological order, and I have taken the liberty of adding punctuation to make them easier for you to read. This is only a small sampling of the letters and documents available in the Belmont Papers at the Columbia University Library.

I hope you find them as fascinating as I did!

J.D. Peterson

Belmont Letters
Sara Swan Whiting Belmont
To
Caroline S. Belmont
January 28, 1883
Paris - Hotel Bristol

My dearest petite-mere,

Oliver and I are writing to you side by side in the most romantic manner! And yet we have been married exactly one day [now] and a month!!

We arrived here about four days ago – My people arrived last night from London and we all arrived together this morning - what are you all doing in New York? [X] let people [X] all about [X]. Tomorrow, Oliver and I are going to Chattily for the day, to [X].

We dined last night with Matilda [X] They are very sweet and [kind] and we had a very nice dinner. Mrs. Gallatin also asked us to a cotillion last night, but I didn't go. She has also asked us to dine this week. [X] a stay - I think it will be [X] and Mrs. D. [Roman] had given us [moments]. I have not yet got a letter from you, petite-mere and I hope you have not forgotten your promise to write once a week. Give my best love to Mr. Belmont and with lots for your dear little self - I am as always your loving,

Sara
All my people send much love to you, my mother in particular.

Belmont Letters
Sara Swan Whiting Belmont
To
Frederika Belmont Howland
March 15, 1883
129 Champs-Élysées, Paris

My dearest Rica

At last a letter from you. Yet you are a joy, however if you do what you say, you will write once a week. I will try and forgive you!

You will be grieved to hear, I am laid up with a vile cold and I have had to back out of lots of nice things. I have just sent word to Mrs. [Adolph] R. that I shall not be able to dine with her this evening.

We went to see Henry 8th [X] last night and I think it is simply beautiful. There are loads of Americans in Paris. The [X] have left Sunday and sail for home 21st April. The [X] are not going home this year. [X] Miller has been in Paris all winter. [X] has now gone to Nice - he will be here soon. We are very comfortable in our apartment and I like it so much more than a hotel. [Kate] [Moore] is flying about with her artist friends and I must say she is quite handsome. [X] Rodgers is in Paris on leave and stopping with the [X]. We are dining there next Monday – they have been very kind ladies but – so have the Rothschilds. How is the dear Helene Beckwith? – and how is [X]? Still [X]? We have heard very little of Freddie [X] lately- what is he doing?

I [do] forgive you and as I feel [ill] my letter will be more than usually stupid.

Give my love to all – and lots and lots for yourself
Alway, dearest Rica,
Your loving,
Sara
If all goes well we expect to sail 14th June.
Remember me to all my friends, please –

Belmont Letters
Sara Swan Whiting Belmont
to
August Belmont
March 16, 1883
129 Champs-Élysées
Paris

Dear Mr. Belmont,

I am so glad you would like to hear from me and I should have written before but was afraid of boring you. The [X] again – I am going to tell [X] and fair [X] of some orphans! Next week Mrs. [Hauteville], Mrs. Plunkett and myself are to have the [X] table – Next Monday we are dining with [X]. We are all more or less excited about the [X] which some people tell us is sure to come day after tomorrow. The anniversary of the [commission] – Oliver is in London on a little visit to Mrs. [Halbreth] and I believe he is coming back with Lewis in a few days – The Rothschilds have all been so very kind to us. We have dined with them all several times and they have also sent us their box at the opera. They all have been awfully nice to us.

We have had terrible weather for the last two weeks but the 17th it is to change I believe – I have had a very bad cold and regret today I am more stupid than usual so please forgive my dull letter – With a great deal of love to all and lots for yourself I am always affectionately yours,

Sara

If it doesn't bore you, please write some soon.

Belmont Letters
Sara Swan Whiting Belmont
to
Frederika (Belmont) Howland
Paris, March 28th, 1883

My dearest Rica.

[X] thanks for your sweet letters. You are as good as gold to write so often. I have no time for anything here until this stupid [X] I am telling, is well not [X]. I have been at it all day and go [X].

How did the great and glorious Fancy Ball come off? What did you go as? I received the papers [today], and was much astonished at the article about my humble self! Please thank him. I am [X] much and give him my love – I am pleased to hear [Leddie G] has settled in his devotion. It was really quite a strain to follow him in his changes last summer. I hear Consuelo is going to spend the summer with the Vanderbilts in Newport – Paris is quite gay and festive. If at the [X] time I wish I was home – I can't tell you how sorry I am that Mrs. Belmont should be offended, but I can do absolutely nothing with Oliver and have tried my very best – I am going to the [X] and speak a little before [X].

fondly [my] dear Rica, with a great deal of love, I am, as always,

your loving,
Sara

Belmont Letters
Mrs. Sara Swan Whiting
To
Oliver H. P. Belmont
Paris, March 29, 1883

Dear Oliver,

I was quite surprised when I came in yesterday to hear that you had left. and I now send you a line to say that I will write you as I promised in reply to your letters.

I hope the change of scene has been of service to you. We have been very quiet today and there is nothing to write. Sara is feeling very tired and not at all well.

In haste,

Sincerely Yours,
S. S. Whiting

Belmont Letters
Sara Swan Whiting Belmont
To
Mrs. Caroline Belmont
March 29, 1883

Dearest petite mere,

I received your short and thoughtful Easter card last evening – You don't know how much it touched me – it seemed a message of comfort to me in my despair! I was confirmed last Sunday. I have been meaning to have it done for a long time, but when the Bishop was in Newport we were always away and so I have not had the opportunity. Oliver has gone to Bordeaux for a few days – I hope he will remain a little while as I have endured already all that I have strength and courage to bear. While in Paris he threatened every day to make a public scandal, which I am afraid at any moment he will do, for he is past listening to reason. My mother has [implored] him at least before doing so, to let his father know of his intoxication, but she does not know if he has done so. I have tried my best to influence him in the right way, and for now at least he has been at the smallest possible [X].

You will never know how it hurts me to write these things to you. [But] his conduct to me leaves me no other choice – I hope you will write me soon. I want to thank you again for your sweet thoughts of me and sending me the Easter card – I am writing you in bed as I am too wretched and ill to get up.

I am as always your loving,
Sara

Belmont Letters
Mrs. Sara Swan Whiting
To
Oliver Belmont
April 4th, 1883
Paris

Dear Oliver,

I received last evening yours of March 2nd [X] – I am sorry to hear that you are still suffering – I say nothing of a nature to worry Sara as she has already had more than she can bear and I think it will be more on four weeks before any [X] of the kind can be discussed – she requires perfect rest – Should you decide not to go to Spain – [X] is a very pleasant place and the air is very bracing, much more so than in the interior – Everyone here is complaining of colds, fever and general malaise – although it is somewhat warmer yesterday and today.

Sincerely yours
S. S. Whiting

Belmont Letters
Mrs. Caroline Belmont
To
Sara Swan Whiting Belmont
April 8, 1883
Newport

My dear Sara [Sallie]

I have been made utterly miserable and wretched by your letter of 28 March. Which came like fearful crash of thunder from a dear [X] – All your letters up to now were so bright and cheerful that I fondly hoped you both were happy and hoped your honeymoon is blissful love surrounded by kind friends.

I consoled myself for the continued absence of my son Oliver by the knowledge of you and his happiness, and now when you are barely married two months to get such news as those [sent] to me, almost breaks my heart. What is to become of you when on the very threshold of your wedded life, such things can happen! You ask my [X] and advice but what can I say over three thousand miles away from you, and how can I [X] you and my child when in utter ignorance of the [X] could have led Oliver to act in the dreadful manner described by you, and which is contrary to all I have known of him from his childhood up. Not only I and his father, but his brothers, sister and the old [X] servants who have been with us since before his birth all [X] to his kindly nature and sweet temper. During his early years, [X] at the naval academy and under Admiral Rogers, who was proper [X] of his [X] loved him for his uniform gentleman-like conduct, and he was beloved by the Admiral's family like a son and brother. You speak of his conduct as that of a madman or one under alcoholic influence, but I can say in all truth that neither his father or I have ever seen or known him under the influence of liquor - he must have sadly changed, according to your account, and that the accusations would come from his young wife, whom you yourself in your letters say that he loves so, will [X] my understanding, and I feel so crushed that I can hardly yet realize the dreadful misfortune of such a state of things between a newly married couple, much less give you advice and comfort. I sympathize with both of you [X] and my heart goes out to you in motherly love and affection.

Whatever my misgivings and those of my husband over your engagement [X] when you both are so young, especially he, they had given way to sincere affection for you, and we both were very ready and anxious to love and cherish you as one of our own children. The fond hope with which I looked forward to your return, would have been inexplicably joy by the happy prospect of your becoming a mother and in all this to be [X] by dreadful difficulties? Are both your lives to be scorched? and is a cold [X] would it writing this [X] of scandal of a [X] before the marriage bells have hardly ceased to ring?

I implore and entreat you my dear Sara [Sallie] to do all that a loving wife and true woman can do to guard against such a calamity. Have patience and forbearance with my dear boy, when he should be at fault. He is your loving husband the father of your yet unborn child, and he ought to be near and dearer to you than all the world.

I cannot write to him because you said that you have not told him that you had written to me.

You ought to return home to your native land as soon as possible. [Your] very pregnancy makes this most [advisable]. We will receive you with open arms and then you must try and find a small cottage, either in Newport or somewhere else in the country. Young people always get along best alone when they have their own snug home which can only be made happy by confidence and love and mutual [X] in important matters, but also in the [X] of each day. Life clouds in wedded life will always appear, but they vanish quickest without the [X] and interference of others, even if they [X] be offered by the tender solicitude of the [X] and dearest friends and relations. While I write to you in all love and candor you will [X] understand that it is not right for me to correspond with you on such a delicate and painful [matter] without the knowledge of your husband. I hoped and pray that long before this reaches you all your [X] between you and him will be at an end. But if it should unfortunately be otherwise, I have to ask from your affection and loyalty that you cable me on receipt of this letter and give me permission to write to Oliver. If most as unfortunate contingency should occur, and you still be at [X] with your husband it is absolutely necessary for Oliver [X] your own, that his father and myself should [X] against him.

In order to avoid delay you need only send the following cable:
Belmont
New York

[That I] may write Oliver, and now I must close this sad letter, trusting that the next mail will bring me more cheering news,

Your most affectionately,
Caroline S. Belmont

Belmont Letters
Sara Swan Whiting Belmont
To
Frederika Belmont Howland
April 14, 1883
Paris

My dearest Rica,

I received a short but sweet letter from you the other day in which you [X] me for not writing [X]. I am tired from shopping and flying around trying to find good clothes. I never want to look at a shop again! Pussy Jones [Edith Jones Wharton] [X] I think is in Paris and she sent me today a lovely silver basket filled with roses. I don't know when she and Harry are to be married. We heard that Mrs. Paran is coming over. [Mr. Greer] is here and he dined [X] us last evening. He doesn't [know] if he is going home this winter or not.

Louis de Tureene often asks after you. What a nice person he is to [X] Frederika!

My letters are not brilliant. Not at all [X] but you know I mean well.

Mrs. Hoffman, I believe sails very soon for America. She is very much cut up at poor [X] death.

What are you doing with yourself? From the great [X] I wish I had been there. It must have [been] so glad of a spree. Give my love to all and do write some again. I like to hear from you.

Always dear Rica,

Your loving,
Sara

Belmont Letters
Caroline Belmont
To
Oliver H.P. Belmont
April 14, 1883
New York

My dear Oliver,

Sara's [Sallie's] letters to me lately, while very affectionate and sweet, seem to evince restlessness and unhappiness. She has confided to me the secret of her condition, and I thought it best as your mother to give you advice, which would guide you in your treatment of your wife under the circumstances.

You must take into consideration the fact that women, particularly those of a nervous nature are sometimes subject to serious misgivings, in the most unaccountable ways, and the fear of the unknown and possibly terrible result of a first confinement preys upon the mind. It is is a time when a husband's gentle and forbearing treatment and devoted attention is put to the test, and above all things alleviates a wife's restlessness and gives her peace of mind necessary to a proper development of her child and its safe delivery. You would never forgive yourself if you were to do anything in ignorance which would cause your wife or your child's ruin.

Let me hear from you dear boy, whether you are tired of Europe and would like to come home to me, bringing Sara [Sallie] with you and then going to Newport to look for a small cottage where you can both pass the summer happily together. I shall be anxious until I hear from you so please write.

Your ever affectionate,
Mother

Belmont Letters
Mrs. S.S. Whiting
to
Oliver H. P. Belmont
April 20, 1883
Paris, France

Dear Oliver,

I received your telegram from Seville and suppose you are now in Tangiers - but think you may return to Seville so will send this note to that place, as a parcel and a letter have been returned here from Bordeaux. We have all of us had such terrible colds that we think of trying a change of air and of subletting the apartment.

I ventured to mention to Sara some things of which you spoke to me in a former letter – The reply she made me was "that she had forgotten absolutely nothing of what had happened."

I will write again in a day or two.

Yours sincerely,
S.S. Whiting

Belmont Letters
Sara Swan Whiting Belmont
To
Caroline Belmont
April 22. 1883
Paris

My dear Mrs. Belmont,

I received your sweet and kind letter two days ago and have been waiting before writing or cabling to think over what you said. I sent you a cable today. Oliver has been in Spain since the last violent scene he gave. He [X] expects to be back in Paris the last of this week. The plan you suggest of taking a cottage next summer and being alone, under ordinary circumstances, would certainly be the best. But as it is, nothing on earth would induce me to be alone with him for an hour, as I am in perfect terror of what he may do. While here, he was perfectly irresponsible. As far as I am concerned, he had no excuse for his unheard of treatment of me, as it was my greatest wish to please him – and my mother and sisters knew absolutely nothing of what I was enduring until my life became utterly unbearable and I went to my mother for protection. This speaks for itself. My astonishment and horror at the change in him, completely [X] me for some time, and the doctor says can be accounted for in no other way than alcoholism, probably absinthe, of which Oliver told me he took a great deal in Bremen.

You can understand all I have suffered and am suffering in this, but to whom can I speak of it, if not you.

With a great deal of love, and thanking you again more than I can say for your sweet letter.

I am always,
your loving,
Sara

Belmont Letters

Telegram one
Oliver H. P. Belmont
To
Sara Swan Whiting Belmont
May 2, 1883
From Paris to Claridge's Hotel, London

Leave for London tonight. How long do you intend being in London? Answer Hotel D'albe.
Oliver

Telegram two:
Sara Swan Whiting Belmont
To
Oliver Hazard Perry Belmont
May 2, 1883
From London to Paris

Do not come for the present. Cannot see you now. Will write
Sara

Telegram Three:
Sara Swan Whiting Belmont
To
Oliver Hazard Perry Belmont
May 2, 1883
From London to Paris

Everything at an end. Cannot see you.
Sara

Belmont Letters
Mrs. Sara Swan Whiting
To
Oliver H. P. Belmont
May 4, 1883
Claridge's London

Dear Oliver

I wrote you several times – to the hotel – Seville Spain – not knowing of any other address. I now write to say we sail on Saturday. The Doctor having advised us to go, as early as possible to avoid for Sara [Sallie] any further excitements. We are all very glad to go back. We had great difficulty in getting cabins at such short notice.

Your Sincerely,
S. S. Whiting

Belmont Letters
Sara Swan Whiting Belmont
To
Caroline Belmont
May 15, 1883 (Thursday evening)
Hotel Brunswick, New York City

My dear Mrs. Belmont

I came very unexpectedly to the "Baltic's" with my mother and arrived this evening. My mother is going on to Newport tomorrow and I am going with her, as I need rest and quiet after a very disagreeable crossing. We leave by the early train and I am so very sorry not to have seen you. I never can forget how sweet you have been to me. I have been and am very unhappy.

With a great deal of love,
your affectionate,
Sara

Belmont Letters
Sara Swan Whiting Belmont
To
Caroline Belmont
May 19, 1883
Newport

My dear Mrs. Belmont,

I am overcome with horror and distress at reading the *World* just now and finding that all my efforts to keep things quiet have been unsuccessful. The first [intimation] I had of anybody knowing anything about it was the note I received in London from Mrs. Gallatin and which I now enclose to you. I did not see her however, and told her nothing. I am sorry that this has come upon you, through no fault of mine. As for me, I am used to suffering now, and my cup is full. Will you please send me Mrs. Gallatin's letter when you have read it. I hope if you have time will write to me, I am so anxious to hear from you.

With much love,
Your affectionate,
Sara

Belmont Letters
Sara Swan Whiting Belmont
To
Oliver Hazard Perry Belmont
May 20, 1883
Newport, R. I.

Mrs. Tiffany has given me your note which surprised me more than I can say. The great personal abuse, the threats, the disgraceful scenes before others, the personal violence to which you subjected me in Paris, the condition you were in a great deal of the time, the manner in which you repeated I was no longer your wife, besides going day and night to places where a man in your position should not have gone, made a [X] of my life perfectly wretched and your presence without [X] perfectly unendurable. And you seem to find fault with me for leaving you – when in my present condition, if you had continued your conduct, it would have been almost certain death – I need scarcely add that it was by the doctor's advice that I left Paris for home – and you know that this is all true –
   I am overwhelmed with grief at your conduct and can say no more.

Sara W. Belmont

Belmont Letters
Caroline S. Belmont
To
Sara Swan Whiting Belmont
May 22, 1883
New York

Mrs. Oliver H. P. Belmont,

I have received your letter of the 19th with an enclosure, which I herewith return. You cannot be more horrified and distressed than I am at the reports and the scandal which your sudden return without your husband has called forth, although they cannot affect me as they do you. I know that my son Oliver has written to you, and I have only to say that things cannot and must not remain as they are now, and that an early solution is demanded by every law of decency and propriety.

Caroline S. Belmont

Belmont Letters
Oliver H. P. Belmont
To
Sara Swan Whiting Belmont
[X] 23, 1883
New York

Mrs. Oliver H. P. Belmont

Your letter of the 20th just has been received. The accusations which you brought against me, I pronounce one and all false, untrue and unfounded in every particular. I can not but hope that you have been led into giving expression to them by the influence of those around you, who have ever since their arrival in Europe stood between you and me and who have aided you in wrecking our married life at its very threshold. My letter of the 19th [X] in which I showed my willingness to forgive the many wrongs done me, and most of all your desertion in leaving Europe without me and without my consent [X] different treatment from an absolute refusal to return to your husband, based on excuses which you yourself cannot believe.

Oliver H. Perry Belmont

Belmont Letters
Oliver H. P. Belmont
To
Sara Swan Whiting Belmont
May 1883

Dear Sara [Sallie]

I arrived by the steamer today - I cannot [X] to you my surprise and my deep regret that you [X] have come to this country with your family in my absence - and without my knowledge.

Nevertheless, I have followed you at once, determined, without considering what has occurred or what injury I have suffered - to do what I can to save us both from scandal and from that which will affect us all our lives.

I cannot go to Newport at once - being on crutches and confined to the home by a sprained ankle, and therefore in order not to lose a single day I write you what otherwise I [X] say in person.

I write therefore demanding as your husband and requesting by all the ties that bind us that you return to me at once. I will [X] apartments for you here or Newport, and I will go any where you prefer to. [I will go to] Newport the moment I am able and locate a house or apartment there.

I make no reference to [X] - but I beg you, now that you have had time for reflection, not to insist on a curse which surely can have no justification in any conduct of mine.

Your husband,
Oliver

Belmont Letters
Caroline S Belmont
To
Mrs. Cushing
[X] 1883
Newport, R. I.

Dear Mrs. Cushing,

You will be glad to hear that your kind and sympathizing letter was received by me this morning with much pleasure. It is a comfort in my deep distress to be assured that my friends whom I love, feel for me in this uncalled for scandal, and unwarrantable behavior on the part of that horrible family. Oliver arrived home on Saturday last and through him, we now know that all the stories which have been circulated about him are utterly false. He had to contend with four women alone, and when he wanted his wife to live with him away from her family, she would not do it, and quarreled with him, and turned away as if she never loved him. They made things so unbearable to him, that he proposed going away for a short time in which Mrs. Whiting and all concurred thinking that a short absence might mend matters and Mrs. Whiting in her plausible way said she would write to Oliver and keep him advised as to their plans. They took that time to undermine his reputation and of ever gaining sympathy among my own friends and they [X] the day he was about to return to Paris, they hurriedly packed up their things, underlet the apartment, and stole over here like thief's [sic] in the night, passing through to Newport hav-ing previously written [X] of their arrival and circulated the wicked stories against my son so that they might gain sympathy here which misled our [X] still [X] of their movements and intention. Oliver's known character from his childhood away his family, friends and classmates and superiors as an honorable, sweet tempered and amiable gentleman, would be in itself a sufficient refutation of their infamous falsehoods, one has given his father, his brothers, and to me, a clean and straight forward account of his whole conduct disproving all the [X] accusations brought against him.

I see few people and talk little on this painful subject, but as you are kind enough to take an interest in us and wish to know something of the facts, I give them to you, hoping that you and Mr. Cushing will always give your friendship.

Mrs. Belmont

Belmont Letters
Sara Swan Whiting Belmont
To
Isabella Tiffany
[no date]
Newport

[Calling Card]

Dear Mrs. Tiffany - can you see me soon – I am so [X] to see you.

With love,
Sara

Belmont Letters
Sara Swan Whiting Belmont
To
Caroline Belmont
Swanhurst, Newport
September [?}

Mrs. August Belmont

I had heard with regret that reports have been circulated that your son, my late husband before [X] marriage had intermarried with another woman and that when he left Paris for Spain in February 1883, he left and traveled in company with a disrespectable woman – That he has married before he married me, appears to me to be so absolutely without foundation in fact, that the report scarcely need be justified with a denial, yet it may not be amiss for me to express to you my belief that this story is utterly devoid of truth or even of a semblance of truth – The reference to the story that he left Paris and traveled with a disrespectable woman, I can only say that I have no belief or reason to believe that that is true, or that it has any more foundation in truth than the story of his previous marriage.

Sara Whiting Belmont

ACKNOWLEDGMENTS

As in Volume One, "Début", I wish to send heartfelt thanks to Kristine Bonner, who worked with me diligently to edit this manuscript. Her time, talent and knowledge of the English language was a tremendous gift toward the completion of the book. In addition, her experience with electronic publishing and computers proved invaluable. Without Kristine's dedication, I don't know if you would be reading this novel now.

I would also like to thank Stella Togo for offering her experience and ideas to the project, and Shane Fowler, who gave advice on content, as well as help with the book's promotion and public relations. Shane's contagious enthusiasm for Sara's story kept me going through long days of writing, editing and promotion.

Finally, a huge 'thank you' to "she-who-shall-remain-nameless", for help with social media, branding and graphic design. I so appreciate all your efforts in helping me publish this novel series.

Although I took great care to be historically accurate, at times, I did take some liberties with history. For example, in Chapter Sixteen, Sara visits her lawyer in the Audrain Building. In fact, the Audrain was built in 1902, and not completed until 1903. I chose this building for the scene after a visit there, as I was much impressed by its aura and architecture.

In Chapter Twenty One, Sara referred to one of "Edith's tragic characters," more precisely, Lily Bart, the main character in "The House of Mirth". In actuality, the novel would not be published until 1905.

Last, but certainly not least, I would like to acknowledge you, dear reader. Your interest and appreciation for Sara's story has given me new energy and dedication to finish the trilogy, therefore completing my task of presenting the truth about this historic scandal.

Thank you, one and all, for your support!
J. D. Peterson

For a full list of acknowledgments please refer to "American Gilt– Début".

BIBLIOGRAPHY

Books

"The King of Fifth Avenue – The Fortunes of August Belmont" by David Black, Dial Press N.Y., N.Y. Copyright © 1981 ISBN 0-385-27194-8

"A Season of Splendor – The Court of Mrs. Astor in Gilded Age New York" by Greg King, John Wiley & Sons, Inc. Hoboken, New Jersey. Copyright © 2009 ISBN 978-470-18569-8

Newspapers

New York Times Archives
New York Tribune
The Brooklyn Daily Eagle
The Washington Critic (District of Columbia)

Online Resources

George Rives Genealogical Notes
New York Public Library

Other Resources

The Belmont Family Papers – Columbia University Rare Books and Manuscripts Library

FOOTNOTE
SOURCES

KFA – "The King of Fifth Avenue - The Fortunes of August Belmont" by David Black

SOS "A Season of Splendor – The court of Mrs. Astor in the gilded age" by Greg King

NYTA - New York Times Archives

NYT - New York Tribune

BDE - The Brooklyn Daily Eagle

WC – "The Washington Critic" – Newspaper from The District of Columbia

GRGN – George Rives Genealogical Notes – New York Public Library

BL - The Belmont Family Letters – Columbia University Rare Books Library, N Y, N.Y.
    CB – Caroline Belmont
    AB – August Belmont
    FH – Frederika Belmont Howland

OB - Oliver Belmont
SSWB – Mrs. Sara Swan Whiting Belmont
SSW – Mrs. Sara Swan Whiting

1	BL - SSWB to CB	1-28-1883	"My dearest petite-mere…
2	BL - SSWB to CB	4-22-1883	""The change in Oliver… accounted for by alcoholism, probably absinthe."
3	KFA	Page 659	"Oliver wanted …a place of their own. Sara refused… and exiled Oliver from her bed. Oliver went wild."
4	BL - SSWB to OB	5-20-1883	"Going day and night where a man in your position should not have gone…"
5	BL - SSWB to CB	3-29-1883	"I can do absolutely nothing with him…"
6	BL - SSWB to OB	5-20-1883	"The way you shouted I was not your wife… Going day and night to places where a man in your position should not have gone…"
7	KFA	Page 660	"He (Oliver) threatened to make a public scan-dal by filing for a separation or divorce."

8	ibid		"Mrs. Whiting begged him to tell his father of his intentions"
9	ibid		"Oliver, feeling ganged up on, left Paris for 'a few days' 'to think things over.'"
10	ibid		"Edith Jones...who's engagement to Henry Stevens... postponed."
11	BL - SSWB to OB	4-22-1883	"I am in perfect terror of what he might do"
12	BL - CB to SSWB	4-18-1883	"Oliver... has never shown any sign of an ugly temper."
13	BL - SSWB - CB	4-22-1883	"The doctor said that the change in Oliver...can be accounted for no other way than alcoholism, probably absinthe, of which Oliver took a great deal in Bremen"
14	KFA	660	"Edith sent Sara a silver basket filled with roses."
15	BL - SSWB to FH	4-14-1883	""Flying around trying to get good clothes."
16	KFA	Page 661	"Mrs. Whiting, who seemed to have taken charge of her daughter's life – wanted a separation or divorce."

17	KFA	Page 660	Edith and Sara were "… sympathetic companion(s) in misery."
18	ibid		"She sought solace in the church…confirmed in Paris"
19	ibid		"Abandoned by her husband on her honeymoon, Sara must have felt humiliated…"
20	ibid		"Oliver's traveling companion was a disreputable French dancer."
21	BL - CB to OB	4-14-1883	"Sara's letters to me have been very sweet…"
22	BL - CD to SSWB	4-18-1883	"How little I can say or do from three thousand miles away…"
23	ibid		"Sara's letters to me lately… seem to evince restlessness and unhappiness."
24	ibid		"take into consideration…serious misgivings in the most unaccountable ways."
25	NYTA	4-27-1883	"All Society in Costume - Mrs. W.K Vanderbilts Great Fancy Dress Ball

26	SOS	page 60	"She (Mrs. Astor) drove in her carriage to Alva's shimmering new palace…"
27	NYTA	4-27-1883	"Chains of orchids and vases… of some ten thousand…roses…"
28	BL - SSW to OB	4-20-1883	"Sara has forgotten nothing…."
29	BL - CB to OB	4-14-1883	"Take into consideration…"
30	BL - CB to SSB	4-18-1883	"to do all that a loving wife and true woman can do to guard against calamity…"
31	BL - OB to SSB	5-2-1883	"Leave for London tonight…"
32	BL - SSB to OB	5-2-1883	"Do not come for the present cannot see you…"
33	BL - SSB to OB	5-2-1883	"Everything at an end…"
34	BL - SSB to CB	5-15-1883	"I never can forget how sweet you've been to me…"
35	KFA	Page 662	"arrived in New York on May 15, 1883… left the next morning for Newport where

			they holed up in a house on Catherine Street until Swanhurst was made ready."
36	BL - CB to SSB	5-22-1883	"an early solution is demanded by every law of decency and propriety."
37	KFA	Page 663	"Oliver arrived in New York – his parents apparently told him to stay in the city...or it would be an admission of guilt, He sprained his ankle..."
38	BL - OB to SSB	May 1883	"Surprise and deep regret that you should have come to this country with your family in my absence and without my knowledge."
39	BL - SSB to CB	May19, 1883	"overcome with horror..." *New York World* prints article."
40	KFA	page 663	"Ironically the first press item about the affair appeared in the *New York World*, the newspaper August so often had used for his own propaganda."
41	BL - CB to SSB	4-18-1883	"Have patience and forbearance with my poor boy, when he should be at fault..."

42	ibid		"Young people always get along best when they're alone in their own snug home…"
43	ibid		"Oliver had never before shown any signs of an ugly temper and if he had 'sadly changed'…"
44	ibid		"What is to become of you when on the threshold of your wedded life…"
45	KFA	page 664	"Sara…didn't believe the story that Oliver was secretly married to someone else before their wedding.
46	BDE	5-19-1883	**"AN UNFOUNDED REPORT AFFECTING THE FAMILY RELATIONS OF OLIVER BELMONT**
47	KFA	Page 664	"Caroline gave dinners, at which Oliver presided, for the older, influential members of their set."
48	BL - OB to SSB	5-22-1883	"…as your husband, by all the ties that bind us that you return to me at once."
49	BL - SSB to OB	5-20-1883	"…your conduct would have been almost certain death for me…"

50	KFA	Page 664	"…her lawyer in a curious coincidence was discussing erecting a statue of the man for whom Oliver had been named…"
51	BL - SSB to CB	4-22-1883	"…I am in perfect terror of what he may do."
52	NYTA	8-18-1883	The Newport Fox Hunt
53	NYTA	9-6-1883	"Mrs. Oliver Hazard Perry Belmont, daughter of Mrs. S.. S. Whiting, of New-York, has just given birth to a daughter."
.54	KFA	page 664	"Oliver was not allowed to see the baby…For the rest of his life he never recognized the child as his daughter.
55	KFA	Page 707	"Mrs. Astor made her hostility to the Belmonts unignorable when she became godmother of Oliver's disowned daughter."
56	NYTA	11-1-1883	"Why they remain in Newport"
57	NYTA	7-6-1883	"Mr. O.H.P. Belmont has arrived at Oakland where he would permanently reside."
58	WC	3-18 -1883	"August Belmont cut Mrs. Astor dead at dinner…"

PHOTOGRAPHIC
CREDITS

Oliver Hazard Perry Belmont	U.S. Library of Congress Used with Permission
Sara Swan Whiting Belmont Vanderbilt Fancy Ball	New York Historical Society Used with Permission
George Lockhart Rives Vanderbilt Fancy Ball	New York Historical Society Used with Permission
Telegrams	Columbia University Rare Books Library Used with Permission
Natica Belmont Rives	New York Public Library Used with Permission
Belmont Letters	Columbia University Rare Books Library Used with Permission

"American Gilt Trilogy" "Absinthe"

Book Two

Book Club Discussion Questions

1. As Sara and Oliver begin their honeymoon in Paris, the future looks happy and carefree.
   a. In light of the challenges of their engagement, how do you feel about the events in Paris?
   b. Sara is now 'Mrs. Belmont'. Do you think her new position in society will work to her advantage?

2. Mrs. Whiting and Sara's older sisters Jane and Milly, plan on joining the newlyweds on their honeymoon to 'announce them to French society'. Sara is the 'baby' of the family as she is the youngest by 14 years.
   a. Why do you think Oliver initially agreed to the living arrangements?
   b. Do you have any experience where your family or personal loyalties collided with other duties or alliances?

3. After a few weeks, Oliver starts going out on his own.
   a. Do you think Oliver is justified in wanting to escape the Whitings?
   b. How do you feel about the clubs he is patronizing?
   c. How do Oliver's activities reflect on Sara?

4. Absinthe becomes a favorite drink of Oliver's, and he joins the ranks of Van Gogh, Oscar Wilde, and Ernest Hemingway, among others.
   a. Do you think the liquor is affecting his personality?
   b. Is absinthe the root of their marital problems? Why or why not?

5. As the situation escalates into violence, how do you feel about Oliver's behavior toward Sara?
   a. Do you think Oliver's anger is justified?
   b. Do you think Oliver truly loves Sara?
   c. Have you ever been in a situation like this?

6. Sara travels to New York City from Paris accompanied only by Bridget, her maid, to attend the Vanderbilt Fancy Ball.
   a. How do you feel about Sara's decision to take this trip, with only Bridget as a companion, taking into consideration the year – 1883?
   b. Do you think Sara is justified in attending the ball alone?
   c. Have you ever traveled alone without your family's knowledge?

7. Alva Vanderbilt refuses to acknowledge Mrs. Astor or Carrie, not inviting them to the ball of the season.
   a. Was Alva justified in her refusal to send an invitation until Mrs. Astor came to her home and acknowledged her into the '400' set?
   b. How do you think this affected the future of upper class society?

8. While Oliver is reportedly seen in Spain traveling with a French dancer, Sara discovers she is pregnant with his child.
   a. What course of action do you think Sara should have taken after finding herself pregnant and abandoned by her husband?
   b. What do you think Oliver should have done upon getting word of the pregnancy?

    c.   At this point, do you think there is a chance for the couple to work through their differences? Why or why not?

9. Mrs. Whiting orders the family back to Newport on the advice of Sara's doctor.

    a.   Do you think Mrs. Whiting's concern for Sara, and her anger with Oliver, entitled her to accept Sara's telegrams and respond to them as if she were Sara?

    b.   Do you think Sara should have waited for Oliver to return?

    c.   What do you think would have happened if Sara had received the telegrams herself?

10. Mrs. Astor cautions Carrie to keep her distance from the Whitings and the Belmonts.

    a.   Do think this was good advice?

    b.   How do you think Mrs. Astor's fondness for Sara will help her reputation?

    c.   Do you think Mrs. Astor's favoritism will hurt Sara's position?

    d.   How do you think the Belmonts' attack will affect Sara's reputation?

11. Upon the Whitings' return to Newport, R.I., Mrs. Whiting goes to the *New York World* newspaper with the story of Oliver's abandonment.

    a.   Do you think this was the right thing to do?

    b.   Do you think Mrs. Whiting should have discussed her plan with Sara?

    c.   The newspaper reports made the situation public. Did this help or hurt Sara?

12. Sara tries to sneak out and meet with Oliver to have a personal discussion.

    a.   Do you think Mrs. Whiting was right in blocking the meeting?

b. What do you think would have happened if Oliver and Sara had been able to talk without the influence of their parents?

c. Do you think Sara should have stood up to Mrs. Whiting and gone to the meeting in spite of her mother's objections?

13. Oliver demands Sara join him at his new estate, Oakland.

a. Do you think Sara should have obeyed Oliver and joined him at Oakland?

b. Are Sara's concerns for her safety and that of her unborn child justified?

c. Do you believe Oliver truly wants Sara to join him?

14. By the end of 1883, instead of celebrating her wedding anniversary, Sara is facing divorce proceedings.

a. Do you think Sara can regain her place in society despite her status as a divorcée and unwed mother?

b. Is Sara's consideration of suicide a betrayal of her baby, Natica?

c. Have you ever felt trapped by a seemingly hopeless situation?

About the Author

J. D. Peterson is an author, singer-songwriter and artist. In addition, she is an alternative healer, certified in multiple modalities. Originally from the East Coast, Ms. Peterson is currently living in Southern California.

For historical photos, documents and more, subscribe to:
www.americangilt.com
Youtube.com: American Gilt
Follow us on:
Twitter: #americangilt1
Like us on Facebook and Pinterest:
American Gilt Trilogy
Previously published as:
Swan Song Trilogy

Made in the USA
Middletown, DE
29 September 2023

39777860R00137